JACKSON MEMORIAL 2

KEITH THOMAS WALKER

KEITHWALKERBOOKS, INC
This is a UMS production

KEITHWALKERBOOKS

Publishing Company
KeithWalkerBooks, Inc.
P.O. Box 331585
Fort Worth, TX 76163

For information write
KeithWalkerBooks, Inc.
P.O. Box 331585
Fort Worth, TX 76163

ISBN-13 DIGIT: 978-0-9967505-5-4
ISBN-10 DIGIT: 099675055X
Library of Congress Control Number: 2017902067
Manufactured in the United States of America

Second Edition

Visit us at www.keithwalkerbooks.com

• • • • • •

When she turned off her car, she checked the bag sitting on the passenger seat. Everything was as she'd left it. There were towels, plenty of gauze, a couple of scalpels, an umbilical cord clamp and scissors. She even packed a bulb syringe to clear her baby's mouth and nose.

In the glove compartment was her husband's snub nose .38. It had been in Bryan's nightstand for so long, he probably forgot he owned it. Naomi didn't want to use the pistol, but it was unlikely the host would lie back and say, "Go ahead, cut me open."

Once Naomi neutralized the donor, she knew she'd have less than ten minutes to complete the operation. She expected it to be very messy.

She wasn't sure how Bryan would react when she came home with a baby. She hoped he'd simply accept it, as he accepted that she was pregnant and later that she might not be pregnant. It would be awkward for a few days, sure, but they would get past it. He'd fall in love with his son or daughter and forget about Mallory. He'd forget that he ever wanted to leave Naomi.

If she was wrong, and he packed his things anyway, Naomi thought she'd be okay with that – because she wouldn't be alone anymore. She'd have her baby. The baby would call her *Mama* and love her unconditionally, because that's what babies do.

This was all good news, but Naomi couldn't stop crying as she peeled the plastic off her next breakfast sandwich. She'd been crying so much, it was a wonder her eyes still worked. They should have been completely dried out by now.

She knew the crying would come to an end soon. All of her suffering would.

Today was a beautiful day.

• • • • • •

KEITH THOMAS WALKER

5

This book is for Dianne Coleman

MORE BOOKS BY
KEITH THOMAS WALKER

Fixin' Tyrone
How to Kill Your Husband
A Good Dude
Riding the Corporate Ladder
The Finley Sisters' Oath of Romance
Blow by Blow
Jewell and the Dapper Dan
Harlot
Plan C (And More KWB Shorts)
Dripping Chocolate
The Realest Ever
Jackson Memorial
Sleeping With the Strangler
Life After
Blood for Isaiah
Brick House
Brick House 2
One on One
Brick House 3

NOVELLAS

Might be Bi Part One
Harder
Primal Part One
The Realest Christmas Ever
Hotline Fling

POETRY COLLECTION

Poor Righteous Poet

FINLEY HIGH SERIES

Prom Night at Finley High
Fast Girls at Finley High
Bullies at Finley High

Visit keithwalkerbooks.com for information about these and upcoming titles from KeithWalkerBooks

ACKNOWLEDGMENTS

Of course I would like to thank God, first and foremost, for giving me the creativity and drive to pursue my dreams and the understanding that I am nothing without Him. I would like to thank my wife for being my first and most important critic, and I would like to thank my mother for always pushing me to be the best I can be. I would like to thank Janae Hampton for being the best advisor, supporter and little sister a brother could ever have.

I would also like to thank (in no particular order) Beulah Neveu, Deloris Harper, Denise Fizer, Michele Halsey Hallahan, Priscilla C. Johnson, Tia Kelly, Melissa Carter, Cathy Atchison, Lanita Irvin, Ramona Weathersbee, Jason Owens, Chanta Rand, Ramona Brown, Sharon Blount, BRAB Book Club, and Uncle Steven Thomas, one love. I'd like to thank everyone who purchased and enjoyed one of my books. Everything I do has always been to please you. I know there are folks who mean the world to me that I'm failing to mention. I apologize ahead of time. Rest assured I'm grateful for everything you've done for me!

CHAPTER ONE
THIRD SHIFT

Welcome back
Where your schemes were your ticket out
Welcome back
To that same old place that you laughed about
Well the patients are all different since you been around
And we got new employees in every crowd
Who'd have thought we'd heal ya?
(Who'd have thought we'd heal ya?)
Just when you thought we'd kill ya!
(Just when you thought we'd kill ya!)
Yeah, we got a lot of crazies
And twice as many folks are lazy
Welcome back
Welcome back, welcome back, welcome back
Welcome back, welcome back, welcome back

"CODE BLUE, MEREDITH BUILDING, SIXTH FLOOR."

"CODE BLUE, MEREDITH BUILDING, SIXTH FLOOR."

The operator didn't sound panicked as she made the announcement overhead, just as 95 percent of the employees who heard it didn't bat an eye. A code blue alarm meant somewhere in the sprawling hospital complex a patient had possibly taken their last breath. But unless the distressed patient was on your floor or an immediate responsibility, no one gave it a second thought.

The nursing supervisor, a petite, quick-witted woman named Lindsey King, sighed as she rose from her desk on the second floor of the Jackson Building. She'd just nuked a Weight

Watchers meal and was eager to get started on it. Her stomach grumbled in protest as she left her office and headed for the staff elevators.

She hoped the operator would cancel the code before she got too far away from her dinner. The thought wasn't farfetched. People set off erroneous code blues all the time. Sometimes housekeepers bumped into the alarm when they cleaned empty rooms. Confused patients were known to push the button themselves. Even visitors could cause panic on a unit by fiddling with their relative's monitor.

The code was still active when the elevator arrived. Lindsey took the lift to the third floor, which was the only floor in the hospital that connected all of the buildings. From there, she followed the hallway to the Meredith Building and took another elevator to the sixth floor. When the doors opened, warning lights were flashing on the Med/Surg unit. Lindsey saw a group of employees, all rushing in the same direction. Her heart rate kicked up a notch as she followed them.

This was what she missed the most about being a floor nurse: The adrenaline rush of high drama and uncertainty. Lindsey believed she was at her best when someone's life hung in the balance.

"What's going on?" she asked an anxious PCT who was moving quickly towards the commotion.

"I don't know," the girl said, barely looking her way. *"She stopped breathing!"*

Her shrill voice caused Lindsey to cringe and roll her eyes. *Well, no shit she stopped breathing. Tell me something I don't know.*

Thankfully she kept those thoughts to herself. The last thing Lindsey needed was another complaint about how she was *rude* and had hurt someone's *feelings*. She often wondered how some of the nurses and techs at the hospital made it this far in life, wearing their emotions on their sleeves all the goddamned time. It had gotten to the point that she couldn't tell them how much they sucked at their job without expecting to get dragged down to Human Resources the following day.

When they rounded the corner, Lindsey saw that all of the hubbub was focused on room 623. There were a few nurses and techs standing outside of the room rubbernecking. When she approached the doorway, Lindsey saw eight more employees inside the room. One was from respiratory. The others were from the floor. In the middle of the crowd was the patient's bed. Sure enough, all of the readings on the heart monitor had flat lined. A nurse Lindsey recognized as the floor's charge was actively doing CPR.

"Where's the doctor?" Lindsey barked, immediately taking charge of the situation. "What happened?"

The charge nurse looked up at her but didn't stop the compressions. Her face was pink and sweaty from her efforts.

"I don't know. She was fine thirty minutes ago, when the tech took her vitals. Next thing we know the alarms are going off. We found her just like this."

"Uh, excuse me."

Lindsey was startled and annoyed when the only person in the room who wasn't an employee approached and tried to squeeze by her. The man looked as spooked as everyone else, but Lindsey saw something else in his dark, sunken eyes and bony features. But he was not her priority.

She stepped aside and told him, "Go. *Move!*"

The visitor obliged, and a few techs made way for Lindsey as she approached the bed. The supervisor's heart squeezed uncomfortably when she laid eyes on the patient for the first time. The woman looked like she was already gone – had been for years. She was thin to the point of frailty. Her eyes floated, half open, in sockets that were as deep and dark as the visitor's. Her long hair was wild and oily. Lindsey also noted sores on her face and arms that were in varying stages of healing. None of this explained why her heart had stopped beating, but together the clues told an interesting story.

"Where's her doctor?" the supervisor asked again.

Every code blue in the hospital brought a certain number of people who *absolutely had to come*; namely the nurses on the floor, respiratory, anesthesia, the nursing supervisor, the doctor, and if all else failed, a chaplain.

"I thought he'd be here by now," the charge nurse said. She was on the verge of panic, but wasn't quite there yet. "Here, can you take over for me?" she asked the nurse standing closest to her.

William Harkins stepped in and began chest compressions when the charge stepped away. Lindsey didn't know William personally, but she knew he'd been working on the unit for more than five years.

"What's she here for?" Lindsey asked. She circled the bed and continued her assessment.

The patient's skin was pale and pasty, but her lips were blue. The discoloration had already started to spread throughout her face. The stench of death was prevalent in the small room; growing stronger by the second.

"Nothing that should be causing this," William said as he pumped her chest.

He rattled off a list of diagnoses, the worst of them being *hepatitis*. For Lindsey, that was the final piece of the puzzle. She lifted one of the patient's arms. There were tracks visible, but they were old. The other arm was the same. Lindsey didn't find what she was looking for until she went to the foot of the bed and lifted the sheets. The needle marks on the patient's legs and feet were fresh. But without a doctor there, she wanted to be absolutely sure before she ordered any medication.

She looked back and asked one of the techs, "That asshole who left when I came in here, who is he?"

"Um, who?" the girl said.

Growing frustrated, Lindsey told her, "What are you doing in here? Is this your patient?"

The girl's confused expression remained as she shook her head.

"*Then get out!*" Lindsey looked back to the group. "Anyone who doesn't need to be in here needs to *leave!*"

After a few more gawkers slipped out of the room, Lindsey asked the charge, "Who was that guy who just left?"

"That was her boyfriend," William interjected. "He's been here with her all night."

"Where the hell did he go?" Lindsey muttered as she exited the room.

Luckily she didn't have to search the whole hospital. The mysterious boyfriend had returned. He stood sheepishly in the hallway. As Lindsey approached him, all of her suppositions rushed back with the strength of a waterfall. Tall, lanky. Sunken eyes and cheeks, matted hair. The asshole was nodding at that very moment. His girlfriend was dying, and he could barely stand up straight.

"What'd you give her?" Lindsey demanded as she marched towards him.

She was more than a foot shorter and sixty pounds lighter, but her tenacity made her appear much larger. The boyfriend backed into the opposite wall. Lindsey closed the distance between them until his funky breath and the stink of his sweat filled her nostrils.

"Wha, what?" he mumbled.

"You want her to *die*?" The supervisor's eyes were wide, her teeth bared. "I know you shot her up with *something*, and I know you took off and got rid of it when I got here. I don't care how high you are right now. I don't even care if you still got dope on you. The only thing I care about is the *patient*. I need to know what you gave her. If you care anything about her, you need to tell me *right now*!"

The alarms continued to wail loudly as the boyfriend considered whether or not he'd say. Lindsey could almost see logic forcing its way into the mush his brain had become.

"Huh, heroin," he finally divulged. His tongue moved as slowly as his mind did. "I – I didn't want to. She begged me to bring it. I... I..."

"Shut the hell up," the supervisor said before turning back to the room. "*We need Narcan!*" she yelled at the charge nurse. "And call security, while you're at it."

The charge took a step towards the doorway and then hesitated. "We, you don't want to wait till the doctor gets here?"

Lindsey's sneer intensified. "*Am I speaking French?*"

The charge may have had authority over her unit, but the nursing supervisor ran the whole hospital during the night shift. Lindsey didn't let the power go to her head, but when it came to saving lives, she did not like to be questioned.

"Okay," the charge said and hurriedly left the room. "I'll – I'll be right back..."

• • • • • •

Ten minutes later, the patient was awake and mostly alert. Narcan was the ultimate opioid reversal. It blew her high within seconds and revived her just as quickly. Dr. Willis showed up a few minutes after the drug was administered. In typical doctor fashion, he took over the scene and attempted to take credit for saving the woman's life. But everyone on the floor knew who the real hero was. The charge nurse apologized after things calmed down, and the doctor left to attend to other matters.

"Sorry I questioned you," she told Lindsey.

"It's fine," the supervisor said. "I'm sorry I yelled at you."

No one was surprised that Lindsey had transformed from bulldog back to her petite, womanly form. Over the years, they'd seen the transformation plenty of times. Lindsey thought she'd get in trouble for *something* she'd done during the code, but she was close to getting her degree as a nurse practitioner. Once she accomplished that feat, she would be off to bigger and better things, and everyone at the hospital could kiss her skinny, white ass.

Two security guards escorted the patient's wobbly boyfriend off the premises. In typical fashion, they did not pursue criminal charges for his role in the overdose. Whether he still had drugs on him or not was not the hospital's concern – for now. If he tried to come back, it would be a different story.

Surprisingly, the patient was more upset about her boyfriend leaving than she was about having no heartbeat for four minutes and forty-five seconds. The supervisor was almost positive a lecture wouldn't help, but she couldn't return to her office without giving the woman a piece of her mind.

"You know you almost didn't make it, right?" She stood on the side of the bed with her arms folded. "Your heart *was not beating*. William was pumping on your chest for five minutes."

"When can he come back?" the woman asked.

Now that she was awake, Lindsey thought the patient looked more disgusting than before. Her voice was ghastly. Her teeth were in horrible shape.

"He's *not* coming back," she told her. "As long as you're admitted, he can't visit you. If he shows up, we're gonna call the police."

The supervisor nearly lost it when the patient's eyes welled with tears.

"What the hell is wrong with you?" Lindsey blurted. "Do you really want him back, or are you upset because you can't get high? Because if it's drugs you want, all you have to do is get out of bed and leave. No one's forcing you to stay here."

The brute honesty caused the patient's chest to hitch. Lindsey's expression softened. Compassion was one of the core values Jackson Memorial expected from all of its employees.

"Girl, you gotta get it together," Lindsey told the patient. "You're here because you came to the ER, and the doctor decided you needed to be admitted. If you want to leave and get high, you're gonna come back in worse shape than you're already in.

"Instead, why don't you take this time to try to help yourself? You're away from your boyfriend and all of the other negative influences. I know you've been shooting up for a long time. But that doesn't mean it has to be a permanent part of your life. You can get clean. We have plenty of social services that can help you. If you want, I'll talk to your doctor tomorrow and get you started on methadone."

The patient didn't respond, but she appeared to be listening.

"It's up to you," Lindsey said with a sigh. "I've seen a lot of addicts in my lifetime. Some can break out of the cycle. Some can't. Right now, you're in the best position to get the resources you need."

She reached and rubbed her shoulder comfortingly before stepping out of the room. The charge and the patient's nurse, William Harkins, followed her out.

"I'm glad you were here," he said when they made it to the hallway.

Lindsey stopped and regarded both of them. William was brawny and handsome; brown skin with light-brown eyes. He'd been growing a beard for the past six months. It was now full and perfectly trimmed. Lindsey didn't know what it was about a man with a full beard that made her panties wet, but William got her every time. Even now, she felt a little weak in the knees as she watched him.

Sometimes she wished she was a floor nurse again, so she could take a shot at guys like him. Nearly everyone at the hospital was screwing each other, but as a nursing supervisor, Lindsey had to be above reproach when it came to things like that. It was important that no employee at the hospital could ever say, *"Oh, Lindsey? That skinny chick? Yeah, I fucked her."*

"Y'all need to keep an eye on her," she told William and the charge. "I don't think she wants help, and things aren't gonna be pretty when she starts going through withdrawal. She may have more dope in her room right now."

Neither William nor the charge suggested going through the patient's belongings, because even in a place where your gown was open in the back, and a tech was always prepared to insert a catheter if you couldn't pee on your own, a patient's privacy was not taken for granted.

"If that boyfriend shows up again tonight, call security first, and then call me," Lindsey instructed. "Don't forget to pass this along to dayshift."

They both nodded.

"Keep an eye on her. Let me know if there's a change in her heart rate," the supervisor added.

"Do you want us to call you if she decides to leave AMA?" the charge nurse asked.

"Yeah, I guess so," Lindsey said with a shrug. "I guess I'll come and try to talk her out of it. If she starts getting restless, remind her that it's 40 degrees outside. Maybe that'll settle her crazy-ass down until morning."

William and his charge grinned at that. Once again Lindsey was struck by how handsome the male nurse was. William had strong forearms with a nice chest and flat stomach. He was short in stature, but that didn't detract from his good looks. What Lindsey wouldn't give to have some dark chocolate in her bed. She thought she might come back and check on him, after her career moved her past the hospital and her reputation there didn't matter anymore.

"I'm going back to my office," she told them. "I haven't had lunch yet. Let me know if you need anything else."

"Okay," the charge said. "We have some cookies in the break room. Janet made them. They're delicious. You should take a few with you."

"No, thank you," Lindsey said. "Trying to watch my weight this week."

"Skinny, little thing like you?" William said with a smile.

The supervisor's face heated. She didn't think he was flirting, but she sure liked the way he was smiling at her. Either way, she held her ground on the cookies.

"No, thank you. Y'all have a nice evening. Hopefully no more excitement..."

• • • • • •

The supervisor may have hoped for a calm hospital for the rest of the night, but for the nurses and techs on William's floor, drama was exactly what they needed to make it through their shift. With the overdose patient safe and not dead (for now), her story was the talk of the unit. Within minutes of the supervisor's departure, the nursing station became a cesspool of gossip and crude jokes. The employees didn't worry too much about anyone being offended by their banter, because at 2:30 am, most of the patients were sound asleep.

Midway through the discussion, William looked to Sherry, his favorite nurse at the hospital, and asked, "You wanna go get lunch?"

She checked the time. "It's a little late. I didn't know if you were still going."

Sherry was top-heavy; with boobs for days and not much going on in the booty department. She was short and a little chunky. She had full lips that she rarely coated with makeup. Today her braids were pulled back in a ponytail. Most people considered her attractive.

"I would've gone sooner, if not for that code," William told her.

"I wonder what they have down there," Sherry mused.

William stood and took a few steps in her direction. "Come on. You know you're hungry."

"Alright." She stood and reached overhead as she stretched her back. The move revealed a piercing above her belly button. William's eyes twinkled when he saw it.

"We're gonna take our lunch," Sherry told their charge nurse.

"Yes, I heard you," the woman said. "Have fun."

William and Sherry left the unit together, holding their comments until they reached the lobby. While they waited for an elevator, Sherry said, "*Have fun*? What's that supposed to mean?"

William stuffed his hands into his pockets and grinned at her. "Um, I think she wants us to have fun."

"Yeah, I wonder what kind of fun she's talking about."

"Why do you care?" he asked.

"You don't care if she knows?"

"I think it'd be weird if she *didn't* know," he replied. "We eat lunch together all the time, always hanging out on the floor. Everybody says you never see one of us without the other."

"So you're okay if she knows?"

"I'm pretty sure *everyone* on the floor knows," he replied. "So what?"

She shook her head but couldn't stop from smiling. "So, that's it?" she asked. "Just like that?"

The elevator dinged, and the doors slid open for them. William stepped on first and pulled her aboard. He leaned down and kissed the corner of her mouth before the doors fully closed.

"Just like that," he said.

CHAPTER TWO
FUNNY VALENTINE

My Valentine
Sweet divine
Come autumn rain or summer shine
He's mine
And HERS
But she's not here
That ring means nothing
When she's not here
My Valentine
Sweet divine
Come Halloween or Christmastime
Thick beard
Beautiful eyes
So smart and funny
Not too tall, but he's fine
No vacations for us
No bed and breakfast
No children sharing our bloodline
For that, he has HER
*But she's not **here***
*When he's **here***
He's all MINE

For lunch that evening, the hospital offered their notorious *mystery pasta*, which came with a roll and two sides. Sherry wanted a full meal, but not at the risk of having bubbly guts a few hours later. She and William made their way to the grill, where they opted for grilled cheese sandwiches and fries instead.

They ate together at a small table for two. The cafeteria was mostly empty at that hour. There were only a dozen or so employees looking for a meal or late night snack. William and Sherry could've taken their lunch back to the unit, as most nurses and techs did, but William enjoyed the private time with his friend. They were cordial to all of their peers who passed their table or stopped to say hi.

William was aware that because they both wore wedding rings, some of the cafeteria staff thought they were married. A few months ago, on one of the nights Sherry was off, the cashier had asked him, "Where's your wife today?" as he swiped his ID badge to pay for his dinner.

Rather than correct her, he simply said, "Oh, she's off tonight."

He considered that a little, white lie that was far less complicated than the look of confusion he would've received if he was honest with the woman.

"Y'all make a cute couple," the cashier had commented as he continued through the line.

William told her, "Thanks," and left the cafeteria with a warm, cozy feeling.

As he enjoyed his grilled cheese with his *work wife*, one of William's friends from security approached their table. The man said, "Hey," to Sherry and "What's up," to William.

"What's up?" William replied.

"Heard you had a little trouble on your floor tonight," the security guard said. William had known him for a few years. His name was Carlos, but he preferred to go by "Sarge," which was his rank in the department.

"Yeah, we did," William said.

Sarge wasn't one of the guards who came to their floor during the code, but William wasn't surprised the news had spread so quickly.

"I'll never understand why somebody wants to get high in the hospital," Sarge said. He stood over their table with his thumbs hooked on his belt.

"Being in the hospital doesn't take away your addictions," William told him. "You've seen all the smokers wheeling their IV poles outside."

"Almost every time an alcoholic leaves," Sherry added, "we'll find Coke bottles in the trash that smell like liquor."

"Did the boyfriend give y'all any trouble when they put him out?" William wondered.

"Naw," Sarge said, shaking his head. "I felt sorry for him, though. He was so high, he couldn't stand up. And he didn't head to any car in the parking lot; just took off walking towards Rosedale. It's a cold night to be on the streets."

"He could've spent the night in his girlfriend's room," William said, "if he wasn't so stupid."

"He'll figure it out," Sarge said.

William didn't share his optimism. Addicts usually didn't *figure it out* until someone found them in a vacant house or under a bridge and put a tag on their toe.

"Well, let me get going," Sarge said. "I'll let you two enjoy your *romantic dinner*," he added before walking away.

William was not surprised to find Sherry's mouth hanging open when his attention returned to her.

"What?" he said, laughing.

"*Romantic?*"

"It is Valentine's Day," William reminded her.

"Yeah, but why would he say that?"

"We've been together for two years. Why are you being so uptight about it tonight?"

"It feels like everyone's throwing it in our face all of a sudden." She grabbed a few fries from her tray and stuffed them in her mouth.

"So what?" William said.

"Is that your mantra now? *So what*?"

"Everybody's cool with it," William insisted. "No one's being malicious."

"Sarge sounds like he's got a little chip on his shoulder," Sherry noticed.

"That's 'cause he likes you," William revealed.

Sherry's face scrunched up. "What? *Eww.*"

William laughed. "*Eww*? Really?"

"How do you know he likes me?"

"He told me – one night when you weren't here."

"And what'd you say?"

"I told him to back off."

She grinned. "You told him that?"

William nodded. "Yeah. What do you think, I'd tell him to go for it?"

"But he knows you're married, right?"

"Yep. And he knows you are too."

"What'd he say when you told him to back off?"

"He said, 'Okay.' Said he wouldn't try anything. But, as you can see, he might be a little jelly."

She shook her head. "You guys are weird."

"I was hoping you wouldn't be mad at me for cock-blocking."

"*Eww*. No way."

"What's up with the *ewws*? People think Sarge is handsome."

"You know I'd never go out with a *Mexican*."

William's eyebrows rose. "Uh, no, I didn't know that. Guess I never asked. Racist much?"

She shook her head and went to work on her sandwich. "No. It's just a preference. I don't mind living next to them, I just wouldn't want one in my bed."

"I see..."

"*Blacks* are the ones I don't want to live next to."

William's eyes grew even bigger.

She laughed. "I'm just kidding."

"I don't know if you're kidding or not. You got a little Uncle Ruckus in you?"

"No. You know I don't."

"A confederate flag tattoo?" he joked.

"I think you would've seen it by now."

"Not necessarily. I've never seen you totally nude. Maybe you have one on your upper back."

"That's weird, huh?" she said.

"What, your confederate tattoo?"

"No, stupid. I was thinking about what you said. We've been together so many times, but never totally nude."

"That's because you won't meet me at a hotel. You always turn me down, so I don't bother asking anymore."

"I would love to, but you know my husband's always up my ass. The only time he trusts me is when I'm at work."

"Isn't that ironic..."

"What do you mean?"

"Nothing," William said. He knew Sherry's wit wasn't on par with his, but that was okay. If he wanted to have an intellectual conversation, his wife was better suited for that.

"Here," he said, reaching into the side pocket of his scrub pants. "Got you something."

Sherry's eyes lit up when he produced a ring box. "Really?"

He smiled and slid it across the table. Sherry's heart rattled as she opened the box. Her thrill was not diminished when she realized there were earrings inside, rather than a ring.

"*Oh my God*!" she exclaimed. "I didn't think you got me anything."

"Why wouldn't I? You're my number one Valentine."

"Number one?" she asked skeptically.

He looked into her eyes and nodded. "Yes, baby. Number one. I love you."

"I love you, too," she said, her eyes watering now. "Here..." She reached into her pocket and produced his gift.

"Sorry. It came in a box, but it was too big. I had to take it out."

William accepted the bottle of Dolce & Gabbana cologne. "Wow. This is nice." He pulled the cap off and brought it to his nose. He inhaled the fragrance and told her, "Mmm. I like it."

"You can take it home?" Sherry asked. "Your wife won't worry where it came from?"

"Nah. She knows I have plenty of girlfriends."

That remark got him a playful kick on the shin that actually hurt.

"*Ow*! I was just kidding."

"Sorry," she said. "I didn't mean to kick you that hard."

"That only means you *did* mean to kick me." William reached under the table to rub his leg.

Concerned now, Sherry asked, "Does it really hurt?"

"Why? You wanna make it up to me?"

She smiled. "It's Valentine's Day. I was gonna do that anyway."

He stared at her mouth. Her lips were full and beautiful. "You have a sexy mouth."

"You're only saying that because you want me to suck your dick," she said with a smirk.

"I do want that. But it's *Valentine's Day*. I want the whole shebang."

"Me too," she said. A delightful heat rolled down her chest and settled between her legs.

"Are you done eating?"

"I been done," she said, though half of their meal remained uneaten.

• • • • • •

The couple left the cafeteria with fifteen minutes left in their lunch break. This was plenty of time. They hopped on an elevator and headed first to the third floor. Once there, they made their way to the Avery Building and took the stairs down to the second floor. The surgical recovery unit was lightly staffed; with only two nurses on third shift. William greeted them as he headed to a linen cart near the nursing station.

"Good evening, ladies."

"Hey, you two," Patty said, barely looking away from her cellphone. "Anything good downstairs?"

"You haven't eaten yet?" William asked. "It's almost three."

"I brought a can of soup," the nurse replied. "I was thinking it would hold me, but I might need a little more to make it through the rest of this shift."

"*Mystery pasta*," Sherry told her.

She waited by the door, while William snatched a blanket and sheet from the linen cart. William also pulled a laundry bag from a huge roll they had on the cart.

The nurse grimaced. "I guess the soup will have to do."

On his way back to the front of the unit, William told her, "One of the nurses on our floor made cookies. We have a boatload. Want me to send you some through the tube station?"

The nurse's face lit up. "*Cookies*? Yeah, that'd be awesome."

"So much for your diet," her coworker said, smiling.

William shook his head. It seemed like every woman in the hospital was constantly dieting. "You should get the cookies in about fifteen minutes," he said as he and Sherry left the unit.

"Okay, thanks, doll," the first nurse told him.

With twelve minutes left, the beaming couple hopped on another elevator. This time they took it down to the basement, where they found a dozen presumably clean hospital beds in an open area. William tossed his linens on top of one of them. He released the brakes and got it rolling towards the Meredith Building.

"Is Natasha doing any better?" he asked, referring to Sherry's oldest child.

"I think so. But with it being Valentine's Day, I'm thinking she might fall back into depression."

"Young love," William said. "Why don't they realize that high school shit doesn't matter?"

"Did you realize it when you were in high school?"

He shook his head, grinning. "Nope."

In the Meredith Building, William pushed their bed to the *service*, rather than staff elevators. After working at the hospital for five years, he knew the service elevators were the only ones that could be stopped for a prolonged period of time without arousing suspicion.

As soon as the doors closed behind them, Sherry spread their sheets across the hospital bed. William pressed the button for the 6th floor, and they began to rise. Sherry waited until he stopped the elevator on the fourth floor before she kicked off her sneakers and pushed her scrubs and panties down her legs. She hopped onto the bed bottomless, while William disrobed from the waist down.

The temperature on the elevator was a little chilly, causing goose bumps to sprout on Sherry's legs. But at the intersection of her thighs, things were hot and already moist.

"Do you want me to take my shirt off, so you can see if I have that tattoo?" she joked as William joined her on the bed.

She was happy to see that he was fully erect. Despite his modest height, William was packing. The sight of his thick, dark meat made Sherry's walls clench in anticipation.

"You never take your top off," he pointed out.

"Yeah, but it's Valentines' Day," she said as she scooted up on the mattress. "I think it would be cool to get totally naked."

"Not here," he said. "I'm still holding out hope that I'll get you to a hotel one day."

Sherry lay with her legs straight, her upper body propped on her elbows. She expected William to straddle her chest, so she could please him orally. But he stopped at the foot of the bed and pulled her knees up. He stared down at her freshly-shaved love box before dropping down to tongue kiss it.

"*Mmmm.*" Sherry was pleasantly surprised by the move. She lay back on the bed, her breaths coming in sweet shudders.

The feel of William's beard on her thighs and genitals was titillating. His hot tongue was magical. He licked her clitoris into a state of pulsating arousal. When it hardened, he alternated between sucking it and thrusting his tongue as deeply into her slit as he could reach. He spread her labia with his fingers as he dined.

The combined sensations of his breath, his beard and every little taste bud on his tongue worked her into a sexual frenzy within seconds. The temperature in the elevator rose steadily as she gripped the sheets and squeezed her throat closed on every moan that tried to force its way up. The sound of William's sucking and slurping was music for her soul.

"*Ooh yeah,*" she whispered. Warm pulses of electricity flowed down her legs. She pushed off the mattress, thrusting herself into his mouth. "*Damn, baby, I'ma cum. I want you inside me.*"

William continued his foreplay, as if he hadn't heard her. After thirty more seconds, he felt the waves of ecstasy flooding her body. He backed away and told her, "Say please."

The sight of her juices glistening on his lips turned her on as much as his tongue action.

"*Please,*" she breathed. "Please, gimme that dick. *Pleeeease.*"

With only six minutes left in their lunch break, William crawled on top of her and took his rightful place between her legs. Sherry was sweating lightly. Her eyes were half-closed. Her mind swirled in a sea of guilty pleasure.

"You smell like pussy," she muttered when they were face to face.

He laughed and kissed her on the lips.

"Eww," she said playfully.

"It's yours," William said and deepened the kiss. His tongue slipped inside her mouth. Despite her protests, she latched onto it and sucked hungrily.

As they kissed, he slipped inside her without protection. She was literally leaking. William's dick was hot and hard. He was larger than her husband. Sherry gasped as he stretched her walls, sending fiery tingles of pleasure up her chest and down her thighs.

William hated condoms. He loved that their relationship was *monogamous*, so to speak. They both had to fulfill their marital duties at home, but other than that, neither of them had another lover.

Sherry was on birth control, so there was no fear of her getting pregnant. If by some happenstance she did find herself with child, they would assume it was her husband's seed and proceed accordingly.

William grunted quietly and pushed in deeper. As the speed of his hips increased, it became difficult to mute the sound of their lovemaking – but they had plenty of practice. William loved the way her kitty squeezed him sensually as her climax peaked. She may have been devoted to another man, but her body belonged to him.

"So soon?" he asked in a hushed voice.

"I – I've been saving it for you," she explained.

The fact that she saved her Valentine loving for him, rather than her husband, pleased William immensely. He tried to do the same, but his wife forced herself on him before he left for work last night. Thankfully his libido was strong, especially around Sherry. Despite being completely satisfied less than ten hours ago, she had him as hard as a rock.

"I love you," he whispered as a powerful shudder rolled down her frame. Her walls contracted even harder, making him feel like her body was milking him, lusting for his seed.

"I love you too," she managed through a wave of ecstasy that was heightened by the date, setting, and their glorious sinfulness. "I love you so much." The profound truth of her statement made her eyes water. *"Happy Valentine's Day, baby."*

● ● ● ● ● ●

In the basement of the Jackson Building, Rosa and Tamara sat behind two dozen monitors that provided a live feed from more than 100 security cameras in the hospital. There was some type of activity on nearly every screen, but at the moment, nothing was as interesting as two nurses who exited a service elevator on the fifth floor of the Meredith Building. The bearded fellow pushed a bed ahead of them, which was his custom.

Rosa used her mouse to switch to a different camera as the nurses followed their usual routine: The female yanked all of the sheets off the bed and stuffed them in a laundry bag. The male pushed their bed against the wall in a quiet hallway and used his foot to apply the brakes. They left the bed there and headed for a laundry chute at the end of the hallway. The female dropped the bag in the chute before the couple disappeared into a stairway.

Their stairwell wasn't monitored, so the girls in dispatch lost track of the couple for a moment. But there was no mystery as to where they were going. Rosa switched to another camera, just as the nurses exited the stairwell on the sixth floor. They were now back on their unit. This portion of Rosa and Tamara's entertainment was over.

"She not even walking funny," Tamara commented, her eyes glued to the screen. "He must not be packing."

"I wish they would put cameras on the *elevators*," Rosa complained, not for the first time.

"You said you were gonna put in a request," Tamara reminded her.

Rosa laughed. "Yeah right. And what am I gonna tell them we need it for?"

"Tell the truth," Tamara suggested. "Tell 'em you wanna watch some freaks get it on."

They both laughed. Their department wasn't very large. As was the case with most areas of the hospital, the number of employees needed to operate it dwindled with each shift. At 7 am, there were four dispatchers, a manager and a supervisor on duty. By second shift there were three dispatchers and a supervisor. By third shift, there were only two people.

"Do you think he gave her a ring?" Rosa asked.

They'd been tuned in to the *Sherry and William Show* since the nurses left their floor for lunch. They weren't allowed to watch movies on Netflix or spend much time on Facebook. But over the years, the ladies in dispatch found that the hospital employees offered the best entertainment. This was reality TV at its purest.

"She would've tried it on, if it was a ring," Tamara guessed. "What kind of ring could it have been anyway? An engagement ring?" she said with a laugh.

"Maybe a promise ring," Rosa joked.

"Yeah, *I promise to marry you whenever I leave my wife,*" Tamara said. "*In the meantime, we can keep fucking every time we work together.*"

Both ladies cracked up.

"I still can't believe how bold they are," Rosa commented.

"Maybe they're in open relationships," Tamara offered.

"If they were, they could fuck anywhere. They wouldn't have to wait until they got to work to do it."

"Wouldn't it be funny if–"

"Wait, there he is!" Rosa said, cutting her friend off.

Her attention moved to a monitor on the left. Tamara wheeled her chair in that direction, so she could get a better look.

"What's this, number *four*?" Rosa asked as they watched a PCT march stiffly down the hallway.

His footsteps quickened when he neared a restroom at the other end. He reached and grabbed the backside of his pants before ducking inside. The girls laughed hysterically.

"Girl, I think he shit hisself this time!" Tamara exclaimed.

"I think so too!" Rosa said. She reached for her notepad and drew another tally mark. "One more trip, and you owe me a dollar."

"He should sue the hospital for tearing his ass up like that," Tamara said with a shake of her head. "What time did he go to the cafeteria? Eleven?"

Rosa nodded. "Yup."

"That pasta got him shitting like that. *Damn shame.* He should just tell his charge he needs to go home sick."

"No, he doesn't! He needs to stay right here, so I can win my dollar."

"Of course *you'd* want that," Tamara said with a smirk.

Her attention moved to another monitor, this one in the cardiac tower. They'd been watching two PCT's have what appeared to be heated exchanges for the past couple of hours. It was rare for a fistfight to break out between employees, but when it came to Jackson Memorial, anything was possible.

Tamara's smile widened when the PCTs rounded a corner, where it was only the two of them. The taller girl put her hands on her hips, and the two started arguing again. The second PCT tried to blow her off with a few choice words and a wave of her hand. The first PCT started working her neck as she offered a rebuttal. The other tech took a step forward, rather than back away from the bigger girl.

"She finna get slapped," Rosa predicted.

Sweet! Tamara wished she had a bag of popcorn.

These were good times!

CHAPTER THREE
CENTRAL SUPPLY

Around the same time Rosa and Tamara watched a PCT rush to the bathroom with a panicked look in his eyes, Central Supply employee Jalen Creel stood at the nursing station on the surgery unit, waiting for the charge nurse to sign off on the wound vac he'd just brought her. While he waited, he chatted with a tech named Tina, who always seemed to have the latest hospital drama.

"They say she was blue in the face," Tina was telling him. "She was almost outta there. Everybody was running around, trying to figure out what was wrong with her, and it turned out her boyfriend had just shot her up with *heroin*."

Jalen's eyes widened. "No shit?"

"Yeah," Tina said. "He was high too. They was up in her room getting *faded*!" She laughed. "Almost cost that dumb bitch her life."

Jalen shook his head. "If you in the hospital, being a dopefiend don't get put on hold, till you get to feeling better. Getting high don't take no vacations. I got some dopefiends in my family. We caught my uncle smoking crack at my granny's funeral."

"For real?"

"Yep. Right in the church. He came out the bathroom with them big, bug eyes, trying to walk up to Granny's casket. We wanted to whoop his ass, but I told my brothers to chill. Black families ain't gotta fight *every* time we get together. We should make an exception at family reunions and funerals."

Tina laughed at that. "Boy, you so crazy."

She reached and touched his arm as she spoke. Jalen's immediate thought was, *Yo, she wants the D!* But he calmed himself. Tina was middle-aged and happily married, as far as he knew. Contrary to his horny thought process, every woman who touched him during a conversation did not want to have sex. Some women were just touchy feely – with no flirting intended.

However, when it came to girls at the hospital wanting the D, Jalen found that his first thought was correct the majority of the time. He stood six feet-one with a short, cropped hairstyle. The waves on the top of his head were prominent. Each day he made sure his scrubs were fresh and ironed. His skin tone was caramel. His face clean-shaven.

Growing up, Jalen was often teased about his *big lips*. But when he got to high school, the girls had nothing but good things to say about his sexy mouth. Jalen wasn't sure if he'd grown into his lips, or if word had spread about his expert kissing skills (both above and below the waist). Either way, he'd been swimming in poontang ever since. He was married now; a responsible family guy, for the most part. Most of the women at the hospital knew that, but it didn't stop some of them from trying their luck.

"Here you go," the floor's charge told him as she returned his iPad.

When he first started working at the hospital, Jalen had to collect signatures on paper when he delivered supplies. Everything was digital now.

"Thank you," he told the charge nurse. To Tina, he said, "Alright, I'll holler at you later."

"Bye, Jalen. I'm glad you're on my shift now."

Her comment gave him pause. *Does she want the D or not??* He kept his feet moving. Unlike most of the cute guys at the hospital, Jalen was not one of Jackson Memorial's infamous whores. He adored his wife and respected their union. They had one child, whom he loved more than anything in the world.

Before he made it off the unit, he was approached by another PCT. This was a friend he hadn't seen in several months.

"Yo, what's up, Jay."

Jalen turned to him with a smile. "What's up, Fred! Glad to see you still here."

"You know I ain't going nowhere," Fred said as the two men grasped hands and embraced briefly.

"What are you doing on this shift?" Fred asked. "Covering for somebody?"

"Nah, this is me now," Jalen said. He stopped near the elevators to continue the conversation.

"You working third shift? Nigga, *why*?"

Jalen laughed at that. After waking up before sunrise for the past four years, staying up all night was a big adjustment. "My daughter started school in the fall. We were having trouble getting someone to take her and pick her up, with me and my wife both working days. Somebody had to switch. Plus it's good to have one of us at home while she's at school – in case she gets sick and has to leave early or something."

"Damn, it sounds like you got stuck with *everything*," Fred noticed. "You drop her off, pick her up, and you gotta give up your sleep if the school calls in the middle of the day..."

Jalen shrugged. "I was the only one who could do it. My wife works at the bank."

"I feel you," Fred said. "Gotta do your daddy thing."

"Already," Jalen said, his chest growing warm with pride.

"So, you liking it?" Fred asked. "Night shift ain't for everybody. That's why you see some of these fools walking around here looking like zombies."

Jalen had experienced a few bouts of drowsiness that night. Coffee helped to counter them each time. But Fred's question ushered an unexpected yawn. It took a few moments before Jalen could respond.

"Damn. Excuse me."

Fred laughed. "See what I'm talking about?"

"It's all good," Jalen said. "I'll get used to it. Plus it ain't nothing but three nights a week."

"Is the work slower on third shift? That could make the time drag."

"It is," Jalen confirmed. "But I'm cool with that. So far the only problem I got is the dude I'm working with."

"Who, Milton?"

"Yeah," Jalen said, frowning.

"That dude's a weirdo."

"Yeah, for real," Jalen agreed. "Working with him ain't gon' be fun."

"But you already knew that, didn't you?" Fred asked.

"Not really," Jalen said. "I never spent much time around him. With my old shift, he'd be leaving when I got here. He'd give me report, and that's it. I knew he was quiet and OCD, but I'm starting to think this fool is straight *crazy*."

Fred laughed. "Everybody on night shift already thinks that. You late."

Jalen shook his head. "I'm about to go see what his crazy ass is up to now. I wouldn't be surprised if he got a bunch of candles lit around the department."

"*Candles*? Why would he do that?"

"I'm not saying he *would*," Jalen explained. "I'm saying he's so weird, nothing would surprise me."

"Damn. Good luck with that," Fred offered.

"Yeah, thanks."

When Jalen got back to his department, he did not find his coworker lighting candles. But Milton Defoor was doing something strange.

"You checking inventory *again*?" Jalen asked him.

His coworker was in the middle of a count and didn't respond right away. When Milton turned to face him, Jalen was struck with a strong sense that something behind the older man's beady eyes was not quite right.

Milton was short and thin. At 65, he was more than twice the age of his new work buddy. Milton was mostly bald up top. He was struggling to hold onto a comb over. His glasses were thick, with what Jalen thought was a 70's style frame. If not for the fact that they had to wear scrubs to work, Jalen was pretty sure Milton would come dressed in church slacks with a checkered shirt and sweater.

Overall he reminded Jalen of his high school history teacher – except Mr. Hudson had a quick wit and a sense of humor. As far as Jalen could tell, Milton hadn't laughed at a joke in years.

Milton's OCD made him remarkably efficient, which was a plus for their department. But he went about everything at a snail's pace. Even now, Jalen grew impatient while he waited for him to respond to a simple question.

"Things are not right," Milton told him. "People, always putting things in the wrong spot. Nobody cares where things go anymore."

Jalen shook his head. He felt sorry for the old fart. Milton had to be close to retirement. Most folks at the hospital would want to take it easy at his age, but he continued to stress himself over insignificant matters.

"Man, you need to take it easy," Jalen said with a grin. "It ain't that serious."

"*It is*," Milton quipped.

Jalen didn't know if he meant to snap at him, but that's the way he received it.

"No one cares about doing things right anymore," the older man said. "Shortcuts... Bad math... Putting things anywhere they want." He shook his head in frustration. "Why work here, if you don't want to do the job *right*?"

"*Me*?" Jalen said. "I haven't even done inventory."

"No, not you," Milton said with a frown. "Well, *maybe* you. I don't know. I just wish they would leave it alone, and let me take care of it."

"Take care of what, man?"

"This, this..." Milton waved an arm across the whole department, which was a virtual warehouse of medical supplies. "Just – never mind," he said. "Never mind."

"*Okay*..." Hoping to salvage some sort of friendly relationship, Jalen asked him, "Hey, did you hear we had a patient shooting up heroin tonight? She OD'd, almost died. That's what that code was."

Milton shook his head, his eyebrows bunched together. "That's gotta be a HIPAA violation; you telling me that."

"Not unless I tell you her name," Jalen said defensively. "I don't even know her name."

"I don't wanna know about that," Milton said. "That's one of *many* problems at this hospital: Too many gossips."

Jeez, Jalen thought. This guy couldn't be for real. "I guess I'll, um..." He didn't have anything to do at the moment, but he was done attempting to be cordial with the ultimate company man. "I'll be back," he said vaguely.

Milton didn't respond before turning back to his inventory.

● ● ● ● ● ●

Fifteen minutes before the night shift employees called it quits at 6:30 am, patient transport employee Carl Redding arrived early for his morning shift. Tall, dark and confident, Carl walked past the ladies at the registration desks in the Jackson Building with a backpack slung over his shoulder.

"Hey, Carl," one of the women called to him.

"How you doing today, Miss Beverly?" he replied. His smile was broad and genuine.

"So far so good," the secretary told him. "Only been here ten minutes, though."

"I'm sure you'll have a great day," Carl said. "God already allowed us to wake up this morning. That's the biggest blessing of all."

"You sho' right," the woman told him. "Thanks, Carl. You always got a good word."

"Morning, Carl," another one of the receptionists said as he made his way down the corridor.

"Hey, Flora. How you doing?"

"Wish I was still at home. But, you know, gotta pay the bills."

"I feel you on that."

"Happy Valentine's Day," she exclaimed. "I was thinking about making enchiladas tonight. You want me to bring you some tomorrow?"

He paused at her desk. "Mmm. You know I can't turn down your good cooking."

Flora grinned and blushed visibly. She was in her late forties and a little overweight. She wouldn't consider herself *hopelessly single*, but her current man-drought was nearing the two year mark. Carl was a couple of decades younger. He was over six feet with beautiful dark skin. His head and beard were shaved low. Flora knew he had a gaggle of admires at the hospital, but he never made her feel like she didn't have a chance at all. Until there was a ring on his finger, he was fair game, as far as she was concerned.

"Okay, I'll bring some – just for you," she said. "You want a whole platter or just enough for lunch?"

"Man, I don't know what I'd do with a whole platter," he said. "I live by myself. I'm afraid it would go to waste. I'll take enough for lunch, though. I won't bring anything else. I'm already looking forward to it."

"Okay," Flora beamed. "I'll make sure to bring it."

"And I'll be sure to come pick it up," Carl said before continuing on his way.

Rather than head to his department to clock-in, he went to the Avery Building and took the stairs down to the basement. On his way to the bathroom, he encountered a housekeeper named Louis.

"Hey, what's up," Carl told him. "You got something for me?"

"Yeah. I'll get it to you in a few minutes," Louis told him. The men shook hands.

"Alright. Send me a text message," Carl told him. "You gon' take it out by the dumpsters?"

Louis nodded. "Wherever you need it to be."

"Bet," Carl said. "Be careful."

"I am," his friend said and headed in the opposite direction.

When he got to the bathroom, Carl was greeted by another employee. He wasn't sure how long Bobby had been waiting there, but the boy appeared anxious. Carl looked him in the eyes as they gripped hands.

"What's up with you?" Carl asked. He noticed Bobby had his backpack with him. Even better, his bag appeared to be full.

"Where you been?" Bobby asked. "You said six-fifteen."

Carl smiled rather than reveal the irritation his question caused. "My bad, baby. I got here as soon as I could."

Bobby grimaced inwardly. He did not like to be called *"baby"* by another man. Fortunately Carl was the only one who did it on a regular basis. Bobby knew his friend was from New Orleans, and the term was part of his speech pattern. Carl didn't mean any harm by it, and he certainly wasn't gay. He even pronounced it differently than the folks in Texas. But still. Bobby only liked it when his girlfriend called him that – or his mother.

"You got something for me?" Carl asked.

"Yeah," Bobby said and frowned. He moved to place his backpack on the bathroom counter. Carl reached to stop him.

"Yo, what the hell you doing."

"Ain't nobody else in here," Bobby complained.

"Maybe not *this second*," Carl said, heading to one of the stalls. "But shit could change in a heartbeat."

"It stink in there," Bobby said as he reluctantly followed him to the adjacent stall.

"It's only gon' take a minute," Carl said. "Quit whining."

Inside his stall, Carl saw that Bobby's complaint was valid. The last person to use his toilet didn't flush when they were done. Out of all the disgusting things men did in hospital bathrooms (this often included jacking off, brushing their teeth or taking a monkey bath in the sink), Carl thought failing to flush was the worst. But unlike his immature co-worker, he knew the business they were conducting was more important than allowing himself to get grossed out over incidentals.

He flushed the toilet before sitting fully clothed on the commode. In the stall next to him, he heard Bobby unzip his backpack and retrieve his offering. He placed a sturdy case on the floor and slid it to Carl's stall. Carl's smile widened when he got his hands on it. The case wasn't very large; about the size one would expect for a cordless drill. But the contents were much more valuable. Carl popped it open on his lap.

"You think I'd tell you I had it if I didn't?" Bobby asked him.

"If you'd buy something without checking it out first, you'd make one hell of a dope man," Carl joked. "Matter of fact, let me know when you get started. I got a whole kilo of talcum powder waiting on your crazy ass."

"Yeah, whatever," Bobby said. "Say, man, we need to talk."

"'Bout what?"

Before Bobby could say, another visitor entered the bathroom. Carl shook his head knowingly. A few moments ago, Bobby wanted to show off his goods at the sink. If Carl had been as anxious as him, they'd both be standing there looking stupid; caught red handed. He closed the case and slid it into his backpack. He leaned forward but couldn't see the new arrival through the small gap between the stall doors.

Next to him, Bobby flushed the toilet and rose to his feet. A second later Carl heard him open his stall and step out.

"Morning, young man."

The visitor sounded old and white. Carl suspected it was a patient, rather than a hospital employee.

"What's up," Bobby said before heading to the sink to wash his hands.

Carl rolled his eyes. Damn kids today didn't have any respect. He was only five years older than Bobby, but he'd been raised differently. He waited until his friend left the bathroom before he flushed his toilet and pretended to wipe his ass and pull up his pants. When he left the stall, Carl saw an older man at one of the urinals.

"Good morning," the man said, looking over his shoulder.

"Morning, sir," Carl told him. "You having a good day so far?"

"My wife's sick again," the visitor replied. "They just brought her down here for a CT."

"Oh, I'm sorry to hear that," Carl said as he washed his hands. "But you can rest assured she's in the best place to get help. The doctors and nurses here are miracle workers. I've seen it with my own eyes."

"Thank you," the older man said. "I wish we didn't have to come, but that makes me feel better."

"No problem," Carl replied. "You have a nice day – you and your wife. What's her name? I'll say a prayer for her today."

Startled, the man said, "Betty. Her name's Betty."

Carl nodded. "Got it. Tell Betty I said get well soon."

"I – well, what's your name?" the man asked.

"I'm Carl," he said with a smile.

"It's very nice to meet you, Carl."

"You too," he said before drying his hands and leaving the restroom.

Outside the door, he found Bobby waiting for him. The boy approached him, still frowning.

"Yo, where my money, man?"

Carl wanted to slap the shit out of him for speaking about their business openly, but his smile remained. The only indication of his annoyance was a slight twitch in the corner of his mouth.

"You know I'm not handing you no money in front of these cameras," he said. They got moving again, this time towards the Meredith Building.

"Man, you act like somebody's watching us *all the time*," Bobby complained. "I heard don't nobody look at those cameras unless something happens; they'll go back and check the film."

"That's fine," Carl said. "Feel free to believe whatever you want. But if you do something stupid on camera, and you get hemmed up for it, don't mention my name, 'cause I already told you."

"You ain't gotta be this damned careful."

"You think I'ma *stop* being careful, just 'cause your silly ass told me to?" Carl said, grinning. "You must be dumber than you look."

Bobby bristled at the comment but didn't let on that he was offended. His appearance had been a topic of conversation as of late, starting with one of the charge nurses in the ER and making its way to his supervisor. The ER charge complained that his scrubs were too wrinkled on some days, and he didn't always comb his high top hairstyle. Bobby didn't appreciate a *white woman* criticizing his 'fro. He couldn't believe his black supervisor didn't come to his defense. He tried to tell her the kinky look is what he was going for.

"I think your hair looks *okay*," Teresa, his supervisor, had said. "But if you wanna stay in the ER, you gotta do something with that head."

Bobby almost told her to go ahead and take him out of the ER. *Fuck 'em.* But he and Carl's hustle depended on him keeping that assignment. And, to be honest, working in the ER was a coveted role in his department. His peers had to move patients throughout the hospital, oftentimes from building to building.

But Bobby was assigned strictly to the ER zone. He only had to transport patients to nearby procedures and then back to their ER room. The workload could be sinfully light on third shift, depending on how many people showed up with an emergency.

When they reached the elevators in the Meredith Building, he told Carl, "Man, we gotta talk."

"About what?" Carl reached to press the UP button. They were surprised when it dinged right away.

"About this work," Bobby said. "I been having..."

The elevator doors opened, and a woman in street clothes stepped off. She looked around in confusion.

"Is this the ground floor?"

"Naw," Bobby told her. "This the basement."

"You just missed it by one," Carl said. "A lot of people make that mistake. They push the button on the bottom, thinking it'll take them to street level."

"Oh." The woman backed up to make room for them.

Carl pressed the **G** button when they were inside.

"This place is so big," the woman said. "I feel like I walked a mile already, just trying to get out of here."

"I know what you mean," Carl said. "It took me weeks to learn where everything is – and I *still* get turned around sometimes." He looked at the elevator buttons and said, "Always look for the button with the *star* next to it. That'll be the ground floor."

"Really?"

"Yeah. I think it's like that in all of our elevators."

He and the woman exchanged smiles as the elevator ascended one floor. When the doors opened again, Carl asked her, "Does this floor look familiar? Are you headed to the garage?"

Behind them Bobby sighed audibly. He had no doubt Carl would walk her all the way to her car, if the woman expressed the slightest bit of doubt.

"Yep, I'm good now," the visitor said, her eyes brightening. "Thank you very much."

"No problem," Carl replied. "You have a nice day."

"You too!"

The woman headed for the exit, while Carl and Bobby walked towards their department.

"Anyway," Bobby said, "I think I'ma need to–"

"Hold that thought," Carl said when they reached Patient Transport. "Let me clock in right quick. We can talk when we leave. Don't you need to clock out?"

Bobby did, but he did not appreciate being put off repeatedly. He couldn't hide his frustration. Carl continued to smile, as if he didn't notice.

Once inside their department, the two men separated. Bobby went straight to the nearest computer to clock out. Carl headed for a different work station. As expected, his stroll through the department took several minutes. If there was someone there Carl didn't say *Good morning* to, Bobby couldn't tell. It was shift change, so there were twice as many employees hanging around than normal. By the time Carl returned to his friend, there was no doubt the younger man was pissed. Carl remained jovial.

"What's the matter? You look like you finna punch somebody in the mouth."

"I feel like I want to," Bobby grumbled.

Bet it won't be me, Carl thought. Most of their co-workers would purchase the wolf tickets Bobby was selling, but Carl had no doubt he would mop the floor with his nappy-headed ass. Not at the hospital, though. He'd be smart enough to catch him somewhere off property.

"You ready to go?" Carl asked him.

"I *been* ready."

"Well come on, then." Carl threw his backpack over his shoulder. "Let's be out."

Before they left the room, Carl reached into his pocket and produced a fold of bills. He palmed it and delivered it to Bobby with a handshake. There were no cameras inside their department, but he still told him, "Don't count it. Just put it in your pocket."

Despite his insolence, Bobby was obedient to that command. He even cracked a smile for the first time.

"Thanks, man."

● ● ● ● ● ●

Outside the weather was a chilly 54 degrees. The sun was on the rise, but it wasn't expected to add much heat that day. Carl and Bobby were dressed identically in black scrubs and sneakers. Their black jackets were provided by the department, so even they were the same. Carl planned to empty his backpack in his car before returning to work, but he accompanied Bobby to his parking spot first.

"Now, what is it you dying to tell me?" he asked as they walked.

With a pocket full of money, Bobby was a lot more reasonable than he was ten minutes ago. "I'm trying to tell you I'm out," he said.

"You out? What you mean? You quitting?"

"I'm not quitting my job, but I think I need to lay low for awhile. I can't keep getting stuff for you."

"Oh, shit. Nah, baby. That ain't no good," Carl said, shaking his head. "What's the problem? Why you wanna do that?"

"I almost got caught this morning," Bobby informed him. "It's been too risky. Every day I feel like I got more and more eyes on me."

"But you got it though, and you didn't get caught."

"I know, but–"

"It ain't easy to get stuff out the ER," Carl told him. "Don't you know how good you got it? Just being in that zone is nice. Everybody in transport want your spot. On top of that you got this little side thing going that's putting extra money in your pocket. This set up is the best you ever gon' have."

"This set up won't matter if I get caught. Then we'll *both* be stuck out."

"I never said there wasn't no risks," Carl said. "I never told you that. That's what you get compensated for. Don't I make it worth your while?"

It was hard to deny that after just getting paid, but Bobby shook his head. "I don't know if the money's worth it."

"Oh yeah? How you figure that. You make eight-fifty an hour, work eight-hour shifts. That's $68 a day – *before* taxes, insurance and your 401K. After all that, what you looking at, two-eighty, two-ninety a week?"

Bobby wasn't sure how he added it up so quickly. He didn't have time to respond before Carl continued speaking.

"You just made $300 for something that took you five minutes to do. You get me one of those machines every day this week, and that's more than you make in a whole month. How that ain't worth it?"

"I can't get one every day," Bobby said. "You think they leave 'em laying around like that?"

"Of course they don't," Carl said. "I was just using that as an example. I only need one or two more of those cases. In the meantime, you can keep picking up the easy shit; otoscopes, blood pressure machines, ECG recorders..."

Not only was there nothing *easy* about any of those thefts, but Carl would only pay a fraction of what Bobby got for the portable ultrasound he lifted this morning. He had only been working for Carl for a few months. That was enough time to learn that the bigger paydays came from expensive electronics.

"Just get me *one more* ultrasound, and we can go back to the other stuff," Carl implored. "I need that. Got people waiting on it."

Bobby didn't bother asking who Carl's customers were. The last time he inquired, he got a lecture about *need-to-know* and *plausible deniability*, whatever that meant.

"I'll try," Bobby said.

"That's what I'm talking about, baby. I got faith in you."

"Yeah, whatever."

"What you gon' do about that hair?" Carl asked before he broke away and headed for his own vehicle.

Bobby stopped and asked him, "What you talking about?"

"Them naps," Carl said. "We ain't gon' have to worry about whether you can get the equipment or not, if you get booted out the ER."

Bobby knew the rumor mill at the hospital was extensive, but he was surprised the complaint had made it to Carl.

"You need to be a little more friendly too," Carl said. "You gotta make people feel like you care about your job and about them."

Bobby's frown was back in full force. "What, you my mentor now?"

"If that's what you need me to be," Carl said. "I'll do whatever it takes to keep you in your position, especially when it's something as easy as taking a comb to them naps." He watched him for a moment before asking, "Why you got a chip on your shoulder, lil' bro?"

At the moment, Bobby had a few grievances. He only mentioned the main one: "I told you; I almost got caught this morning."

"But you *didn't*, and you got paid. If I sit here complaining about all the shit that almost happened to me, we'd be here for days. I almost drowned in Katrina. I almost got shot a dozen times. I almost slipped in the shower and broke my neck this morning. But I *didn't*. I'm here making money, and so are you. Count your blessings, nigga."

Bobby didn't agree with Carl on a lot of issues, but he agreed with the wisdom in that statement. He had a lot to be grateful for. He couldn't stop from cracking a smile.

"That's the spirit!" Carl said and gave him a slap on the back. "Don't forget to straighten out them naps before you get to work tonight!"

Bobby's smile dropped just as quickly. Carl didn't notice. He had already turned and walked away.

CHAPTER FOUR
ENTREPRENIGGA

By lunchtime Carl was in full work and hustle mode. His job required him to transport patients, either by wheelchair, stretcher or bed, to various areas in the hospital. His hustle required the same amount of walking – with far better pay and less effort. He was well known and popular throughout the hospital, no matter what unit he visited. His accomplices, or *employees*, as he preferred to call them, perked up each time they saw him. Carl constantly had to remind them that unless he texted them first, he wasn't on their floor for business.

"Oh, I just wanted to let you know I been busy," a PCT named Matt said after Carl dropped off a patient on the urology unit.

"What you got for me?" Carl asked.

Matt trailed behind as Carl pushed an empty stretcher to the staff elevators.

"Twenty drainage bags, ten bedpans..."

"*Twenty*? How you pull that off?"

"Got the whole box," he told him. "Snatched it a couple of days ago."

"They not looking for it yet?"

"They already did. The dayshift charge doesn't remember where she put it when it got delivered. They already got some more from central supply."

"You say they still in the box?"

"No. I had to ditch the box. I got 'em in my bag; in my locker."

"Bet," Carl said. "What about that foley tray I been asking you about? You haven't seen none of those?"

"I'm trying, but they're hard."

"Don't stress yourself, baby. If you can get it, that's cool. If not, no biggie."

"Are you gonna get these bags today?"

"Yeah. I'll text you when I go to lunch. I need some more gloves too; medium and large."

"Damn, you always need gloves."

"Can you get 'em?"

"How many boxes?"

"As many as you feel comfortable with."

"Alright, I gotcha."

When he clocked out for lunch, Carl grabbed his backpack and began making his rounds. He picked up the smaller items first.

From surgery, a tech named Marsha hooked him up with gauze, forceps, scalpels and an assortment of syringes. Carl thought he could make $150 from the supplies, so he gave her 30 bucks.

"Thank you!" she said. "Same time next week?"

He nodded. "Yes, ma'am."

"I told you to stop calling me *ma'am*," she replied.

The tech was in her late sixties. Carl didn't think he could stop calling her that, even if he tried. He told her, "I'm sorry, Miss Marsha. I keep forgetting."

On the ortho floor, a tech named Caleb surprised him with half a dozen leg braces. He managed to get the high-tech ones; with metal hinges and straps. Carl knew he could get $25 apiece for them, so he gave the tech $50.

"Can you get some more?" he asked him.

Caleb shook his head. "No. Not for a while at least. They haven't realized these are missing. When they do, the manager's gonna be pissed."

"What about the neck collars?" Carl asked. "I need those *Vista's*; the ones with the space for a tracheotomy."

"They're hard to get out of here, because I can't fold them or nothing."

"If you can swing it, I'll give you twenty bucks apiece." The last time Carl got his hands on one of those collars, he was surprised to find it retailed for $70.

"I'll try," Caleb said. "What about gloves? You need some more of those?"

"Always," Carl said. "Medium and large. I'll holler at you later."

They gripped hands before Carl continued on his way.

By then his backpack was full. He took it to his car and drove off property. He went to the 7-11 around the corner and emptied the contents in the trunk. He returned to the hospital and made a few more pickups, until his bag was full again. He took it to the hospital's fitness center, where he had a second locker. He traded the full backpack for an identical one that was empty. He visited several more of his employees and then dropped the backpack off in his other locker in Patient Transport.

In less than 45 minutes, Carl had picked up $1,500 worth of medical equipment and paid $300 for it. He still had four employees whose goods wouldn't fit in his backpack. He planned to meet them after work and collect the supplies off property. Counting the portable ultrasound he got from Bobby that morning, he was poised to make $3,000 for one day's work.

● ● ● ● ● ●

Growing up, Carl never fancied himself an entrepreneur. His mother was poor, his father was in prison, and his brothers sold crack cocaine. When the hurricane ravished their New Orleans neighborhood, Carl was hopeful about the new start he'd get in Texas. He landed a job at Jackson Memorial and planned to break away from the curse of poverty and incarceration that had plagued his family. At the hospital, anyone could come into an entry-level position and work their way all the way up. Even if you wanted to be a *doctor*, the hospital would pay for your education.

The positive vibes began to fade when Carl's uncle, another New Orleans native, let his diabetes get the best of him. The surgeons took Uncle Curley's toes and then his foot and finally amputated his leg above the knee. Curley still weighed over 300 pounds without the limb, so mobility became a problem. To add insult to injury, Uncle Curley's home was burglarized one night, while he was fast asleep. The thieves didn't find much of value, which may have been the reason they decided to make off with his wheelchair – either that, or they used it to haul their stolen items. Carl visited his uncle a few days after the burglary and was presented with an indecent proposal.

"Say, don't you still work at the hospital?"

"Yeah, Unc. You know I do," Carl had told him. "What's up? Is it something you need me to get for you?"

"Yeah," Uncle Curley said, his eyes tinged with glaucoma and despair. "I needs me a wheelchair."

"A *wheelchair*? What, what you mean, Unc? Don't you got insurance for that?"

"They giving me a hard time, 'cause I didn't report the break-in. I guess they think I stole it. I don't know why they think I want *two* wheelchairs, like I'm selling them bitches or something. But they got my order wrapped up in a bunch of fucking red tape. I needs me a wheelchair *now*. I can't even get to the corner store to get my squares. Got me stuck in the house, like I'm on house arrest again."

"Maybe that ain't such a bad thing, Unc. You don't need to be smoking anyway," Carl joked.

"I ain't got too many years left," Curley said seriously. "If I wanna drink whiskey and smoke squares with the time I got, can't no doctor or insurance company tell me I can't. Just wait till your days are short, and The Man try to treat you like a child. You'll see what I'm talking about."

Carl didn't like the idea of his uncle considering his own mortality. It wasn't something he wanted to think about either. He told him, "I'll see what I can do," and put the problem on the back burner until he returned to work.

At the hospital, he found that not only were wheelchairs plentiful, but as a patient transporter, he had unlimited access to them. He began mapping out a plan while rolling a new mother out to the dismissal area. He noticed his fellow transporters were a lazy bunch. Rather than return the wheelchairs to the department after use, they left them everywhere; by the valet, the parking garages and sidewalks.

Carl spent the rest of his shift studying the security cameras on the outside of the Jackson Building. He didn't find any blind spots there, but the Meredith Building didn't have a camera mounted near the Subway restaurant that was attached to it. Carl's heart revved like a motorboat when he pushed a wheelchair past the monitored zone. His pulse began to race again when he finished his shift and went to check on it. The wheelchair was still there.

A million things could've gone wrong, but growing up with hustlers had taught Carl a very important rule: *If you don't look like you're doing something wrong, chances are no one will pay you any attention.* With that in mind, he went to the parking garage, got his car, and pulled to the side of the road next to the wheelchair. He popped the trunk, collapsed the wheelchair and placed it inside. When he drove away, no security personnel followed him. No one at work questioned him about it the next day.

Carl's thievery may have ended there, but his uncle gave him interesting news a few weeks later.

"Say, Carl, the dude at the store wanna know if you can get another wheelchair."

"What?" His eyebrows bunched together in anger. "You told somebody about that shit?"

"Watch your mouth, youngin'. Yeah I told somebody, but only 'cause I see a way to put some money in your pocket. Half the shit in that A-rab's store come off the streets. He's straight."

"He sell wheelchairs outta that store?"

"Naw," Curley said with a chuckle. "I don't know what the hell he need it for. I don't need to know. Just thought I'd pass it on to you. Could turn out to be something worthwhile."

Against better judgment, Carl met with the store owner prior to embarking on another theft. Sure enough, the man said he'd pay $100 for a wheelchair.

"If you can get some other medical stuff, I'll buy that too," he had said.

"What kind of stuff?" Carl wanted to know.

"Whatever; gloves, gauze, syringes."

"What you'll pay for that stuff?"

"Bring it, and I'll make you an offer."

Intrigued, Carl got a second wheelchair and five boxes of latex gloves for the store owner, who he later came to know as Rafal. The compensation was fair. Carl carried out a few more thefts over the next month before a simple Google search told him how much his stolen items were worth. Not surprisingly, Rafal was only paying 20-25% of the items' value. It took another month for Carl to put together a plan to bypass Rafal and eventually become Rafal himself. His uncle helped him with a lot of the logistics.

"If that A-rab can do it, nigga, yo black ass can do it too!" Curley told him more than once.

Four years later, Carl's enterprise was very profitable. He wasn't foolish enough to think the scheme could go on forever. He saved as much of his ill-gotten gains as possible, knowing he might have to shut down at any moment.

Before his death, Uncle Curley marveled at how far Carl had come since stealing his first wheelchair. "Look at you, boy! You done come up! You a *entrepreneur!*"

"Nah, Unc," he said. "Entrepreneurs don't come up like this. I'm more of a *entreprenigga.*"

Curley laughed and said, "Shit, sometimes, that's the best a nigga can hope for. I'm proud of you, nephew."

"Thanks. But I don't know how long I'ma be able to keep it going."

"It won't be you that mess it up," Curley had warned. "It'll be a hating-ass nigga. Watch out for him, and you'll be fine."

Carl nodded. "I will, Unc. Don't worry."

● ● ● ● ● ●

Towards the end of his shift, Carl transported a patient from oncology to the Continued Care Unit on the 4th floor of the Avery Building. Neither he nor the patient acknowledged it, but the move was not a good sign. Continued Care was for patients who were on their way out: There was no cure for what they had, and the family had chosen hospice at the hospital, rather than let their beloved die at home.

The benefits to being on that floor were around-the-clock care and morphine out the wazoo. A downside was watching your neighbors get carted off by a mortician's crew. Even if they closed your door, and you didn't see it happen, you'd know the room across from you, which had been occupied for months, was suddenly vacant and fresh-smelling. And you'd know why.

After unloading his patient and notifying the charge of his arrival, Carl rolled his empty wheelchair towards the staff elevators at the end of the unit. He didn't make it far before one of his favorite PCTs approached him with a big smile and a hug.

"Hey, buddy!"

Carl had always considered Danielle an oddity at the hospital because of her flagrant hoodrat mentality. He knew plenty of women like her in New Orleans. It was rare for them to pull it together long enough to establish and maintain employment. Passing a drug test was usually the requirement that kept them at bay.

But Danielle had been working at Jackson Memorial for over three months. She was tatted-up, weaved-up and reeking of Newports after every break, but she hadn't done anything horrible enough to get fired. She had officially made it past her probation period.

Even better, Danielle had to be one of the finest women at the hospital. She had dark skin, thick thighs and a *glorious* ass. Carl fought to keep his hands to himself as she squished her swollen breasts against him.

"Damn," he muttered. "Shit, happy Valentine's Day."

"*Happy Valentines' Day*!" she repeated. She backed away and licked her lips, grinning. "What'd you get me?"

"Same thing I got you last year."

"Whatever! I didn't even know you last year. You didn't get me nothing!"

"This year I got you a brand new one!"

"I swear y'all niggas ain't shit," she replied with a shake of her head.

"Whatever, girl. You got a man. Ain't that what you always telling me? You shot me down so many times, I done stopped trying to get with you."

"You didn't wanna be with me anyway," she said. "You just wanted to smash."

"True," Carl said. There was no point in lying about it. "Still do."

"Oooh! I swear y'all ain't shit!" She laughed.

Carl didn't know if she was referring to the men at Jackson Memorial or the ones she knew outside of work, but he figured they all treated her the same. Nearly every single man at the hospital wanted a piece of her – the black ones for sure, but not brothers exclusively. Whenever Carl ran into Danielle outside of her floor, she had a different guy trailing behind.

"Did you hear some lady died of an overdose last night?" she asked him.

Carl laughed. "Yeah, I heard about the OD – but she didn't die, though. Who told you that?"

"One of my friends," she said. "I should've known *you* heard about it already. You always in everybody's business."

"*Me*? You the one trying to spread a rumor that ain't even true! At least I got my facts right, baby."

Danielle propped a hand on her hip. "Well, what happened then?"

Carl told her what he knew about the drug addict and her wayward boyfriend.

Danielle laughed. "Did he try to come back?"

"I don't know. They told him they'd call the police if he did."

"Man, these dopefiends up here outta control!"

"They outta control everywhere."

"You right about that," she agreed. And then she lowered her voice and said, "I got something for you."

"Oh yeah, what you got for me?" Carl asked, his tone now conspiratorial as well.

"Boy, stop looking at me like that," she said, slapping his arm. "It ain't what you think."

"I bet it *is* what I think," he commented. "You ain't giving up no ass, so it could only be one other thing."

"I got you some *gloves*," she said, beaming as if she'd done something extraordinary.

When it came to Carl's operation, latex gloves were always needed, but their value was one of the lowest. A box of 100 retailed for $7.50, so Carl was only willing to pay three bucks for them, which he considered generous. That worked out well for those who didn't want to take bigger risks. As an entreprenigga, Carl needed both big and smalltime hustlers on his payroll.

"I'll come get 'em before I clock out," he told her. "How many you got?"

She surprised him by saying, "*A whole case.*"

"No shit? How you gon' get 'em out of here?"

"You just said you'd come get 'em."

"A'ight. I'll bring one of those transport wheelchairs..."

The transport wheelchairs were big and bulky, made of plastic. Patients couldn't drive them independently; they had to be pushed from behind. Carl liked them because they were made for dismissals, so they had plenty of cargo space. Most of it was concealed by whoever was pushing it.

"I'll text you before I head back up here," he said and got his wheelchair moving again. Danielle followed him to the elevator.

Before they got there, their attention was drawn to one of the patients' rooms. The door flew open, and a PCT, known affectionately as *Miss Daisy*, rushed out. Her cheeks were rose-colored. Her eyes, normally no larger than slits, were open wide. Her chest rose and fell as she struggled to catch her breath.

"Dang, Miss Daisy. What's wrong with you?" Danielle asked, her face lit with amusement.

The tech looked around fretfully, as if she didn't know if she should say. Carl looked on with obvious interest. Miss Daisy was of Asian descent, he wasn't sure which country. She was middle-aged, with dark, shoulder-length hair. Carl didn't know her personally, but he knew she was soft-spoken and modest. She never wore makeup or behaved in a manner that would make her stand out in a crowd. The look on her face now was the most emotion he'd ever seen her exhibit.

Miss Daisy looked back at the patient's room before approaching Carl and Danielle. He looked over her shoulder, wondering who the hell was in there and what had happened.

"Mr. Frierson," she said, her voice hushed, "he a nasty man! *So nasty!*"

"*Whaa?*"

Danielle's eyes widened. She was all for this type of drama. Carl was too. It was hard to keep a straight face while he watched Miss Daisy. Her thick accent, coupled with her surprised, indignant expression was comical.

"What he do?" Danielle asked. The fresh gossip had her drooling.

"He..." Miss Daisy looked around again. Her eyes locked on Carl, and the crimson in her cheeks grew even deeper. She shuddered and decided against whatever she was going to tell them. "I – I can't say." She shook her head. "No, it's too *embarrassing!*"

"Shit," Danielle exclaimed. *"What'd he say?"*

They all looked back at the patient's room. The door was still open. Carl was tempted to take a peek inside, just to see what the guy looked like.

"He never say nasty things to you?" Miss Daisy asked Danielle.

"He did when he first got here," Danielle confirmed. "But it was only one time. I thought he was playing. I told him if he didn't cut it out, I'd tell his wife the next time she came up here. He didn't say nothing else after that."

Miss Daisy nodded. "Okay. That's what I'll do. I'll tell him I'll tell his wife."

"But what he say?" Danielle pressed.

Miss Daisy shook her head briskly. "Probably same thing he tell you," she said before walking off.

Danielle laughed again. "I'ma make her tell me," she told Carl.

"What'd he say to you?" he wondered. "She said it's probably the same thing."

"I *know* it ain't the same thing," Danielle said matter-of-factly. "He told me I have a nice ass. Miss Daisy ain't got *no ass at all!*"

Carl checked out the Asian woman and chuckled. It was true. Miss Daisy was flatter than the palm of his hand. He hadn't seen Danielle's assets that day, so he tried his luck with that.

"You don't have a nice ass."

She rolled her eyes. "Shut up. You know I do."

"Nuh-uhn. Lemme see."

She told him, "Nigga, you ain't slick." But she turned her back on him anyway. She only gave him a quick look, but it was enough to make him smile warmly.

"Damn," he muttered. It was amazing how many times that worked for him. If there was one thing he knew about women, it was that they were all exhibitionists; some openly, while others tried to hide it. Either way, they didn't wear booty shorts and pushup bras just so their homegirls would tell them they were fine.

"If you gon' let me look at it, you might as well let me—"

"Boy, gone," Danielle said, pushing him towards the elevator. "Don't forget to come back with that cart."

"Alright. You know you a tease, though, right?"

She said, "You just don't know."

Carl found that response intriguing, but he didn't ask what she meant.

CHAPTER FIVE
BABY SHOWER

Congratulations!
You had sex!
You spread your legs and did it well!
Now look at that belly
It's full of donuts!
Just kidding!
We know why it's starting to swell
What will you name her?
Or is it a boy?
Are you ready?
Did you buy blankets and toys?
Did you get a room prepared?
You'll need plenty of diapers
For your brand new bundle of joy
And formula too
That stuff's expensive!
How much do you make?
Ooh, that's gonna hurt
You got a car seat and crib?
I'd give you my old stuff
But I gave it to a lady at church
You feeling sleepy?
Get used to that!
You can rest when your baby turns **eighteen**
You say your husband's talking about leaving?
What a jerk!
Child support is what you need!
Anyway, here, I brought you these cutie booties!
They're yellow
So they'll work for a girl or a boy

You look a mess!
Go get some rest
Congrats on your new bundle of joy!

One of Carl's last runs for the day was to transport a patient from MRI to the cardiac tower. When he got there, he noticed the sweet aroma of snacks and pastries. He dropped his patient off and followed his nose to the unit's break room. The door was closed and windowless, but Carl heard voices coming from inside. He backed away and approached a nurse he was friendly with.

"What y'all got going on in there?" he asked him. "A Valentine's party?"

The nurse shook his head. "Nah. Well, kinda. It's a baby shower for one of the techs. They kinda rolled it into a Valentine's party, but really it's for her. They brought her a bunch of presents and stuff."

"Oh," Carl said. "I was gonna run in there and see if I could snag a cupcake or something."

He was hoping that was still an option, but the nurse said, "Maybe you can come back after everyone eats. The women are in there now. I don't think they'd appreciate you crashing their baby shower – especially if you don't have a gift."

"That's cool," Carl said. "Who's pregnant? Somebody I know?"

His friend shrugged. "She's been here for a while, but I don't know if you know her. *Naomi...?*"

The name wasn't familiar. Carl shook his head. "What she look like? She fine?"

The nurse shook his head right away. "No, sir. Not at all."

Carl laughed at that. "That's probably why I don't know her!" He snickered as he headed for the elevators.

Inside the break room, the woman of the hour, a PCT named Naomi Gilcrease, beamed beneath the fluorescent lights and adoration of her peers. The room was beautifully decorated with streamers and baby shower banners. Little bottles and booties hung from the ceiling.

Naomi was not very popular – at or outside of work. She'd never been, and she didn't think her baby shower would change that. But at that moment, everyone was there for *her*. They were looking at her and smiling at her, doting on her protruding belly.

Well, to be honest, her belly hadn't really protruded that much. She was 249 pounds before she got pregnant and had only put on seven more pounds in the past eight months. Her coworkers thought it was a blessing that the baby didn't add much more weight. Naomi didn't know if they said that because she was already fat, or if it would've been a blessing for a skinny girl too.

Because she and her husband didn't want to know the sex of their child until its birth, all of the gifts Naomi received were unisex; diapers, bottles, wet wipes, yellow blankets and onesies. The ladies who had children regaled her with wonderful stories about what motherhood would be like. Naomi didn't have much information to share in return, but she was gracious, answering all of their questions as best she could.

"What are you gonna name him – or *her*, if it's a girl?" her charge nurse wanted to know.

"I don't know," Naomi said honestly. She was a short woman, with broad shoulders her husband Bryan once made the mistake of referring to as *manly*.

He'd followed that up with, "I should take you to the football game, so you can help the Cowboys with their offensive line!"

In response to those comments, Naomi shook the hell out of the next beer she brought him. How dare he criticize her figure? It wasn't like he was gracing the cover of romance novels. Bryan was just as fat as her, and he damn well knew it!

He cursed her out royally when his beer exploded in all directions, including on the TV screen, where his beloved Cowboys were actually winning for a change. But Naomi didn't regret the trick she played on him. Nope. Not one bit.

"You really haven't decided on a name?" her charge nurse asked incredulously. "I can understand not wanting to know the sex, but I thought you'd at least have a couple of names picked out."

Naomi's face heated. Ever since she got pregnant, everyone had expectations of what she should be doing. Didn't anyone ever look the baby in the eyes first and decide if it looked like a Fred or a Jacob?

"Bryan wants a junior," she told them. "But I don't like how his name is spelled with a *Y*. I wanna name him Jacob."

Naomi had an unmistakably southern accent. Most people thought Mississippi, but she was actually from Georgia. Her hair was short and straight. She never wore makeup, not even on her wedding day.

"What if it's a girl?" another nurse in the room asked.

"Ooh, I hope it's a girl!" another squealed.

Naomi's smile spread across her face. She couldn't believe Tabitha was so excited about a baby that wasn't even hers. None of these nurses had ever been this nice to her. Even when they begged her to *pretty, pretty please* clean up a diarrhea patient for the third time in one shift, they never seemed grateful for it afterwards.

Her baby had changed everything. Naomi envisioned play dates with their children. Tabitha sounded like she wouldn't mind babysitting every now and then. Naomi never had real friends like that before. Who would've thought all it took was one lucky sperm cell hooking up with her magical egg?

"I wanna name her Glenda, after my grandmama," she said.

"Ooh, that's a pretty name!"

"I like that," one of the PCTs agreed. "That name is rare these days."

Naomi couldn't stop grinning. She thought so too.

"Did you get the baby's room fixed up yet?" their charge asked.

Naomi nodded. "Yeah, we finished it this weekend."

"What color did you paint the walls?"

"Baby blue."

"Really? What if you have a girl?"

"I think it looks nice either way."

"Baby blue will work for a boy or a girl," another tech agreed. "If you had painted it pink, that'd be different."

"Did you get all of your furniture yet?" someone else asked.

Naomi nodded. "Our crib is beautiful. It's solid oak."

That brought a few *oohs* from the ladies crowded around her.

"We got perfect, little curtains," she told them. "Everything matches. It's *beautiful*!"

"*Pictures!*" Tabitha said. "Where's your phone?"

Naomi's face heated again. There was so much she didn't know about motherhood. "I didn't, I didn't think to take pictures of it. I'm sorry."

"Oh, no, it's fine," the nurse said. "You can take some tonight and show us tomorrow."

"Okay."

"Is Bryan as happy as you are?" their charge asked.

"He is," Naomi said, her smile back in full flair. "It's all we talk about. This is the best thing that's ever happened to us."

"*Awww!*"

One of her coworkers gushed so much, she had tears in her eyes.

● ● ● ● ● ●

When she got home, Naomi struggled to tote all of her gifts. She had to make two trips. Thanks to her neighbors, she couldn't find a parking spot right in front of her building. Getting off at 6:30 meant all of the nine-to-fivers got home before her. Plus there were a lot of Section 8 units in her apartments; with mothers who didn't work at all. Most of their cars were parked right up front; exactly where they were when Naomi left for work this morning.

By the time she got everything inside, Naomi had broken out in a sweat, despite the cool February temperature. Her breathing was rough as she cleared off the dining room table. Most of the debris was mail and other documents that may or may not have been important, so she stacked it on one of the chairs rather than throw it away. When she was done, she smiled as she arranged her gifts on the mostly clean table. Mr. Tucker, one of her ten or so cats, tried to hop up on the table immediately to inspect the nice-smelling boxes and gift bags. Naomi shooed him away.

"*No!* Not for you!"

The cat bristled before making his way to the chair on the far side of the table. Naomi would have to move a number of things to get to him there, and he knew she wasn't going to do that.

With a dozen more feline eyes watching her from various locations, Naomi went to the kitchen to start dinner. Even here, her day didn't get any easier. Both the dishwasher and the sink were full of dirty dishes.

"Dammit Bryan," she muttered as she searched for her casserole dish. She found it on the counter; caked with the remnants of her last spaghetti bake. There was no way it would come clean without a good pre-soak, so she abandoned it as well as her plans for a special dinner.

She pulled a pack of wieners from the fridge instead and found a can of chili. Ten minutes later, her chilidogs were ready. She was dismayed to discover she didn't have any shredded cheese to sprinkle on top. She didn't have time to shower and change out of her scrubs before she heard her husband arrive home from work. She made it to the living room just as he noticed their gifts on the dining table.

"What the hell is this?" he grunted.

"No! *Get down!*" Naomi yelled at Mr. Tucker.

The cat had made his way to the middle of the table and was snuggling against one of the baby's new stuffed animals. Mr. Tucker growled at her and initially stood his ground. Naomi noticed one of his eyes was half-closed with a slight, green discharge. She raised a hand to swat him, but he jumped down and took off down the hallway.

Naomi turned to her husband and smiled. "Hey, baby."

She wrapped her arms around Bryan's waist; which was no small task. Her gut, coupled with his girth, meant she had to stretch her arms extra wide. Bryan did not reciprocate when she kissed him on the cheek.

"What's all this?" he asked again.

"What does it look like?" she said, stepping away from him. She giggled as she approached their gifts. "I told you we were having a baby shower at work. Look what everybody got me – I mean *us*. This is all for the baby! Isn't it wonderful?"

Bryan didn't share her enthusiasm or appreciation. He stared at the items on the table as if there was a catch: If they opened anything, someone might show up tomorrow and demand they pay for it, like those sneaky hotel mini bars.

"You should've seen the way they set everything up in the break room," Naomi told him. "They had banners on the wall, little bottles and stuff hanging off the ceiling. They brought cake and cupcakes and–"

"Did you bring any cake?"

Naomi sighed and shook her head. "I told you I'm not bringing anymore sweets home from work – not after what happened last time."

Last time was their office Christmas party a couple of months ago. Naomi visited the break room several times during her shift to stuff her face. One of the nurses – a *black* woman named Sephora – chuckled when she saw her exit the room with another full plate.

"Girl, you must really like those cookies!"

Naomi thought the look on her face was pure evil. It was one of those condescending looks only a *black bitch* could pull off – not that Naomi had a problem with black people. A lot of their women just happened to be bitches, that's all.

Before Naomi left work that day, the charge nurse was practically begging people to take food home, so she wouldn't have to throw it away. Of course *Sephora* had to throw in her two cents again.

"You can give those cookies to Naomi. She can't get enough of them!"

But she was wrong about that. Naomi didn't take any desert home that day, and she vowed to never do so again.

"Well, what's for dinner?" Bryan asked.

Naomi rolled her eyes. She wasn't surprised that he was being so ungrateful, but it still hurt to see it.

"Chilidogs," she told him.

"With fries?"

"No, chips."

"Chili *cheese* dogs?"

"No. We ain't got no cheese."

Bryan sighed. "Well, I'm ready to eat."

"Come in here," she said. "I don't wanna eat on the couch today."

She thought his shoulders slumped, but he didn't respond before following her into the kitchen.

● ● ● ● ● ●

Bryan worked as a courier for an auto parts store. He wasn't a total lard-ass, but that was only because he was taller than his wife. They weighed roughly the same. His height helped distribute the bulk more. His fat settled mostly in his gut, which didn't look that bad on him. Naomi wasn't a fan of his long, greasy hair, but she'd long since given up asking him to cut it. She was grateful he pulled it back in a ponytail most of the time.

After watching him scarf down four hotdogs, she said, "We have to start eating better, when the baby gets here."

Her husband hmphed but didn't have a comment for that.

She waited a few beats before asking, "Did you hear me?"

He swallowed the chips in his mouth and said, "Yeah."

"Yeah – *what*?" she pressed. "What do you think about it?"

"You're the one feeding me," he replied.

Naomi had a feeling he'd blame her. "What about all the food you eat at work – and on your way to work? And all of your beer? I don't have nothing to do with that."

Bryan lowered his head and shook it slightly. He looked up at her and asked, "What else you got to complain about?"

"I'm not complaining. I'm just saying; we should make some changes, for the baby."

Bryan's eyes returned to his plate, which was mostly empty. He began to scoop up the remaining chili with the few chips he had left.

"So, um, Happy Valentine's Day," she said.

He looked up at her, his eyes now registering guilt. "I didn't get you anything," he said. "Sorry, I couldn't afford it."

No surprise there, but Naomi still got a sinking feeling in her chest. "You could've got a card," she offered.

He lowered his gaze again.

"Here," she said.

She reached for a card that had been on the other side of the table the whole time. Her husband looked even more sheepish as he accepted it. Naomi watched his expression change when he opened the envelope. He stared at the front of the card for a few moments. She could tell he was not pleased when he opened it and a Subway gift card fell onto his plate. He made no attempt to retrieve it. Naomi reached across the table and plucked the card from his leftovers. She used a paper towel to wipe the chili off it.

"What's your problem?" she asked.

She thought he'd protest her forcing healthy eating habits on him. He surprised her by complaining about the card instead.

"Why'd you get this? I'm not a *Dad*."

She frowned. "You will be soon, in less than a month."

He blew out a pent up breath and shook his head as he read the inside of the card.

"I don't get you," she said. "Why you so grumpy?"

"It's – nothing." He closed the card and looked up at her. "Thank you." He did not take his gift card before leaving the table.

● ● ● ● ● ●

Twenty minutes later Naomi had made some headway on the mess in the kitchen. Washing all of the dishes was too much of a task, but she straightened out everything in the dishwasher and got it started. When she returned to the living room, her husband was parked in front of the television in his recliner. Rather than the remote, he had his Playstation controller in hand.

Naomi stood next to his chair for a few seconds. She waited, but he didn't look away from the TV.

"Can you help me with the baby's room tonight?" she finally asked.

No response.

"You said we would fix it up last week," she reminded him. "You've been saying it for months."

He frowned and told her, "You do it."

"I can't clean that whole room by myself," she complained. "It's mostly your stuff."

"No, it's not!"

"Yes, it is," he groaned. "You and them damn cats."

"Where's the baby gonna sleep when it gets here?" she asked. "Do you even care?"

"Why don't you get all of *your stuff* out of there *first*, and leave whatever you think is mine," he offered. "Until then, leave me out of it."

Naomi's cheeks reddened, but her husband was unmoved. He hadn't looked away from the television since she approached him.

With tears in her eyes, she stormed out of the room. Her heavy footsteps were thunderous in the narrow hallway. The smaller cats quickly cleared a path for her. She stopped in front of the spare bedroom and tried to collect herself before she stepped inside. It didn't help. The sight of their baby's room caused her tears to spill freely.

The walls were painted white, just as they had been when they first moved to the apartment. As far as Naomi knew, the property manager would balk at the idea of them repainting it baby blue. There were no cute curtains, either. When they moved in two years ago, they put sheets over the windows. It didn't make sense, at the time, to buy new curtains for a room no one would occupy. The sheets still hung in their original position, except they were a lot more dingy and sun-bleached now.

Even worse was the amount of clutter the couple had allowed to accumulate in the room. *Hoarder* was such an ugly word. Naomi deflected it with a passion. But there were few other ways to describe what she was looking at. All of their winter coats, extra clothes and too little clothes were in there. Boxes of discarded auto parts lined one of the walls, along with two full sets of tires. There were dozens of trash bags. Most were stuffed with clothes. Others were filled with recyclables they never found the time to drop off.

There were papers; boxes of them that had varying degrees of importance. Naomi would have to go through them individually to find out why they never got thrown out. Beneath the rubbish was a twin-size bed that she couldn't see at all. There were two dressers regurgitating even more clothes. The top half of a treadmill was visible on the opposite side of the room. There were clothes draped on it as well.

Naomi's heart thumped painfully as she accepted the full magnitude of the work that lie before her. She swallowed roughly and wiped a fresh coat of sweat from her brow. Disposing of all of this would be hard enough. Even worse was the smell she'd have to contend with as she dug through the madness. Most of her cats had found refuge here. Naomi used to put out a fresh litter box for them twice a week, but she hadn't done that in months. The whole room was their litter box. The stench of cat shit and piss singed her nostrils.

Naomi wondered if it was safe to be in there without a full hazmat suit. Was that something she could borrow from work? The thought of a newborn sleeping in the room was horrifying.

Tears streamed down her face as she took a few unsteady steps into the muck.

She grabbed one of the boxes near the door and lugged it out of the room without inspecting it. She was strong enough to lift it, rather than drag it. She left the box in the hallway and went back for another. Nearly-feral feline faces watched her curiously. When she returned a third time, her lungs burned from the exertion. Her face and neck were slick with sweat.

With only two items gone, the odor in the room seemed to intensify. The further she stepped into the wasteland, the more overpowering it became. This was more than just moldy clothes and cat feces. There was something absolutely *wrong* in the room.

Naomi abandoned her efforts to clear the debris until she found the source of the odor. She had to climb over piles of paper and trash bags, but she finally traced it to one of the dressers. The middle drawer was half-open. Beneath a layer of clothes was a large indentation that looked like a rat's nest.

She lifted a shirt and gasped when she saw two furry bodies beneath it. It took her brain a moment to process the fact that the deceased critters were kittens rather than rats. They were very small and very dead – had been for a good while. The stench wafting from them forced its way into her mouth and down her throat.

"Jesus."

The only bright spot Naomi could note was it was too cold for flies, therefore there were no maggots. If there were maggots, she would've lost her dinner for sure.

Naomi backed away from the dresser, her nose now running in addition to her eyes. She might not need a hazmat suit, but she definitely needed a pair of gloves for this disgusting project. She was pretty sure they had some in the bathroom.

She wished she could say her tears were for the dead kittens or the condition of her baby's room, but there was more. Naomi wept because the walls were closing in on her, and time was running short. In one month everyone would know what an unforgivable liar she was – unless she managed to produce a baby. But after ten years of trying, it was clear God wasn't going to bless her with a miraculous pregnancy. Even if it happened now, it was too late. Everyone thought she was a month away from delivering.

Naomi's heart squeezed uncomfortably as she considered all of the horrible things that would happen if the truth came out. Her marriage, her job, her sanity – she could kiss all of that goodbye.

Thankfully there was an out. She'd been thinking long and hard, and a solution came to her a few weeks ago. It was so simple, she was a fool for not thinking of it sooner.

She worked at a hospital. And, as luck would have it, babies were born there every day. Beautiful, blonde, blue-eyed babies.

Of course *taking* one of them was a horrible idea. It was ludicrous to even consider it. But if Naomi didn't come up with a newborn, her life was over. So either way she was screwed.

If God wasn't going to bless her with a child, then she had to fall back on the understanding that God helps those who help themselves. She could've had any number of crappy jobs in the past five years, but God found a way for her to work at Jackson Memorial; an acclaimed *baby-making machine*. If that wasn't destiny, then there was no such thing.

Naomi wiped the snot under her nose as she emerged from her future baby's room. Thinking of the newborns at the hospital brought a smile to her face, even as tears rolled down her cheeks. It was a strange, perverse grin.

Jacob

Glenda

Those were both wonderful names for her precious child.

CHAPTER SIX
MOONLIGHTING

Welcome to the city of the cutthroats and deathblows
You ain't seen no fucking ghettos
Like these motherfucking Meadows!
You ain't seen these crack and heroin babies
Eating popcorn for dinner
We ain't got a lot of heroes here, man
But we got a lot of sinners
All these dope boys is winners
Fiends be coming 'round the clock
Don't try to short-stop on my block
You'll get blasted, cuz
I got this on lock
It's J Crook from the 'Brook
I came up from that dirty nigga with a snot nose
Now I'm gleaming
Bitch, look at my diamonds!
I run the motherfucking Meadows!

On Friday night, the atmosphere at Club Paradise was ripe with testosterone, marijuana smoke and the unmistakable scent of stripper oil. Danielle and her boyfriend Jamien, who was more commonly known by his stage name *J Crook* or simply *Crook*, sat together at a table near the DJ booth.

"Y'all hear this beat right here?" the DJ said as a hard baseline made his speakers jump. "This right here is *817 Murder Meadows* by Overbrook Meadows' very own *J Crook*! If you didn't know, *Crook is in the building tonight!* If you a nigga, don't run up to him smiling and shit, like a lil' bitch! If it ain't about money, just tell him '*What's up,*' and keep it moving. But *ladies*, you know how to make our local celebrities feel welcome. Show him some love! Check out this track y'all, while we bring *Larissa* to the main stage. Larissa, *bring yo fine ass up here!*"

A redbone with thick thighs, a pudgy belly and beestings up top made her way to the stage, while Crook's new single played at a deafening volume.

Welcome to the city of the cutthroats and deathblows
You ain't seen no fucking ghettos
Like these motherfucking Meadows!

Despite the DJ's request for the ladies to show Crook a little hospitality, no one approached his table – not right away, at least. Crook already had a fine woman sitting next to him. None of the dancers wanted to be disrespectful.

Danielle rocked her head slowly to the beat as she watched Larissa start her routine. The dancer was a bit chubby, but she could climb the pole with the best of them. Unfortunately, none of the customers approached the stage to get a better look and drop a few dollars.

There were nearly fifty patrons in attendance. That was a good crowd for 11 pm on a Friday. Danielle expected twice as many people to crowd the club by one am. The moonlight not only brought out the crazies in Overbrook Meadows, but it tended to bring out the horny as well.

Midway through Crook's song, Danielle began to rap along. The music was so loud, no one standing more than five feet away could hear her. But they certainly saw her. As she got hype, her hands flew up in the air. Her gestures were gangster; bold and threatening. She flashed her boyfriend's gang signs, though she was not in a gang herself.

Danielle's eyes were low from a blunt she and Crook had smoked. She had also snorted a line of cocaine that had her blood running hot and fast. This was the drug balance she preferred, especially on nights like this, when she worked a full shift at the hospital prior to coming to the club.

"Fellas, if you ain't tipping, what the hell you doing here?" the DJ belted. "Gone and pick one of these lovely ladies for a lap dance!"

The DJ's guilt trip worked sometimes, but no one rose from their seat. Crook looked over and grinned at his woman. He loved the way Danielle vibed to his song. The guys in the room didn't know it, but they were being subconsciously influenced the whole time they were in the club. If they got a lap dance while his song played, their brain would associate the song to the pleasure they felt at that moment.

When his tune ended, Danielle beamed at her man. "That's the best song you ever made, baby! You 'bout to blow up!"

Crook nodded, barely acknowledging her statement.

Danielle didn't mind his lackluster response. She knew he had a *gangsta* image to uphold. Smiling or not, she thought Crook was the finest man in the building. He had fair skin, a bald head and big, bowling ball size fists. He didn't work out, but his chest was swollen. His arms were strong and toned.

As the DJ transitioned to a new song, he introduced the next dancer.

"Coming to the main stage is *Enchantress*! Come on, girl. Get yo fine ass up here. Fellas, get yo tips ready. Don't nobody like a broke-ass nigga!"

Danielle looked the DJ's way. He grinned and winked at her. She turned to Crook, who was nodding to the beat of the new song. He was as cool as a popsicle.

Danielle rose to her feet to reveal her G-string and long, sexy legs. Her six-inch stilettos had her ass looking nice and bulbous. Up top, her breasts weren't spilling out of her bikini, but she had more than a handful. Her nipples were erect, visible beneath the thin fabric. Many eyes followed her as she strutted to the stage. No one paid Larissa any mind as she made her tired-ass exit.

Danielle didn't like the song the DJ selected for her, but that didn't matter. The important thing was she had three and a half minutes to perform. Her goal was to entice; lure men to the stage like a black widow. She wanted them to give her all of the money in their hands and their pockets. She needed them to believe that as hot as the action got on stage, it would be ten times better if they paid $30 for a lap dance.

When she got on stage, Danielle didn't waste any time losing her top. She watched her first customer across the room as he rose to his feet, his eyes fixated on her dark nipples. As soon as he approached her, she seductively danced her way to him. He was only clutching about $10 in ones. That was okay. If she made $10 per minute, she'd be balling by the time the club closed at five am.

She dropped to her knees in front of the mark. She could tell he was mesmerized by her curves and her tattoos. She leaned forward, until his face disappeared between her chocolate breasts. She felt no emotion when he motor-boated her, but her eyes said otherwise.

Eye contact was key.

She maintained his gaze as she backed away and lowered herself on the stage. She spread her legs wide, and he began to drop dollars like they were burning his hand. His eyes were glued to her sex, so she reached and moved her G-string to the side – just for a second – exposing her freshly shaved kitty. His eyes grew even wider, and he dropped the rest of his money.

Danielle smiled and mouthed, *"Thank you, baby."*

The customer smiled too and reached into his pocket. He produced another handful of bills. This wad was four times as big. A quick count told Danielle he had gotten change for two twenties from one of the servers. She pretended not to notice his money as she plotted to get every dime.

Another customer appeared on her left. Danielle knew that would happen, because when she lay back on the stage, the first guy blocked everyone's view. She checked to make sure the second man had money in his hand before she rolled to her knees and backed her ass into his lap. He began to drop bills onto her gyrating spine.

She reached to peal her panties down. Slowly. The new customer threw at least $20 in the air as he watched her. The sight of her asshole got him fully erect. His mouth watered when her muffin was fully exposed.

The first customer felt neglected. He tossed five bills her way. Danielle looked over her shoulder and smiled at him, but he didn't throw anything else, so she continued to shake her goodies for the guy on the left.

She reached between her legs and moaned as she rubbed her snatch. More dollars fell like snowflakes. She lowered her upper body and used her fingers to spread her labia. The second customer stared at her sweet pink and swallowed hard. More money dropped from his hands. When they were empty, he reached for her hips and pulled her closer. Danielle watched in the mirror in front of her as he dry humped her.

"*Ooh, yeah,*" she moaned, her eyes half closed, her bottom lip between her teeth. "*Mmmm, work it, daddy.*"

At end of her set, Danielle guessed she'd made nearly $50. She had to tear herself away from the men as she exited the stage.

Smiling, she told them, "I'll come find you later," before heading backstage. That was a promise she intended to keep. If they were willing to spend that much at the stage, her chances of talking them into a lap dance were around 100 percent.

She did not look Crook's way, because her customers wouldn't like the fact that her boyfriend benefitted from her dancing. They knew the money they tipped her would end up in his pocket at some point, but they wanted to believe it was just for her, and they were now special to her. Danielle wanted them to believe that too.

This was her fantasy island.

● ● ● ● ● ●

For the rest of the night, Crook had enough sense to keep his distance, while Danielle worked the floor and got paid. The club had several burly security guards who were always on the lookout for drunks who might get aggressive or too frisky. Danielle knew they had her back, but she felt even more protected with Crook there. He may not have been in love with her, but she knew he cared for her. Plus she was the breadwinner in their household. For that reason alone, Crook would make sure she made it home every night.

Rather than trust the lockers in the changing room, Danielle dropped her money off with her boyfriend in intervals. She tried to make sure none of her steady customers saw her, but when you walk around in a G-string, there were always a lot of eyes on you.

As was the case with most of the dancers, Danielle could not do her job sober. She constantly drank alcohol with her *dates*. She wasn't particular about what kind they had, as long as it was hard liquor. She popped pills too, but only if she got them from

Crook or one of the girls. You could never trust a pill from a customer.

Danielle also had a personal supply of cocaine in her locker. That, more than anything, gave her the energy to get through her shifts. As an added benefit, the coke made her horny, so she wasn't always lying when she told a patron, *"Damn, baby. You got me so wet right now."*

Whenever she wasn't on stage, she worked the room; flirting and chatting with the men. She felt Crook's eyes on her each time she led a guy to the back for a lap dance. He never accused her of anything heinous, but he was no lame. He knew guys tried to push the limits back there, and some of the girls allowed it.

Danielle paid his jealousy no mind until one of her regulars showed up at two am. She knew Patrick worked a night job and got off at one. On the weekends he came straight to her after work.

Most of her customers were unmemorable, but Danielle's eyes lit up for Patrick. He wasn't bad looking, and he was good for a hundred bucks each time she saw him. She knew he'd fallen in love with her. Despite Danielle's unwillingness to divulge her phone number or very much personal information, he believed she loved him too.

She watched him from the bar, as Patrick found an empty table. She resisted the urge to run straight to him, even though there were a few dancers itching to steal his affection. She waited for him to spot her and wave before she made her way to his table.

"Hey, baby, I missed you," she said as she sat on his lap.

He rested his head on her shoulder and hugged her with both arms. "I missed you too."

Judging by his breath and the open bottle he brought with him, she knew he was already lit.

"You been drinking already?"

He nodded and smiled sheepishly. "Yeah."

"Why you get the party started without me?"

He shrugged. "I been thinking about you a lot this week."

She wasn't surprised to hear that. Valentine's Day had just passed. That was a hard holiday for the lonely.

"Been thinking about you too," she said.

He told her, "I almost didn't come tonight."

"Really? Why?"

"Because I... I'm starting to feel like I want more," he complained. "I want a *woman*, Danielle, someone I can take home with me."

She hated that she had told him her real name. It made his grievances sound more personal.

"You know I can't leave the club with anybody," she reminded him. "I'll get fired."

"You can meet me outside of the club any day," he offered, not for the first time. "No one here has to know."

"I wouldn't feel comfortable dating anyone I met at the club," she insisted. "I'm sorry. That's a rule I made a long time ago, and I haven't changed my mind about it."

He shook his head and sighed. He looked like he might cry. That was the last thing Danielle wanted. This was why she preferred *real* men like Crook, rather than pussies like Patrick.

"Come here, baby." She stood and took his hand. "Let's get a dance. I'll make you feel better."

He stood and wrapped his arm possessively around her waist as she led him to the private area. Despite his inner turmoil, Danielle felt good about what she'd accomplished. No girl in the club could finagle a lap dance so quickly. None of them could trade heartbreak for a sexual tease so effectively.

Her heart froze when she looked back and saw Crook watching them with what she would say was real jealousy in his eyes. But, as always, the show must go on.

● ● ● ● ● ●

All told, she talked Patrick into four dances in a row at thirty bucks a pop. She was completely nude the whole time. That wasn't a problem, but Patrick was a lot more aggressive than usual. He wanted to kiss her on the mouth. She turned away and let him suck her neck instead.

He tried to rub her slit. She blocked his attempts until the fourth dance, and then told him, "Naw, baby. You gotta pay more for that."

Patrick quickly produced another twenty. She took it and allowed him to grope her downstairs. She blocked him again when his finger slid between her labia.

"Please, Danielle."

"You gotta pay—"

Two more twenties appeared.

She looked around and didn't see anyone watching them. She took the money and told him, "Okay. Hurry up."

Patrick did not hurry up. He fingered her for the duration of the last song. She would've stopped him, but he was good at it. She stroked his erection through his pants, while he pleasured her. Soon his fingers were slick with her essence. Her heart thundered. Her body trembled as her clitoris sang for him.

This was not the first time she had climaxed at the club. In the midst of passion, she had to look out for both the club manager and Crook. If either of them saw what was going on, her ass was grass. The fear of being found out made her orgasm that much sweeter.

Her head was still spinning when the song ended. She felt Patrick's dick go limp in her hand, and she knew he had cum too.

He told her, "Thank you," and moved to kiss her again.

He had spent nearly $200 in fifteen minutes, so Danielle allowed it – but only a peck.

When they left the champagne room, she was relieved to see Crook was no longer at his table. This wasn't unusual. He was a hustler, and Friday night was prime time for dealers. She was grateful he didn't see the dreamy look in her and Patrick's eyes. She knew he'd be back to pick her up when the club closed.

Danielle stashed her money in her locker and got back to work.

● ● ● ● ● ●

Crook returned a few minutes before five to give her a ride home. She couldn't have been more ready. Her dogs were barking, and even the coke could no longer fight her fatigue. She'd made over $500 that night, which was a great haul. It was more than she made in a whole week at the hospital.

Crook was mostly quiet as he drove. Danielle had experienced this before. The conversation always went a certain way when she asked him what was wrong. But pretending not to notice his brooding started to get on her nerves.

She reached and turned down the radio before asking, "What's your problem?"

Crook took a moment to consider his approach. He asked her, "What's up with that hoe-ass nigga that keep coming to the club?"

Danielle sighed quietly. "Who you talking about?"

"You know who I'm talking about." His eyes remained glued to the road. "The one that show up every time you work. That fool with the button-down."

"You mean my *best customer*? What about him, Crook?"

"That nigga wanna be with you. He treat you like you his woman."

"They all wanna be with me. All of 'em treat me like I'm their woman. *That's the plan.*"

"Naw, but he different," Crook said, shaking his big, bald head. "He wanna be with you *for real*. The rest of them know they can't have you."

"So what if he think that? That make him pay more."

"You was in there with that dude for a long-ass time. I had to leave. Couldn't sit out there waiting on you. It was fucking with my head."

"No one told you to wait on me. You ain't gotta come at all."

He looked her way. His eyes were filled with malice, but he knew he didn't have a leg to stand on. He turned back to the road and asked, "What was y'all doing in there?"

"*A motherfucking lap dance!*" Danielle said. "Why? You want one when we get home?"

He grimaced. "You need to watch your mouth."

"No, you need to chill with all that jealousy shit. Why you even come, if you can't stand to see me work."

"I ain't got no problem with it. I'm just saying; what's going on with you and ol' boy is different. You know it is."

"He ain't the only one I got sprung," Danielle informed him. "If you was about your paper, you'd be hoping I get twenty more niggas wrapped around my finger like that, instead of sitting here complaining about it. You met me at the club, *remember*? You didn't have a problem with what I was doing then."

"Yeah, I know I met you at the club. That's how I know you'll fuck one of them niggas."

"I'm with you every night! And you know I can't fuck nobody *in the club*, so what's the problem?"

That statement gave her clitoris a guilty aftershock. Outside of what happened tonight, she had sex in the club twice last year. It was never something she planned, it just happened. The first time was when a customer started eating her unexpectedly during a private dance. She told him to stop, but he grabbed her ass and started sucking her clit with everything he had. She came in his face within seconds.

The second time Danielle was not ashamed to say she initiated it. The customer was packing nine inches of thick meat. When she saw it bulging next to his thigh, she didn't think it was real. But it was hot to the touch when she grabbed it.

She had told him, "Let me see it," and he obliged.

She then asked him, "You got a condom," and he did.

The club manager strolled by while she was in the midst of that freaky episode, but from his vantage point, it looked like any other lap dance. He thought Danielle was *pretending* to ride him, when in reality, the customer was nine inches deep in her cookie jar.

But that was before Crook came along. Since then, she tried to be a good girl.

Crook continued to stare at the road as he told her, "I'll be glad when you quit this job and focus on the hospital."

Danielle was tired of hearing that, even though working at Jackson Memorial was her idea.

When she didn't respond, he looked over at her and said, "Oh, I guess you forgot you was trying to get your kids back."

Danielle seethed. That was a low blow, especially after she'd been getting loaded and shoving her vagina in people's faces for the past seven hours.

She had three children. Surprisingly they all had the same baby-daddy. Shalisa and Shaleah were four-year-old twins. Lemarcus Jr. was two. Danielle and Lemarcus Sr. were ride-or-die for years before he got locked up for drug pedaling. Their life together was never a walk in the park, but she wasn't prepared for how hard life was without him. Stressed and dead broke, Danielle made the mistake of dropping the kids off with his mother for a few days that quickly turned into six months. When she finally decided to pick them up, Grandma flat out refused.

"They been here this long. Why you want 'em now?"

Danielle was indignant. "*'Cause they mine.*"

"You wasn't thinking about that while you was running the streets. What you gon' do with 'em, girl? Leave 'em in some motel room, while you shaking your ass at the titty club? You know you can't take care of 'em. They better off here with me."

"You can't keep my kids!" Danielle had snapped, her claws extending.

Grandma tried a more rational approach. "Girl, let me keep them. I'm retired. I ain't got nothing to do all day but take care of 'em. Don't you want them to have some kind of *life* – a roof over their head that ain't going nowhere?" Danielle was almost inclined to agree with her, until she added, "If you take them, they gon' end up just like you."

With that, the gloves came off.

"Well, you raised *Lemarcus*, and look how he ended up," Danielle snarled.

Grandma wanted to slap her for that; Danielle could see it in her eyes. But the older woman knew a custody battle was on the horizon. One of them had to act like she had some damn sense.

"Call the police if you want to," Grandma said, her nose in the air. "Take me to court. You left these babies over here for more than *six months*. That means this is their *established residence*. You can look it up, if you want to. I already did. Take me in front of the judge and explain why yo stripping ass is a better parent than me. I would love to see you pull that off! Ain't had a real address in five years. You ready to piss in a cup, to prove you ain't getting high?"

Danielle's blood boiled. She wanted to kick Grandma's ass, but at the time, she was still faithful to Lemarcus. Plus her kids were in the house somewhere, and she didn't want to freak them out.

She left that day without her children – not because she didn't think she *could* take them, but because deep down she knew Grandma was right about her. Danielle did live in a motel. Her piss was always dirtier than a cup of lean. A year later, the only thing that had changed was Grandma had more ammunition. The kids had been with her for a year and a half now. And although she allowed Danielle to visit them anytime she wanted, she rarely did.

It was Crook who got the ball rolling again. When they hooked up, he said he'd do whatever it took to help get her babies back and raise them right. But the bulk of the work fell on Danielle's shoulders. The first step was to get a regular job. Her cousin got her on at the hospital and even hooked her up with a bottle of clean urine to get through human resources.

Now that she was past her probation period at Jackson Memorial, all Danielle had to do was stop stripping and wean herself off drugs. As with anything else, that was easier said than done. Every time she gave it some real thought, her head started to hurt. She hated her job as a PCT. Nothing felt better than getting faded and making *real* money at the club.

Crook was the only person in her life who gave her a hard time about it. *You had a **goal***, he'd tell her. *This supposed to be about them kids.* At times, she hated him for it. It wasn't like he was living the straight and narrow. He was a no good dope dealer, just like Lemarcus. Plus his motives to get her out of the club were tinged with jealousy. That weakened his argument and made him look like a punk in Danielle's eyes.

● ● ● ● ● ●

When they got home (this week it was the Sunset Motel), she wanted nothing more than to get off her feet and chill.

"You got some brown?" she asked, referring to powdered heroin, rather than the cocaine that kept her wired all night.

Crook sat on the bed and pulled a huge wad of cash from his pocket. Most of the bills were ones. "Where the rest of it?" he asked. "What you make after I left?"

Danielle produced another stack of cash, minus the $50 she always kept for herself, and tossed it on his lap. Crook added the money to his wad and resumed his count.

"Nigga you heard me ask for a bag." Danielle propped her hands on her hips and sneered at him. "Gimme some fucking dope."

Crook sneered back at her as he reached in his pocket and found what she wanted. He gave it to her and said, "Your habit's getting expensive."

"I know you ain't fix your mouth to say some shit like that." Danielle turned her back on him and approached the dresser, where her plate and razor were right where she had left them. "As much money as I'm giving you," she continued, "you shouldn't have *nothing* to say when I ask for something. You must think I'm one of them dumb-ass bitches. You got me fucked up."

"You better watch your mouth."

"Or what? Fuck you." Danielle paid him no mind as she prepared her line. "How much money *you* make tonight, nigga?"

"I sold out. I gotta score in the morning."

"You always say that shit. But you don't never seem to have the money from whatever you sold. Ain't that how it's supposed to go? You score. You sell the shit, and you score again with the profit. Where your fucking *profit*, Crook? Is you stacking any of this money? Where it's at? You shouldn't never need my money to score again."

"Bitch, you know I gotta pay for my studio time, this room, everything we eat. Ain't none of this shit free."

"We ain't living in the fucking *Hamptons*, Crook. You know what, that's why they call you that, ain't it? You ain't nothing but a *crook*; a thief-ass nigga that don't know how to sell dope. You lucky you can rap, 'cause you ain't good for shit else."

He wasn't surprised she was acting so ballsy. Taming Danielle was a feat he'd yet to accomplish. If she didn't make so much money, he would've been long gone by now. "I told you to watch your mouth," he growled.

"Watch it do what?"

"I'm finna watch it suck my dick!"

"Yeah right, nigga. You ain't done nothing to make me wanna suck your dick." She paused to snort both of the lines she had scraped together. Unlike coke, the heroin didn't hit her immediately. When it did take hold, it would be soft and smooth, like the mellow kiss of death. "You can damn sho' eat this pussy, though," she continued, as if she'd never stopped speaking.

Crook was certainly not about to do that – not unless she took a bath first. But after watching her entice men all night, he'd be lying if he said he wasn't eager to be the one – *the only one* – who could slide inside her. Staring at her ass as he sat behind her got his dick hard before he rose to his feet.

Danielle heard him rise from the bed. Anticipating violence, she started to turn and go on the offensive. But she looked back and saw the look in his eyes and relaxed. He pushed her forward roughly, forcing her to lean with both forearms on the dresser. She sneered as he yanked her skirt up and her G-string down. He unfastened his pants and pushed them down his hips. He kicked her legs apart like a police officer and entered her erogenous zone with no hesitation.

"Why you so wet," he breathed, "if them niggas at the club ain't turning you on?"

The dick and the heroin hit Danielle simultaneously, making it difficult to respond. She closed her eyes and inhaled deeply as she rode both waves.

"Yeah, I finally shut yo ass up," Crook said.

His strokes were slow, but hard. His aim was to punish her, but Danielle felt nothing but pleasure. He was right about her getting turned on at the club. One of the customers she danced for tonight was so fine, Danielle wanted to pay *him* for the way he was touching her. She closed her eyes and imagined the stranger was fucking her in the champagne room.

"*Yeeeah,*" Crook grunted. "*Yeah, bitch. That's what I thought.*"

CHAPTER SEVEN
SUSPICION

The following week, patient transporter Bobby Grant had another harrowing experience during his night shift in the ER.

The ultrasound department was open 24 hours, but due to the high demand for their services, portable ultrasound devices were available in the ER for doctors to use. They were usually kept at the nurses' stations, well out of reach from Bobby's thieving hands. But because of the fast-paced environment, the ultrasounds sometimes got left in the exam rooms after a patient was discharged or sent for a procedure.

In those cases, a PCT or nurse would come to retrieve the expensive equipment. If they missed it, the housekeepers were sure to find it when they prepared the room for the next patient. If a housekeeper accidentally bundled something valuable with the sheets and sent it down the laundry chute, an employee in that department would send it back to the ER.

But before any of that could happen, Bobby was on the lookout for the ultrasound Carl requested. The portable ones came in a case that wasn't very big; about the size of a small laptop bag. As a transporter, Bobby had access to all areas in the ER. His only limitations were knowing when an ultrasound would be used and getting to it before anyone had a chance to return it to the nurses' station.

For this, Bobby had to do a lot of walking throughout the emergency room and a lot of peeking around curtains. He hoped not to arouse suspicion, but even he would admit his behavior was odd that night.

The first person to question him was a PCT. Her name was Angela. She was a notorious slacker, so Bobby didn't consider her a threat.

"You doing a lot of walking tonight," she said as she sidled up to him. "You got a Fitbit?"

He shook his head. "What's that?"

"I guess you don't have one then. Who you looking for?"

He shook his head again. "Nobody."

"Just trying to stay awake?" she offered.

That seemed like a good excuse. He nodded. "Yeah."

"We just made a fresh pot of coffee," she told him. "It's in the break room. You want me to get you a cup?"

Bobby knew the girl had a crush on him, which was another reason he didn't consider her a threat. Unfortunately for her, he already had a woman. Plus Angela was short, and she didn't have much of a neck. Even if Bobby was interested in cheating, he wasn't attracted to women who didn't have necks.

He checked his phone and said, "It's too late for that. I don't drink coffee after two, 'cause I have trouble sleeping when I get home."

"Me too," Angela said. "I was just letting you know it was in there. Some of these nurses will drink up to the last minute – and take a cup with them when they leave. I don't know how they do it."

"Yeah," Bobby said vaguely, hoping to cut the conversation short. He didn't need a tagalong for this mission. He came to a complete stop and then reversed course. "I think I'ma go outside for a minute."

"The cold air will help," Angela said. "I do that sometimes, when I feel like I'm about to pass out. I would go with you, but I just got back from my break."

Didn't nobody ask your troll-looking ass to go with me, Bobby thought. "Alright, I'll catch up with you later," he said.

The next person to notice his peculiar behavior was one of the housekeepers. After running into him three times during their shift, she asked bluntly, "What you looking for in here?"

"What you mean?"

"You keep running in these rooms after the patient gone," she noticed. "What you need?"

Due to the employee hierarchy at the hospital, Bobby wasn't concerned about Juanita's perceptions. They both had entry-level positions, but transporters were slightly higher on the totem pole.

"Why I gotta be looking for something?" he asked her.

"Ain't no patient in here. What other reason you got to be in here."

"Maybe I wanna help you clean this room."

"Well, shit, grab some gloves," she said. "They got me working my ass off tonight. I wish somebody *would* help me."

"Not now," Bobby said. "Maybe later. I got something else to do."

"Then what you come in here for?" she asked again, but Bobby had already continued on his way.

When the charge nurse spied him later that night, Bobby noticed her eyes narrow as she stepped in his direction. A dark chill rolled down his spine. He wanted to take off, but he'd been leaning against a wall when she saw him. She'd be even more curious if he tried to get away.

Inside the room he was waiting on, a pregnant woman was complaining of abdominal pain. Rather than transfer her to ultrasound, the ER doctor had *finally* requested one of the coveted portable devices. The sight of it had made Bobby salivate. The look in the charge nurse's eyes took his emotions in a different direction.

"What are you doing?" she asked directly.

"Nothing." His tone was different than the first two times he was questioned. He even stood up straighter.

When it came to rank at the hospital, the ER charge was at the top of her department. The nursing supervisor could still come and bark orders at her, and the doctors sometimes didn't give her the respect she deserved. But all of the other employees understood that if you got on Roslyn's bad side, she could get you out of there immediately. You could complain to Human Resources later, but they weren't likely to override her decision.

"Are you on a run?" she asked as she stepped closer.

Bobby's whole body felt tense. He liked Roslyn. Not only was she smart and pretty, but she was a sister too. That was one of the things he loved about the hospital: They didn't just claim to celebrate diversity. They backed it up with plenty of minorities in leadership roles.

"No, I'm not on a run," he told her.

The nurse looked up at his hair before responding. The move was subtle, but it gave Bobby pause. He thought the complaints from the ER had come from the other charge nurse; a white woman named Patricia. It had never occurred to him that a black woman wanted him to do something about his nappy hair. He didn't know what to think of Roslyn now.

"Could you not stand here, in the middle of the hallway," she replied. "It's a lot going on here. You in the way."

Bobby felt his temper rising as he looked up and then down the hallway. *In the way? Of what?* The night had been calm. At the moment, no one was frantically wheeling a patient in his direction. If this was the *other* charge, he would've asked what the hell she was talking about. Some people simply can't stand to see a lower-level employee not working. Bobby hated people like that.

"Plus it looks suspicious," Roslyn added. "We've been having some thefts in the ER. If people see you standing around, not doing nothing, they might start to wonder if you had something to do with it."

Bobby's irritation dissipated, and he broke out in a cool sweat. The charge seemed to notice his unease – or maybe he misread her. In any event, she stepped past him and looked into the room he was waiting on. When she backed away, her eyes narrowed again.

She stared at him for a couple of seconds before saying, "We lost one of them a few weeks ago; that portable ultrasound..."

Her assertions were so dead-on, Bobby couldn't respond. His heart began to kick with enough force to make his shirt jump. If she couldn't hear it, surely she saw it punching through his chest. She also had to see the sweat on his brow, because Bobby felt it accumulating. If he stood there much longer, one of the droplets would bead and roll down his face. She'd know he was guilty then.

But maybe he was wrong about that, because the next thing she said was, "Have you seen anyone carrying one of those cases around – someone who's not a nurse or tech?"

Bobby shook his head. He had to clear his throat before he responded. "I don't even know what you're talking about. What case?"

His voice was shaky. He wanted to convince himself that it wasn't, but Roslyn's expression changed again. This time her head tilted slightly, and one of her eyes was wider than the other.

She asked him, "What you so nervous for?"

"I..." This was it: Bobby was about to lose his job. This was the worst-case scenario he'd been worried about since the first box of gloves he pilfered for Carl. *Fucking Carl!* This was all his fault!

"I don't wanna get in trouble," he said honestly. "I know y'all already mad at me, 'cause I didn't cut my hair. Now you telling me I can't be standing here chilling. I feel like y'all out to get me."

The best thing about his lie was it was based on truth, so his pained expression was genuine. His comments explained his sweaty face too. Bobby wasn't normally a good liar, but this one was genius. He watched as Roslyn's suspicion morphed into sympathy.

"Ain't nobody trying to get you in trouble," she said. "If anything, I'm trying to help keep you *out* of trouble. If you think people out to get you, why would you want to be hanging around *chilling*? Don't you know that's just gon' give them more ammunition to use against you?"

She was only ten years older, but Bobby appreciated her motherly tone. She sounded like she actually cared about him.

"As far as your hair, you got the right to be as nappy as you wanna be," she said with a smile. "But we have the right to decide we don't want you in the ER because of it. We have standards in this department. If you don't feel the need to adhere to them, that's your choice. You can stand on your principles all day long, even if your principles put you out the ER."

Bobby was still confused about which charge nurse had complained about his hair, but at the moment, it didn't matter. He had talked this one out of believing he was a thief – that was the important thing.

"Alright, thank you," he told the nurse. "I feel what you're saying. I'll do my best to stay busy. I don't wanna get fired."

"Boy, ain't nobody gonna *fire* you," she replied. "The worst that'll happen is you can't be a transporter *in the ER*. You can always go back to working the rest of the hospital. They don't give a damn what y'all look like over there." She laughed.

Bobby found it amusing how different units in the hospital took shots at one another. Listening to her, you'd think the ER was a totally separate entity. But workplace rivalries aside, he had to get the hell away from her, before Roslyn put two and two together again.

"Alright, I guess I'll go find something to do," he told her. He turned quickly when he felt the first droplet of sweat roll down his cheek.

"Okay," she called after him. "Good luck with that."

● ● ● ● ● ●

Another transporter, Carl Redding, arrived thirty minutes early for his shift that morning, because he never knew when he'd have to return to his car to drop off loot before he clocked in. He'd texted Bobby prior to entering the building and was not pleased to hear his employee had come up short with his thievery. Carl was even more dismayed when he met Bobby in the Meredith Building and saw how spooked he was.

"Yo, I'm out."

"What you mean you out?" Carl asked him. The men walked leisurely through the lobby, in the general direction of their department.

"I said I'm out," Bobby repeated. "I don't wanna do it no more."

"Nah, baby. You can't be out," Carl said with a grin. "What's the problem? What's got you looking like you seen a ghost?"

"You can't tell me I'm not out, if I say I'm out," Bobby complained. "I can be out whenever I want to."

"Alright. Calm down," Carl said. "Tell me what's wrong."

They stopped near a crowd of vending machines that offered everything from ice cream to pork rinds. Not many first shift employees had arrived yet, so there was no foot traffic moving around them.

"Man, I almost got caught today," Bobby whined.

"You saw another one of them cases?"

"Yeah, but I couldn't get it. It was a lot of people watching me. I think they know what's up."

He explained what happened between him and the ER charge.

Carl's mood remained chipper when he replied. "They not on to you. You just bringing too much attention to yourself; the way you hanging out, waiting on people to leave a room."

"What was I supposed to do? I told you they not leaving those things laying around no more. As soon as the patient's gone, they take everything."

"They'll slip up," Carl assured him. "They can't be on the ball every time. You just gotta play it cool."

"Man, you ain't listening. I'm sick of looking for them cases all the time. I feel like that's all I do. Everybody's asking why I walk around so much. I look suspicious."

"That hair's drawing more attention to you than anything else," Carl countered.

"This ain't got shit to do with my hair!" Bobby said, growing aggravated. "You ain't even listening to what I'm saying."

Carl ignored his outburst. "I hear you loud and clear, young blood. But you the one not listening. If you was smart, you could finesse this situation. But that starts from the ground up – including what you look like. Have you ever tried flirting with that charge nurse? She'll probably hand the damn case to you, if you give her some dick."

Bobby rolled his eyes at that. "Fool, she married, and I already got a girl. Plus she way older than me."

Carl shook his head. "Don't nobody give a damn about none of that. Not at this hospital. A lot of these women are lonely. They don't do nothing but work hard and pay bills. You wouldn't believe how many have offered to buy me cell phones, take me on vacation, whatever I want. You think they'd think twice about giving me something that belongs to the hospital; something they not even responsible for?"

"I ain't with that," Bobby said. "I don't cheat on my woman."

Carl shrugged. "That's on you."

"Anyway, ain't none of this changed my mind about getting that box for you. I can't do it. I'm out."

"You *out* out, or you just don't wanna get that case?"

"I can get the little stuff," Bobby conceded. "Those ear scopes, blood pressure machines, sutures... I can get that all day long. But if you can't accept that, then I'm out."

"You know I can accept that," Carl said. "But that's just pocket change for you. How you gon' go from getting three hundred a pop to getting ten, twenty dollars?"

"When that was all I was getting, it was enough," Bobby said. "I was cool with it."

Carl sighed. "Okay. Just get me *one more* ultrasound, and then you can go back to the little shit."

Bobby couldn't believe the way this conversation was going. "Say, man, you need to stop telling me what to do. I told you what I'm willing to do for you. You can either take it or leave it."

"Yeah, I hear you, baby. I just need one more ultrasound. I got people waiting on it. If you can get it this week, I got $400 for you."

That was a hundred more than Carl gave him last time. But it wasn't enough.

"Nah, man."

"*Five hundred*," Carl said. "You need to man up, baby. Get this money."

Bobby stared at him, wondering what the ceiling on this payment was. He knew Carl was reselling the stolen equipment, but he didn't know who the buyer(s) was. He was pretty sure another hospital wouldn't purchase equipment from an individual.

"Alright," he decided. "For five hundred, I can get you another one."

"That's what I'm talking about," Carl said. He gave him a pat on the back before walking away. "Text me when you got it."

"Where you going?" Bobby asked, noticing he was not headed towards their department. "You not gon' clock in?"

"I'll be there in time to clock in," Carl assured him. "Gotta check on something first..."

● ● ● ● ● ●

After meeting with Bobby, Carl headed to Central Supply in the Jackson Building. His heart sighed when he entered the department. For him, the room was like an oasis. There was nothing but hospital equipment from wall to wall. There were rows of tall shelves packed so tightly, you couldn't stretch your arms while standing between them.

Carl had tried to transfer to the department a couple of times over the past year, but each time he checked, they only had openings on the night shift. In retrospect, it was probably good that he didn't work there. Carl wouldn't have been able to resist plucking pricey items off the shelves on a daily basis. He would've gotten caught long ago.

But he didn't have to work there to get the items he wanted. All he needed was at least one thief implanted. He looked around and spotted his employee seated at a desk near the front of the room. Carl approached him and patted his shoulder.

"Yo, what's up? How you been, bro?"

Jalen looked up at him and offered a quick, if not sleepy smile. "What's up, man? You just getting to work?"

"Yeah. Thought I'd stop by to say what's up. How's everything with you? You liking your new shift?"

"Naw. Not really," Jalen said honestly.

"Having trouble staying awake?" Carl asked. His smile was radiant.

Jalen didn't think he'd ever met anyone who remained as upbeat as Carl.

"Yeah, it's kinda hard," he acknowledged with a yawn. "But it's not that."

"I can't imagine what the downside is," Carl said, looking around the room. "Everything looks sweet to me. Wish I was in your shoes."

"I told you they had an opening on nights."

"Can't do that. But if a spot opens up on dayshift, let me know."

"You'll be the first person I call," Jalen said.

"How's business?" Carl asked him. "You got something for me?"

Jalen shook his head. He swiveled his chair and gestured towards the back of the room. Carl followed his gaze. He didn't see anyone, but now that he was paying attention, he heard a few sounds coming from that direction.

Rather than ask who it was, Carl said, "Well, let me know if you still wanna sell your old phone. I better go clock in, before I mess around and be late."

"Alright. I'll catch up with you later," Jalen told him.

The men gripped hands before Carl took off.

A few minutes later, Jalen's coworker Milton emerged from the shelves with a clipboard in hand. Thanks to the new iPads they got for the department, he could check their inventory without a pen and paper. But Milton was old school. He preferred to write everything down and then transfer the numbers to the computer.

"I see you're still double-working yourself," Jalen called when the men locked eyes. "Why you fighting so hard against technology?"

Jalen thought Milton cut his eyes at him, but with those thick glasses, it was hard to tell.

"You probably got an old TV at home," Jalen joked, "a big, heavy one, with knobs that fell off, so you gotta turn the channel with pliers." He laughed.

Milton shook his head as he took a seat behind his computer. This time his look of irritation was clear.

"I'm just playing," Jalen told him. "You ain't gotta be so uptight, man. The shift will go by a lot quicker if you loosen up."

"It goes by just fine," Milton replied. "All you have to do is stay busy. Give yourself a to-do list with more things than you can accomplish during the shift. That way you'll always find yourself running out of time."

Jalen was surprised by how much sense that made. But, "How am I supposed to do that? I do whatever jobs they put in the system. If don't nobody need nothing, I ain't got nothing to do."

"Most of the people in this department wouldn't mind that," Milton said. "You could find somewhere to take a nap, for all I care. As long as I don't see it..."

Jalen frowned at that comment. Since he'd been working the night shift, Milton made it clear that he didn't want him around. Almost every conversation they had ended with Milton trying to get him out of his hair.

The two didn't speak again for the next five minutes. Jalen was grateful when the dayshift started to trickle in at six-thirty.

Not only did their arrival mean it was time for him to go home, but he was happy to have *normal* people in the department.

"Hey, boo! How was your night?" Misty asked. She approached him and gave him a quick hug.

When they worked together, Misty was Jalen's best friend in the department. She was cute and single, but she never tried anything inappropriate. She knew how much he loved his wife and daughter.

"I'm cool," Jalen said. "I miss you, though. I miss everybody on dayshift."

"We miss you too! But I know you gotta do what you gotta do for your family. How's nights going? You not having trouble staying awake?"

"I haven't fallen asleep yet," Jalen boasted.

"*Yet*?" She giggled. "Does that mean it still might happen?"

"I don't know," he said with a grin. "Milton says I can go take a nap if I want to. He said he'll cover for me."

"Really?" Misty's smile was infectious. "You told him that?" she asked their coworker.

"I don't care what he does," Milton said without looking away from his computer. His tone did not match their joviality.

Misty raised her eyebrows as she turned back to Jalen. She gave him a *Trouble in paradise?* look. He nodded, his eyes saying, *Yeah, this is what I'm dealing with.*

A few minutes later, their supervisor arrived, just as Jalen was clocking out.

"Can I talk to you for a second?" he asked and followed Corey to his office.

Corey was a tall, chunky man who had been working at the hospital for three decades. From the back, Jalen noticed his body was completely flat. But when he rounded his desk and turned to face him, Corey was extremely fluffy. He didn't try to hide his bulges. His shirt was tucked neatly under his big belly.

"Hey, Jalen. What's going on?"

"Can I get the door?" Jalen asked. He turned and closed it, without waiting for a response. His supervisor's expression was curious as they both took a seat.

"Is everything alright?"

"Yeah, I guess so," Jalen said. "I wanted – is it okay if I talk to you about Milton?"

Corey nodded. "Sure. What's going on?"

Jalen had a good rapport with his supervisor, so he was straightforward. "You know that guy's a weirdo, right?"

Corey laughed. "He's a little eccentric, yes."

"No, not just *eccentric*," Jalen said, shaking his head. "That dude's a nut job. I never met anyone more OCD than him. He does inventory every night. It doesn't matter if we get a shipment or not. He's always going through the shelves; counting and rearranging stuff. He don't even use the iPad. He does it all on paper."

"Yes, I know," Corey said. "He's been like that for years."

"He never leaves the office," Jalen went on. "I do, pretty much all the runs on our shift."

Realizing he was serious about these complaints, Corey's smile faded. "Milton's been working nights by himself for a long time," he said. "We decided to put another person on the shift to help him out. He's getting older, and he can't run around as much as he used to. But I thought that's what you wanted: You like to walk and talk to people, while he prefers to stay in his little cave and do inventory. I thought that would work out well for both of you."

"He doesn't like me," Jalen pressed. "Every time I touch something, he says I put it in the wrong spot. I've been doing this job for a long time. I know where everything goes, just like he does. Just because I put something in a different place than he wants it doesn't mean he's right and I'm wrong."

"Why don't you let him put things where he wants them?" Corey suggested.

Jalen's eyes widened. "Really? That's your solution; for me to let him have his way?"

"Sorry, I – I guess I don't understand what the problem is," Corey said. "Nobody else wants to do inventory and stocking. But Milton loves that crap. And he's good at it. If he's willing to crunch numbers all night, and all you have to do is leave him alone and let him do it, that sounds like a win-win. Doing the runs should keep you busy."

"Sometimes it doesn't," Jalen said, growing frustrated. "Sometimes there aren't enough runs in the system, and I don't have anything to do."

"And that's *bad*? Jalen, I don't think I've ever heard anyone complain about not having to work. If there are no jobs, feel free to take a break. Go to the cafeteria. Visit some of your friends in the hospital. I would never give you permission to take a *nap* – but as long as you're awake when someone puts a run in, I'm not too concerned about what you do with your downtime."

Dammit. Jalen realized how lame his arguments must've sounded. He wished he had a more valid complaint, but his supervisor was right. He should be grateful that Milton was such a pencil-pushing nerd.

The problem was Jalen couldn't make his money on the side with Milton watching his every move. Last night he tried to make two fetal monitors disappear. Because of Milton, they were both still on the shelf, safe and sound.

Jalen knew he'd put himself in this predicament by becoming dependent on Carl's money. In the past six months, 100% of his car payments came from funds he got from stealing. He'd already adjusted his budget to account for this.

But all hope was not lost. Jalen rarely encountered a problem he didn't eventually figure out. This Milton situation would be no different.

"You're right," he told his supervisor. "I don't know what I'm tripping for. If that fool wants to do all the hard work, I might as well let him."

"That's the spirit!" Corey's smile returned as Jalen exited his office.

CHAPTER EIGHT
THE FRIERSONS

Towards the end of second shift, Danielle was treated to a major scandal on the Continued Care Unit. While working at one of the hallway computers, she was surprised to see Miss Daisy, a demure PCT, suddenly rush from room 408. The look on her face was similar to the first time Danielle saw her run out of Mr. Frierson's room, except now Daisy appeared more fearful than embarrassed. The reason for that became apparent when another woman stormed out of Mr. Frierson's room and gave pursuit.

"Get back here, you whore! *Where the hell do you think you're going?"*

Danielle's jaw dropped as she took in the scene.

Mr. Frierson had been on the unit for months. Danielle recognized the screaming woman as his wife. She was usually a sweet lady; always quick to smile at the staff taking care of her husband. At the moment she was unrecognizable. Her cheeks were red, her teeth bared. Danielle stood frozen in shock as Miss Daisy sprinted past her.

"What the hell..."

She looked back in time to see Daisy duck into the employee break room. Mrs. Frierson gave chase, but she didn't catch up before Daisy slammed the door closed. The older woman found the door locked when she tried to follow her inside. After twisting and yanking on the knob to no avail, she began to pound it with her fist.

"Open the door! ***I know you're in there, bitch****!"*

"Oh shit," Danielle mumbled as she watched the scene unfold.

The commotion drew more employees from all over the unit. The break room required a four digit code to get in, so Daisy was safe for now. But Danielle knew she'd have to leave the room at some point. Their charge nurse was perturbed when she rounded the corner and saw several people standing idly by while the drama escalated.

She hurried to the visitor and asked, "*What's going on here? What are you doing?*"

Mrs. Frierson spun on her so quickly, the nurse recoiled.

"*This, this fucking Chinese **bitch** was in there giving my husband a blowjob!*" Mrs. Frierson spat. "*I saw the dirty whore with my own eyes!*"

Danielle didn't think things could get any more bizarre, but that was the absolute *last* thing she expected the woman to say. *Miss Daisy?* Giving a patient a BJ? Danielle wouldn't have believed that in a million years, if she wasn't hearing it firsthand.

She knew Mr. Frierson was a pervert, because he made a freaky comment to her when he first arrived on the unit. Last week Daisy said he said something inappropriate to her, but she wouldn't go into detail. She had seemed pretty upset about it at the time.

Danielle wondered when Daisy transitioned from being offended to agreeable. And even if she was agreeable, what would possess her to give a patient *head* at the hospital?? Daisy was one of the most seasoned and respected techs on the unit. None of this made sense.

Their charge nurse, Maria, was just as flabbergasted. Her face went completely white as she stared at the patient's wife. Her mouth fell open, and she worked her jaw for a couple of seconds before she could get the words out. "She, wh, what are you talking about? No one's doing anything like that on this floor."

"How are you going to tell me what I just saw with my own goddamned eyes?!" Mrs. Frierson barked. She advanced on Maria, until they were nose to nose. "Make this bitch come out of there, and she can tell you what she did!" She turned back to the door and tried the doorknob again. She gave it a hearty kick when it still wouldn't open. "***Whore!***" she screamed at the wooden barrier.

"*Stop it!*" Maria demanded. She boldly stepped between the visitor and the door. "*You're making a scene!*"

"No, your nasty tech is the one making a scene! What the hell kind of hospital is this? *You people are disgusting!*"

"Come to my office," Maria beckoned. "Whatever happened, we can talk about it in private. What you're doing right now is *completely unacceptable.* If you keep it up, I'll have to call security."

"You wanna call security on *me*?" Mrs. Frierson was incredulous. "*What about what your fucking tech did*?"

"Come to my office, and we'll get to the bottom of it. *Please*! You're making a scene!" she repeated. Maria looked around and saw that a few patients had limped from their beds and joined the gawkers. "Is Daisy even in there?" she asked one of her nurses.

The nurse shrugged, and Danielle spoke up. "Yeah. I saw her run in there."

"*Yeah, she's in there!*" Mrs. Frierson yelled. The veins in her neck stood out boldly. "She ran in there to get away from me!"

"Alright, come on," Maria said. "We'll get to her in a second." She took the woman's arm and was able to pull her away from the break room.

As she followed her down the hall, Mrs. Frierson kept looking back angrily, hoping the door would open, and Daisy would have the nerve to show her face again.

When they were out of sight, Danielle was the first to burst into laughter. Kelly, another PCT on the unit, approached her with a huge grin and big, disbelieving eyes.

"What the hell happened?"

"I don't know," Danielle said. "That lady just ran Daisy out of the room."

"You saw it?"

"Yeah, I was standing right here!"

Realizing there was only one eyewitness, the onlookers began to crowd around Danielle.

"Did she really do that?" Kelly asked. "Miss Daisy's like, she's so shy and quiet. And she's *married.*"

"Mr. Frierson's a *pervert*," Danielle told her. She was oblivious to the fact that other patients were listening, and her comments could get her in trouble.

"Did he try something with you?" Kelly wondered.

"He said something about my ass once," Danielle confirmed. "But I didn't take him seriously."

"He offered to buy me a car," Kelly said. This revelation got everyone's attention.

"Really?" Danielle said. "You never told me that!"

Kelly shrugged. She was an attractive woman, in her mid-twenties. She had fair skin and an exceptional set of knockers. Danielle would've been jealous of her, if Kelly wasn't so damn skinny. Below the waist, Kelly had no curves at all.

"It was just a stupid comment," Kelly reported. "At least, I thought it was at the time. I was helping him to the bathroom, and he asked if he could kiss me. He said he would make it worth my while, if I gave him some *loving*."

Danielle brought a hand to her mouth as her jaw dropped again. "No shit."

"Yeah." Kelly nodded. "I told him, 'Oh yeah, how you gonna make it worth my while?' But I was just playing. He said he could buy me a car. I thought he was playing too."

"*Daaamn*," Danielle exclaimed. "I guess he *wasn't* playing. Do he got money like that?"

Kelly shrugged. "I have no idea. I didn't even think about it. I told him he'd better watch his mouth, or I'd tell his wife."

"That's what I told him too!" Danielle recalled.

"They do have money," another nurse who was watching the back and forth commented. "Y'all never heard of the *Frierson's*? They're a pretty big deal in the city. They had that leather company in Everman."

Kelly's eyes widened. "No way."

"Yup," the nurse said. "That's them. The leather company closed a long time ago, but there's still a lot of money in that family."

"Shit," Danielle said. "You telling me I could've got me a car out of him?"

They all laughed, and then Kelly asked, "Do you want one bad enough to do what Miss Daisy did?"

All eyes returned to the break room door, which was still shut tight.

"Y'all think she really did that?" the nurse asked.

"I saw his wife when she first got here," Danielle informed them. "She was only on the floor for about ten seconds before

Miss Daisy came running up outta there. I'm starting to think she really was in there giving that man a blo–"

Danielle looked around and realized how many people were listening to them. Kelly and the nurse followed her eyes. Four patients were hanging on their every word.

"I don't know *nothing*," Danielle said abruptly. "Whatever happened in there is between that man, his wife and Miss Daisy."

It wasn't that easy to make the conversation go away, but her coworkers let her off the hook.

"Yeah," Kelly said. "I didn't see nothing, and I don't know nothing. Matter of fact, I'm finna get back to work."

"Me too," the nurse said.

Danielle thought it would be best if she followed suit.

• • • • • •

Fortunately Danielle's work didn't take her off the hallway. She was still near the break room when the door cracked open five minutes later. As Danielle approached, Daisy's face appeared in the opening. The tech started to close the door again, but she relaxed a little when she saw who it was.

"Miss Daisy!" Danielle exclaimed. "Are you okay? What happened?"

The panicked tech's eyes darted from right to left. "Is, is she still here?" she asked. Her voice was shaky, her lips trembling.

"Who, Maria?" Danielle asked, referring to their charge nurse.

Daisy shook her head. "No. *Mrs. Frierson*." She spoke in a whisper, even though it was just the two of them standing there.

Danielle fought to maintain a serious, concerned expression. A fit of laughter rumbled in her chest, but she managed to keep it down.

"She's in the office with Maria," she informed her.

The news didn't ease Daisy's tension.

"Miss Daisy, is it true what that lady said?" Danielle asked. "Was you doing something with her husband?" She couldn't stop a slick smile from stretching her lips then. This was simply too much. Danielle knew everyone had a different side of them that few people knew about. But even her secret stripper job paled in comparison to this.

Rather than respond, Daisy opened the door and squeezed by as she exited the break room. Danielle thought she was going to Maria's office, but Daisy moved quickly in the opposite direction. Danielle realized she was heading to the elevators.

"Wait!" she called after her. The hilarity of Daisy attempting to escape this indignity got the best of her. Her laughter came loud and boisterously. *"Miss Daisy! Wait! Where you going?"*

When she reached the elevators, the tech jabbed the down button repeatedly. As luck would have it, one of the elevators dinged, and the doors slid open. But it wasn't empty. To their surprise, their *manager* stood burly and angry, dressed in street clothes. Danielle didn't know Ramona was in the building, but she must have been. There was no way she made it from home that quickly.

Danielle wished she could've seen the look on Daisy's face when she and Ramona locked eyes, but the tech had her back to her. She did get to see her expression when the tech suddenly performed an about-face. Daisy's rosy cheeks were sheet white now, as if she'd seen a ghost. The disgraced tech got her legs moving again, this time much faster than before.

"And where do you think *you're* going?" their manager barked. She was a large woman with a deep, authoritative voice.

Danielle couldn't stop laughing as Daisy broke out into a full sprint. She thought she was running back to the break room, but Daisy sped by her, all the way to the opposite end of the hall. The tech didn't look back as she yanked open the door of the stairway.

"*Hey!*" Their manager gave chase. She looked just as comical as she clomped down the hallway.

By then several more employees converged on the scene. They didn't arrive in time to see Daisy make her escape, but they did get to see their manager snatch the stairway door open and yell at the freaky tech.

"You might as well come back, Daisy! You're fired either way! You hear me? You're fired either way!"

Behind her, Danielle doubled over with laughter. She had witnessed or heard dozens of outrageous stories since she started working at the hospital. This was officially the new number one. She couldn't wait to tell everyone she knew.

● ● ● ● ● ●

Danielle didn't know William or Sherry, two nurses from the sixth floor of the Meredith Building, but the story made it to them just the same. Ten hours after Miss Daisy's fantastic flight to freedom, they sat together in the hospital's cafeteria. It was two am, and they were both starving. This week the unconventional couple only had one shift together. Neither of them could wait to pick up a bed after lunch and make their way to their favorite elevator.

"Would you do it?" William asked as he watched his work-wife dunk a French fry in a pile of ketchup.

"Do what?" Sherry asked.

"Suck a guy off for a new car."

She rolled her eyes but grinned. "You're nasty."

"Yeah, that's what I thought," he said with a nod. "What kind of car would you ask for?"

"Shut up! I didn't say I would do it." Rather than eat her fry outright, she sucked all of the ketchup off first, slowly. "I'll suck *you* off for a new car."

"Whatever," he chuckled. "You'd suck me off for a can of Coke."

She giggled. "Maybe for a 20-ounce."

William laughed too. "What do you think is gonna happen to her?"

"You mean besides getting fired?"

"Yeah. Do you think she'll lose her license?"

"I don't think PCT's have licenses."

"I mean her certificate, or whatever."

"I doubt it. What if she doesn't even get fired," Sherry ventured. "Is there anything in our employee handbook that specifically says we can't have sex with a patient?"

"I think that's, um, an *unwritten* rule," William said. "Like we can't take a shit in the middle of the nurses' station without cleaning it up."

Sherry laughed. "So it's okay to take a shit, as long as we clean it up?"

He nodded. "I think so."

"I'll have to try that."

"Gross."

"It was your idea."

"Hey, what if she says the blowjob was for *holistic healing*," William offered.

"I don't think that would fly," Sherry said with a giggle.

"It might. You know the dick bone is connected to the—"

"Hip bone?"

"Not unless you're *deformed*. But think about it; if you offer the balls relief, maybe it will relieve other ailments in the body."

"I heard the old freak has cancer."

"If I had cancer, I'd want a blow job."

Sherry couldn't stop smiling as she watched him. She loved their time together, even if it was fleeting. She loved William's hazel eyes and his beard. She loved his wit and his sense of humor. If she wasn't married already, she'd marry him in a heartbeat.

"I wanna suck your dick," she revealed. "I feel like I haven't done that in a while."

William looked around comically and confirmed no one was in earshot. "It has been a while," he agreed.

"It's only been a week."

"Like that old chili commercial used to say: '*Well, that's too long.*'"

She smiled but said, "I don't remember that commercial."

William wasn't surprised to hear that. At times he felt like he and Sherry had nothing in common. She wasn't as bright as him, so a lot of his jokes were wasted on her. Still, they were compatible. Or was it only their genitals that were compatible? William had long ago decided it didn't matter. He once heard Albert Einstein's wife was a simple woman with an average intellect. Yet she fulfilled everything he needed in a spouse.

He reached across the table and placed his hand on Sherry's. She looked up at him and smiled endearingly.

"I love you," he told her.

His affection heated her whole body. Her smile deepened. "I love you too, baby."

"William?"

He looked up and did not panic when he saw a familiar face standing next to their table. The woman wore street clothes, rather than scrubs, which made sense because she did not work at the hospital. William's eyes narrowed as he stared at her, but he couldn't figure out where he knew her from. Sherry casually withdrew her hand from his. The stranger caught the move. She looked down and watched their interactions openly.

"Um, sorry," William told the woman. "I know your face, but..."

"Claudia," she said. "I'm friends with *Jennifer*. You came to a barbecue at my house last summer."

Sherry's heart stopped beating when she heard his wife's name. To make matters worse, Claudia looked down at her when she said it –

Jennifer

– *as* if the word was an arrow that would pierce her soul. But William remained cool and collected. He smiled and didn't miss a beat.

"Oh, hey, Claudia!" He rose to his feet and gave her a side-to-side hug. "What are you doing here? I hope it's nothing serious."

The woman was taken aback by his demeanor. His attitude didn't match what she thought she just saw.

"I'm, uh..." She frowned. "It's my father. We brought him to the ER tonight."

"Oh no," William said. "Is everything okay?"

"He..."

The woman looked down at Sherry again and shook her head slightly. William could tell her father wasn't the only thing she wanted to discuss. But he and Sherry hadn't maintained their relationship for this long by panicking every time they were found out. Their boldness seemed foolish at times, but it might have been the glue that held their affair together.

"He's gonna be okay," Claudia said when her eyes returned to William. "My husband and I – we've been so stressed since we got here, it didn't occur to us how hungry we were until everything settled down. I'm glad this cafeteria is open all night."

"It's is convenient," William agreed. "Just make sure you avoid the pasta – whenever they're serving it – unless you enjoy your bathroom time."

Claudia smiled politely, and then her attention returned to Sherry.

"Oh, I'm sorry," William said. "Claudia, this is Sherry. She works on my unit. Sherry, this is my wife's friend, Claudia."

"Hi," Sherry said. Her heart was beating so hard, she could see her fingers shaking when she reached to shake her hand.

Claudia said, "Hi," as she returned the gesture. She did not offer William's coworker a smile. "Well, I'd better hurry up and get our food, before my husband comes looking for me."

"Okay," William told her. "What room is your father in? I'll stop by when I get off this morning."

"C324," Claudia said. "It's in the heart tower." She turned and gestured in the general direction. "Over there somewhere, I think..."

"I know where it is," William said. "Are you spending the night with him?"

"I am, but my husband might leave soon."

Sherry thought she was repeating the word *husband* more than was necessary. Surely it was a jab at their apparent affair.

"Okay." William nodded. "In the meantime, I'll be praying for your father's recovery."

"Thank you," Claudia said. She offered him a genuine smile, but it faded when she looked down at Sherry. "Nice to meet you," she told her. "What did you say your name was again?"

Sherry's heart raced even faster. She knew Claudia had but one reason to remember her name: She wanted to make sure she got it right when she gave William's wife a call. But it wasn't like Sherry could withhold the information.

"Sherry," she said. "I hope your father gets well."

Claudia didn't respond to her before she turned and walked away.

When she was gone, Sherry reached and rubbed her forehead. "Oh my God," she breathed.

"What?" William said as he sat down.

"Really? Are you telling me you're not worried about that?"

He shook his head. "No. Why should I be? My wife knows I have friends at work."

"William, we were practically holding hands," Sherry said in a hushed voice.

"I'll find some way to explain it – *if* Jennifer asks," he promised. "I'll tell her your dog died, and I was comforting you."

Sherry rolled her eyes. "Yeah right."

"Are you ready to go?" he asked. He began placing their food debris on a tray. "I don't wanna be here when Claudia comes through the line. And we don't have a lot of time to get a bed."

"*A bed*?" Sherry's eyes widened. "You can't be serious. After what just happened?..."

"What happened?" he said. "I ran into a friend of my wife. It's not the end of the world. I'm still horny."

Sherry couldn't help but chuckle at that. "Oh my God, William. I can't – I don't even know what to say about you."

"You don't have to say anything," he replied. "Just lay back and enjoy the ride."

She shook her head. "I can't. That lady took me completely out of the mood."

"But, but you promised," he pouted.

"What did I promise?"

"You said you wanted to do what that tech did for her patient, remember? You said you feel like you haven't done it in a long time..."

"Are you telling me you still want a blow job?"

"My wife might leave me when I get home," he kidded. "A blow job would make me feel a lot better about that."

"*Jesus*." She shook her head but couldn't help but smile. Her work-husband was a certifiable screwball. "Okay. Fine."

"*Sweet*! Do we need to stop and get a towel, or..."

She sighed but her smile remained. "No. I'll swallow, William."

"*Score*!"

When he stood with their tray, she noticed he was already getting an erection.

"*William, are you serious*?" she hissed as she stared at it.

"It might be a tumor," he said. "That's why I need *holistic healing*."

"Damn," Sherry said as she rose to her feet. "You really don't give a fuck."

"Life would suck if I did," William agreed.

CHAPTER NINE
VIRGIL

Make his jaw fall to the floor
Make his dick get real hard
Put his accounts in overdraft
Make him use his credit cards
Drop that ass down to the floor
Spin on that pole
Do it real slow
Tease his ass
Tease
Tease
His ass
Don't show the nookie till he comes back
Champagne room is where it pops off
Squeeze my ass
Baby, it's soft
Titties real
Tweak my nipples
I'ma ride you like I fuck
Real slow
Damn, you got me hot
I'm finna cum
This pussy sweet like bubble gum
Your girlfriend tripping?
She ain't got no ass?
I'll be your private dancer
If you got the cash

Later that night, Danielle was hard at work at her second job at Club Paradise. As was the case with every Saturday night, the ballers and hardworking men were plentiful. Most were tipping well, because this was the fourth weekend of the month, which made it payday for everyone who got their checks bi-weekly. That was the pay schedule at Jackson Memorial, so Danielle wasn't too surprised to see a familiar face enter the building. It was inevitable, really. The hospital employed over 3,000 people. It was foolish to think none of them would ever come to her strip club.

That understanding, however, didn't make it any less awkward. Danielle was seated at a table with her boyfriend when she spotted Virgil Bason stroll into the building with two other men. Virgil worked in patient transport at the hospital. He came to Danielle's floor at least once a day to drop off a patient or pick one up for a procedure. Ever since she'd known him, Virgil had been annoying, so Danielle expected the same tonight. She sighed inwardly, hoping to avoid him if possible.

The club was BYOB, so Virgil and his crew headed straight to an empty table, rather than approach the bar. In less than a minute, a server approached them and asked if they needed ice or cups for their drinks. The server wasn't a dancer, but she had plenty of cleavage exposed. Virgil grinned like the pervert he was as he conversed with her.

Danielle shook her head and turned back to her boyfriend. Crook hadn't noticed anything. She considered giving him a heads up, but she didn't want to hear his mouth. Plus there was a chance Virgil would be discreet when he realized she was one of the dancers. It was a *slim* chance, but Danielle had to latch on to something. The alternative was already starting to creep her out.

A few songs later, the DJ called *Enchantress* to the stage. Danielle had a queasy feeling as she rose to her feet. She felt like she might throw up any alcohol she attempted to consume, but she was too damn sober to pull this off. She wished she'd gone to the locker room to snort a little more white when she first laid eyes on Virgil. Nothing gave her that *I really don't give a fuck* feeling like cocaine did.

She did not look Virgil's way as she made her way to the stage. But, as expected, he was staring straight at her when she turned to face the crowd. Initially he expressed shock, and then he smiled. His expression jumped to lusty excitement when Danielle started dancing and took her top off. He damn near ran to the stage when she shed her G-string.

With him standing at her feet with a fistful of cash, it was no longer possible to ignore him. Danielle dropped to her knees to give him a closer view of her breasts and also to deliver a private message. She hoped Crook wasn't watching them too closely.

"Listen, boy: Before you do anything dumb, I'ma let you know that my boyfriend's here, and he won't put up with no stupid shit. He'll stomp the shit outta your goofy ass."

Virgil's smile didn't fade. He started to turn around, but Danielle reached and took hold of his head. She pulled his face between her breasts and said, "Don't look at him, *dummy*! I'm just telling you, 'cause I know how childish you are. I don't want you to get fucked up."

When she released him, Virgil's smile widened. He wasn't bad looking. He had dark skin and a strong jawline. He wasn't muscular, but he wasn't fat, either. Danielle wouldn't have had a problem with him at work, if he wasn't so immature. But he was only 22, so maybe that was to be expected.

"I didn't know you worked here," he finally said.

Danielle continued to dance for him. "Yeah, I know you didn't."

"Why you didn't tell me?"

"Probably because I don't want people I work with to see me naked."

"Shit, it's too late for that now!" Virgil said. He looked her up and down. "Girl, you fine as hell! I think I'm finna go broke up in here!"

Danielle rolled her eyes. *Great.*

"It's okay if I touch you?" he asked.

She wanted to tell him it wasn't, but it wouldn't take long for him to realize she was lying. "It's fine, if you tipping," she said. "But don't you think that would be weird? We work together. We're like, cousins, or something."

He shook his head. "Shit, no the hell we ain't! I *been* wanting to get with you. I don't mind spending money to see what you working with!"

"Why you ain't spending it then?" she asked and stood to her full height.

She backed away from him and continued her routine. Virgil threw five ones on the stage and waved her back to him.

"Come closer," he said. "You said I could touch you, right?"

"*Yes, Virgil.*" Her annoyance was unmistakable, but he wasn't bothered.

"Bring that ass over here," he demanded. "Put that ass on my lap!"

Danielle grimaced. She wondered if the club manager would give her a pass, if she told him she didn't want to dance for this particular customer. Then again, what difference did it make at this point? Virgil had already seen her naked. He would continue watching her all night long, even if she didn't dance for him directly. He would take the story to the hospital regardless of how their night played out.

Danielle decided to get over her hang-ups and do her fucking job. She knew the risks when she first started working there. Virgil's money was just as valuable as anyone else's, and he was obviously an easy mark. If she didn't take advantage of him, then she wasn't the coldblooded hustler she thought she was.

She dropped to her knees again and turned her back on him.

"Hell yeah!" he shouted.

She watched him in the mirror in front of her as he ogled her bare ass and genitals. With her legs spread, he could see *everything*, even with the dim lighting in the club. He tossed more money as she gyrated for him. When he dropped his last dollar, he grabbed both of her butt cheeks. Danielle continued to dance as he squeezed them, like he'd been wanting to do at work for the longest time. His mouth hung open. He stared unabashedly at her goodies.

She could tell he didn't want to give up the view, but his desire to simulate a sex act was too strong. He reached for her hips and pulled her closer. The height of the stage was perfect. With him standing, her ass landed in his lap at the optimal position for doggy style. She could feel his rock hard erection as he grinded against her.

A minute ago Danielle felt like she was at his mercy, but now she felt powerful. Virgil looked like he was going to bust a nut in his boxers – all because of how fine she was and how good she felt to him. Her exhibitionist side was riding a new high. She scanned the mirror behind the stage until she spotted Crook in the crowd. She delighted in the fact that her boyfriend was watching one of her coworkers dry hump her, and there was nothing he could do about it.

She was a coldblooded hustler after all!

She crawled away from Virgil and entertained another customer who had come to the stage. She rolled onto her back this time and spread her legs wide. The new guy made it rain as Virgil looked on.

Danielle looked the customer in the eyes and smiled mischievously. "Thank you, baby."

The man reached into his pocket for more cash, but Danielle's song came to an end. She had to relinquish the stage to another dancer. She collected her money and asked the second customer, "You wanna get a dance later?"

He nodded eagerly. "Yeah. For sure!"

"I want a dance too," Virgil said, feeling left out.

She told him, "That's cool. It's thirty dollars."

"I got that," he said. "I'm a baller."

Danielle started to tell him, "*No, sir. You are not!*" She knew how much transporters made at the hospital. But emasculating him wouldn't put a dime in her pocket, so she said, "Alright. Catch up with me later."

Both men stared at her naked ass when she headed to the dressing room.

• • • • • •

"You know that nigga?"

Danielle only wanted to drop off her money with Crook. She didn't sit with him after midnight, because the club was packed by then. Having an obvious boyfriend there was bad for business.

But Crook took her hand and pulled her down to the seat next to him. Ignoring him was not an option. By then Danielle had snorted more than a little bit and was as high as a rocket. She had plenty of *I really don't give a fuck* for the customers and enough for her boyfriend too.

"What nigga?" she asked him.

Crook turned in his chair and faced her fully. "You know who the fuck I'm talking about." His demeanor was dark and serious, but Danielle wasn't worried about him getting out of line at the club.

"It's almost two hundred people in here," she countered. "I don't know who you talking about."

Crook looked around angrily, until he spotted her friend in the crowd. Virgil was at the same table he and his friends picked out earlier. There were two dancers flirting with them, but Danielle knew her coworker was saving his money for her.

"*Him*," Crook said, nodding in his direction.

"Oh, yeah. He work with me," she said casually.

"*Work with you?*" Crook's eyebrows bunched together. "*At the hospital?*"

She nodded. "Where else you think I'm talking about? You know he don't work here."

"Say, I told you I'm sick of your goddamned mouth."

"Whatever, Crook. I gotta get back to work. You done?"

"Naw, I ain't done. What that nigga doing here? You told him you work here?"

"No. He just showed up. He didn't know I was here."

"Bitch, you lying."

"*No, I ain't, Crook*! Why would I want somebody from the hospital to come here? He gon' go back and tell everybody, then they all gon' start coming." Danielle realized she had unwittingly added more fuel to the fire.

"That's what you want?" Crook asked. "You want all them niggas to start coming here?"

"*No, boy*! I didn't want *that one* to come. It just happened."

"And you gotta dance with him and shit? Throw yo pussy all in his face?"

"That's my job, Crook! I can't avoid him, just because I know him."

"This some bull shit," he grumbled.

"I gotta go," she said.

When she stood, he grabbed her wrist again. Danielle looked around and got the attention of one of the club's bouncers. Rudy was bald and bulky. He never had to defend Danielle from her own boyfriend, but he was up for the task if need be. Crook followed her eyes and realized he was about to get kicked out of the club. He released Danielle's arm and seethed as she sauntered away.

● ● ● ● ● ●

Virgil didn't make an ass out of himself that night, but Danielle found him unshakable for the next two hours. He showed up at the stage every time she danced and felt her up to his heart's content. As he drank more of the apple Ciroc his crew brought, he became more cocky.

"I can't believe I'm looking at your pussy," he commented as he stared down at her.

Danielle was on her back at the time, with her legs high and wide.

"It's just a pussy," she said. "You acting like you never seen one before."

"They all different," he replied. "I ain't never seen *yours*. Yours is special, 'cause I been wanting to see it for a long time. This is like a dream come true."

"Too bad you gotta put an asterisk on this little memory you're creating," she said.

"How you figure?"

"It ain't like you won my heart, and I'm gonna make love to you. The only reason you get to see my pussy is 'cause you paying for it. As a matter of fact..." She snapped her legs closed. "You been standing there talking, but I don't see no tipping going on."

"Whatever..." Virgil placed his hands on her knees and tried to pry them apart.

Danielle resisted and told him, "Don't play. I'll get you kicked out of here for fucking with me."

She looked to her left, where another bouncer was standing close enough to hear their conversation. Virgil looked that way, and the two men locked eyes.

"Oh, for real?" Virgil said to Danielle. He withdrew his hands. "You gon' do me like that?"

"If you out of money, you might as well go sit down," she told him. "Better yet, you can go home."

"I already paid to get in here," he complained.

"That don't mean you can touch me for free."

"But I can stand here and watch you, right?"

"*No, nigga!* You can take your broke ass back to your table and watch me from over there!"

"Is there a problem?" the bouncer said, stepping closer.

"Naw," Virgil said. He reached into his pocket and produced $20 in ones. "You doing me dirty," he told Danielle. "You know I don't get paid that much."

"Better go to the topless club next time," Danielle suggested. "Everything over there is cheaper."

"Naw, I'm here 'cause I wanna see the *whole thing*," Virgil said, grinning now. He placed his hands on her knees again. "Can we get these open now?"

"Holding money in your hand ain't the same as tipping," she informed him.

He laughed and dropped five ones on her stomach. Danielle's legs magically fell open. The bouncer backed away and gave them some privacy.

● ● ● ● ● ●

At two am Crook was still in his seat. Danielle had seen him talking and texting with people all night. She suspected he was slacking on his drug dealing, so he could keep an eye on her and Virgil. That was a bitch-nigga move. It was more irritating than having Virgil there in the first place.

To avoid further conflict, Danielle stopped dropping her money off with him. She had to keep it in her locker instead, but that wasn't the safest move. All of the dancers were hustlers and connivers. Some of them were thieves. Danielle hoped she wouldn't have to kick a bitch's ass for tampering with her locker. So far, each time she checked everything was as she left it.

By two-thirty Virgil was drunk and down to his last forty bucks. He'd been holding off getting a lap dance from Danielle, because he knew she'd break him down to his last dime. He stood unsteadily and marched across the club in her direction. Danielle was sitting with another gentleman, but he hadn't agreed to a lap dance, so she was agreeable when Virgil stepped to their table and told her, "I'm ready for that dance now."

"Are you sure," she asked, flirting. "You had me waiting all night..."

"Yeah, I'm ready," he said. "Here." He hiccupped and produced a wad of singles. "I counted it already."

Danielle had been getting paid in ones for so long, she could tell it was thirty dollars.

"Alright, boy." She took the money and then gripped his hand, so he could help her to her feet. "Let's go get your little dance."

"Naw, ain't *little*," Virgil said, slurring his words. "Ain't nothing little about me. I want a *big* dance."

She laughed. "What the hell does that mean?"

"You know what it means," he said. "Come on. Where we need to go?"

"Right over here," Danielle said. She led the way to the private area.

Virgil's lap dance wasn't spectacular. It wasn't as eventful as the one she had with her regular customer Patrick last week. But it was nice. Danielle wasn't attracted to him at work, but on the couch in the "Champagne Room," her appreciation for his masculinity grew. She liked the way he gripped her ass while she rode him. She didn't bother stopping him from kissing her breasts and nibbling her nipples.

Virgil was fully erect the whole time. She stroked him through his pants and could tell how big he was. Crook was bigger, and she preferred her boyfriend's personality. But she was no longer vehemently opposed to screwing around with her coworker, if the opportunity ever presented itself.

Most likely because of his inebriation, Virgil repeatedly tried to take the dance further than the club allowed. Danielle blocked his horny hands.

"You can't touch me between my legs. I don't know where your hands been."

"Come on," he pleaded. "They clean."

"Hell no, Virgil! You not finna go back to work and tell everybody you grabbed my pussy."

"I ain't gon' tell nobody," he promised. "How much you'll charge me – just to touch it one time?"

Danielle felt she was sliding further into whoredom by responding, but money was the only thing that mattered while she was at the club. Hopefully Virgil was so drunk, he wouldn't remember any of this when they got back to work.

"Thirty more dollars," she said.

"*Damn*! Just to touch it?"

"If you ain't got it, then keep your hands on my ass or my tits."

He pushed up, so he could dig in his front pocket. He came out with his last bill. It was a ten.

"Nope." She shook her head. "Better go to the ATM. They got one in the lobby."

"Girl, you gon' have me living on the streets. I can't spend no more money in here tonight. I spent a hundred already."

"You didn't spend all that on me."

"I gave you at least *seventy*."

Danielle thought he was probably right about that. She still should've stuck to her guns, but there was something about taking a man's last dollar... It gave her a rush that was comparable to the cocaine.

She plucked the ten out of his hand and said, "Alright. *Hurry up*."

Virgil smiled and reached between her legs as their song came to an end. Like all men, he went further than she said he could. His quick touch turned into a prolonged groping that lasted ten seconds. Danielle allowed it because he didn't try to penetrate her with any of his fingers, and his caress started to feel good.

When they left the lap dance area, she noticed Crook had moved to a seat closer to them. Despite the move, he couldn't see inside the Champagne Room, so Danielle wasn't sure why he bothered. The only thing he accomplished was to make himself look more foolish – and angry. He looked like a bull with its balls in a vice.

Danielle rolled her eyes at him and headed for the locker room. Before her shift started, she told him to give her a whole 8 ball, so she wouldn't have to get more coke throughout the night. Thanks to her foresight, she had no reason to speak to his jealous ass until they left at five am.

● ● ● ● ● ●

The ride home from the club was as tense as Danielle expected.

"You a straight up ho."

"How I'm a ho, Crook?"

"I seen the way that nigga was following you around all night. How you gon' get down like that with some nigga you work with?"

"I told you I didn't know he was coming! What was I supposed to do?"

"You looked like you liked it," Crook said. "Yo ass wasn't uncomfortable at all!"

"Of course I looked like I liked it! That's my job. That's what I do! I make all them motherfuckers think I like them! I want them to think I love the shit out of they ugly ass."

"You know he gon' run back to work telling all your business. And then what? You gon' have every nigga at the hospital showing up at that damned club!"

"So what, Crook? As long as they got some money, I don't give a damn!"

"What? Bitch, you know that make you a ho!"

"I'm doing the *exact same thing* I was doing when you met me! *The exact same thing*! You wasn't calling me a ho when you got your first dance! If I'm a ho now, I was a ho then too! That mean I been a ho the whole time we been together, so why you wait till now to start complaining about it?!"

Crook didn't have a response for that, so he kept his mouth shut for the rest of the drive. While he sulked, Danielle fumed. She regretted giving him all of the money she earned that night. If he was calling her a ho, then taking her money made him her *pimp* – and she wasn't a damn prostitute!

When they got to their motel room, she was ready to blast off with her heroin high and forget about all of this until tomorrow, but Crook threw a monkey wrench into her plans.

"Naw. You need to leave that shit alone. You can't be snorting boy and girl all night and think you finna get your kids back. You gotta start getting right, girl. You gon' quit working at that damn club, focus on the hospital and get your life together."

"Whatever, nigga! I'll quit stripping when *I* feel like it – not you! Gimme a bag!"

He turned away from her before saying, "I ain't got it."

Danielle was so pissed, she started to punch him in the back of the head. Instead she grabbed his shoulder and jerked him back around. "Quit lying, nigga! You just said you wanted me to quit snorting. Now you talking about you ain't got it. It's either one or the other!"

"It's *both*!"

"Then go get it!" she demanded.

"I gotta use that money to score some hard."

"Man, fuck that! You not gon' play me, Crook! You'd have enough money to get *both*, if yo ass wasn't chilling in the club all night; trying to keep an eye on me. Either go get it, or give me my motherfucking money, and I'll get it my damn self!"

"What about yo *kids*?" he snapped. "When you gon' put them ahead of all this bullshit? You act like you don't even want 'em back!"

"You ain't worried about my motherfucking kids! You worried about niggas looking at my pussy, and that make you a *bitch-ass-nigga*! Why don't you rap about *the real you* next time you go to the studio: *I'm a **bitch**, so I gotta follow my girl around all night.*"

Danielle had been in abusive relationships before, so she wasn't surprised when Crook bared his teeth and took a swing at her. What Crook didn't know was those abusive relationships taught Danielle a thing or two about defending herself from a man twice her size. She ducked, and his punch caught nothing but air. When she came back up, she brought a straight right with her. Her punch landed squarely on his lips.

Crook stumbled backwards, shocked that he missed her with his strike and she caught him with hers. He ran his fingers over his quickly swelling lips and was even more surprised when he tasted fresh blood.

"*Bitch*."

"You tried to hit me first!"

Danielle stood before him with her fists balled. Her fighting stance was official. She was still wearing her stilettos, but Crook realized he couldn't take her sexy appearance for granted. She had dodged his punch like a brawler and hit him like a man. Rather than go toe-to-toe and risk getting beat up by a female, he lowered his head and charged forward, catching her in a bear hug. As feisty as she was, Danielle didn't weigh enough to avoid getting taken down to the floor.

"*You bitch-ass nigga!*" she screamed. "*Fight me! Why you wrestling? Stand up and fight!*"

Crook wanted no parts of that. He was having a hard enough time getting his punches in while lying on top of her. Each time he let go of her arms, she struck out and either scratched his face or punched him in the mouth again.

Growing frustrated, he told her, *"Bitch, I'ma kill you!"*

"Do it, nigga! Kill me!"

She began to kick wildly in addition to throwing punches upwards. Crook started with offense, but he quickly found himself on the defense – despite his superior position. Danielle was like a Tasmanian devil. He tried to grab her arms and restrain her, but she was too quick. He needed two hands for one of her arms, which left her other hand free to punch and claw his skin.

"Gimme my money!" she screamed, over and over again. ***"Gimme my money, Crook!"***

She popped him in the mouth again, and Crook lost all willingness to preserve their relationship or her pretty face. He let go of her arms and stood on his knees. Before she could react, he began to pummel her head with blows hard enough to subdue a man. Danielle managed to block most of them, but two powerful blows got through. The first connected with her forehead. The other impacted her chin.

It was the second one that finally shut her up. Her arms dropped like a heavy load, and her eyes rolled to the back of her head. Her face went completely slack.

Crook didn't consider himself a woman beater. The guilt he felt as he looked down at the damage he'd done was real. He made it to his feet and staggered to the bathroom. Even when he checked the mirror and assessed the injuries she'd inflicted on him, he still felt sorry for Danielle.

He stood over the sink breathing hard and sweating profusely. His blood flowed freely into the basin. She had cracked his bottom lip so badly, he knew stitches were required to close the gaping wound. His shirt was ripped, almost completely off. He had so many scratches on his face, it looked like he'd raped someone.

"Shit," he muttered. "Goddammit, what I do?"

His reflection didn't offer an answer. To make matters worse, he wasn't the only one who wanted to know what had happened.

BOOM! BOOM! BOOM!

"What the hell's going on in there?"

The pounding on the motel's door sent his heart into overdrive. Even in the heat of the moment, Crook realized the visitor did not identify himself as a *policeman*, so there was still time.

He tore the rest of his shirt off and used it to wipe the blood from his face. His lip immediately began to gush again. There was no time to tend to it. He returned to the front room and hurriedly packed his belongings in a duffle bag. He threw his jacket on without a shirt and bolted from the room.

He nearly ran over the motel manager, who had come to investigate the disturbance. The manager was stunned by Crook's ghastly appearance. Running a motel in that neighborhood brought him in contact with the lowest lowlifes the city had to offer. The manager had seen shootings, stabbings, overdoses and beatings – but *rapes* were always the worst for him. He hated to see a woman violated in that manner.

"Hey, what the hell did you do?" he asked the bloodied man.

"*Get back!*" Crook barked. He had his hand in his jacket pocket. He gripped his car keys, but the bulge resembled a pistol.

The manager's hands flew into the air.

"*Don't shoot!*" he screamed. "*Just leave. Don't shoot!*"

Upon hearing a gun was on the scene, a dozen tenants ran in every direction. They were lured to the room by Danielle's screams. None of them wanted their nosiness to send them to the morgue.

Crook didn't mean to insinuate that he had a weapon, but he was smart enough to take advantage of the misunderstanding. He booked it to his car and hopped inside without opposition.

He knew there were a lot of eyes and cameras on him as he sped out of the parking lot. Hopefully everyone would calm down when they realized there was no rape; simply a domestic violence offense. His injuries were worse than Danielle's, so he might be able to convince the police that *she* was the aggressor.

In the meantime, he needed to find a place to stash his money, drugs and weapons before he went to the hospital to get his lip stitched up.

CHAPTER TEN
OBSTACLES

My pencil
My pen
My notebook
My chair
There's another computer over there
Please don't sit in my chair
Did you sniffle?
Are you sick?
Don't touch any of my things!
Don't open those boxes
I'll take care of the inventory
Everyone knows that's my thing
Where's my pen?
Are you touching it?
It's yours now
Take it when you leave
Did someone use my notebook?
When I left it, the top was facing six
Now it's clearly facing three!
Did you sneeze?
Why are you here?
I need germicidal wipes
What do you need?
A monitor? A razor?
An optical laser?
Here
You're welcome
Please sign for it and leave!

On Monday, February 27th, Naomi's shift at work was stained with anxiety. Ever since the baby shower on Valentines' Day, her pregnancy (or lack thereof), had been eating away at her like termites. The daily stress had accumulated in her gut. Now she felt it directly in her womb. It sat between her ovaries like a putrid cantaloupe; undigested and rotting, slimy and smelly.

It hurt so badly, she'd sometimes clutch her stomach in an attempt to alleviate the pain, or at least provide temporary relief. That Monday, her charge nurse happened upon her in the midst of one such crisis. Naomi sat alone in the break room. The pain in her belly was so intense, she had doubled-over, in addition to gripping her bowels with both hands.

The floor's charge stopped short when she saw her. The smile slipped from her face as the break room door closed silently behind her. She rushed to her PCT and placed a hand on her back.

"Oh my goodness, Naomi! Are you okay?"

Naomi looked up at her. She reached to move the hair out of her face and realized her forehead was slick with sweat. She wiped it and forced a smile.

"I'm fine. Sorry. Did you need something? I didn't hear you calling me."

"No," Velma said. "I didn't need anything. I was just coming to see if we had any sandwiches left. But, you don't look so good. Is it..." The color drained from her face. "*Is it the baby?*"

Naomi's eyes widened. She released the grip on her stomach and wiped the sweat from her palms on her scrub pants. "No, I'm fine," she told her. "It's nothing. I think, I think I felt a few kicks, that's all."

Velma's look of worry did not diminish. "Honey, are you sure? Are you having abdominal pain? You looked liked you were grimacing. The way you were grabbing your stomach..."

"I must've ate something that didn't agree with me," Naomi offered. "Between the baby jumping around and whatever I ate not sitting right, my stomach does feel weird. But I'm fine." She wiped her forehead again. "Just a little hot..."

Velma's tension eased a little, but the worry didn't leave her eyes. "Well, this is something you'll experience more and more as your due date approaches. When is your big day again?"

"I don't have an exact date yet," Naomi said. "I should get an update when I see the doctor again."

"You haven't had any bleeding, have you?"

Naomi shook her head, though she had been bleeding every month like clockwork. In fact, her period started that morning. The cramps played a role in her abdominal distress, but she knew that wasn't the kind of bleeding her charge nurse was referring to.

"If you have any bleeding *at all*," Velma stressed, "you need to get it checked out. You can go to the ER right now, if you want to."

The mere thought of that encounter made her stomach spasm so suddenly and so violently, Naomi almost clutched her womb again. But she couldn't do that – not with her charge nurse watching.

She could imagine the stunned report the ER doctor would give after performing an ultrasound:

"Um, ma'am, did you know that you're not pregnant? Er, um, you probably should've been tipped off by your menstruation cycle – and the fact that we have no record that *any* doctor has *ever* said you're with child. To be clear, the mass lodged in your womb is a *rotten cantaloupe*. We don't know how it got there or how long it's been there. But it's really gross. You'll surely die if we don't remove it. In the meantime, we've already told everyone on your floor that you're not pregnant; you're just a big, fat, ugly liar. When you get out of surgery, they want you to return all of the gifts you received for your *liar, liar, pants on fire* baby shower..."

"I'm fine," Naomi insisted.

She looked her charge in the eyes and offered a weak smile. Velma seemed to accept it.

"Okay, well, if there's anything you need," Velma said, "just let me know. My kids are all grown now, but I remember what it was like; all the icky and uncomfortable things that come with pregnancy. It'll all be worth it in the end, when you have that sweet, little baby in your arms."

The nurse's smile was endearing. Naomi hoped hers was too, even though her mind's eye wouldn't let go of the cantaloupe. She imagined herself swaddling the putrid fruit in the nursery, with her friends and family gathered around her. In her vision, no one said her baby was too black, bald, slimy or stinky, because all babies are beautiful, even the made up ones.

• • • • • •

By lunchtime, Naomi's anxiety had returned with a vengeance. But it wasn't the same as before. Rather than knots in her stomach, it was her head that throbbed as she stepped off her unit. She told the charge she was going to the cafeteria, but Naomi had another errand to attend to. This was a fact-finding mission that took her out of the Cardiac Tower to the seldom-visited Clark Building.

When it came to women's services at the hospital, the Clark Building was the hot spot. This was the only building where one hundred percent of the patients were female – with the exception of newborns, who might be boys or girls. In addition to pregnancies, some of the patients in the Clark Building needed hysterectomies, mastectomies or other GYN surgeries.

But, of course, it was the baby-making floors Naomi was most interested in. If she was to get an infant out of the hospital within the next few weeks, it was time to map out a plan.

On the second floor of the Clark Building was the Mother/Baby unit. Naomi had never visited the floor, but by definition she knew there were newborns there. The problem with that unit was the *mothers* were there too. It didn't seem likely that she could wrestle a baby out of one of their arms. She might be able to snatch an infant when it left mama's side for a procedure, but she'd have to know too much about the baby's medical regimen to pull that off.

Instead, Naomi knew the best place to acquire her child was from *Labor and Delivery*. She had never visited that unit either, but she knew that was where all of the magic took place. Mothers entered fat and uncomfortable and left with a baby in their arms. Naomi suspected the unit was somewhat chaotic, because there were a lot of births each day, and the mothers didn't get to keep their newborns right away. Even if the baby was completely healthy, they still had to go to the nursery for a while.

This was the gap Naomi hoped to exploit. So far, her plans for *Grand Theft Baby* were uncomplicated: Enter Unit. Select Baby. Leave With Baby. Common sense told her she'd probably have to add more steps than that. But until she encountered a problem, Naomi's best bet was to keep it simple. By working at the hospital, she already had an advantage over any stranger attempting the same thing. Her employment status gave her *credence*. Her ID badge opened virtually any door in the hospital.

Naomi was greeted by warm sunlight when she exited the Cardiac Tower at 1pm. The high temperature that day was 69 degrees. If not for the storm clouds that had been hovering over her for the past few months, she would've considered the weather perfect. It was only a short walk, but she found herself sweating again when she reentered the hospital through the Jackson Building.

Most of the hospital employees knew that although the buildings were all physically connected, you could not travel between them on every floor. To do that, you had only two options: You could remain on the ground floor and access each building from there. Or you could take advantage of an architectural design that connected all of the buildings via the third floor. Naomi weighed her options as she neared the Avery Building.

If she entered the Clark Building on the ground level and took the elevator up to Labor and Delivery, she'd emerge in the lobby. She would be greeted by a secretary, and she'd most likely have to pass the nurses' station before she made it to the babies. She'd have to explain herself to several people before she made it that far.

Naomi headed for the elevators instead, knowing it would be better to enter on the third floor. From that entrance, she'd emerge near the back of the unit. That would put her in the midst of the action. From there, all she had to do was find the babies, grab one and flee the scene.

Her plan sounded foolproof, but that didn't stop her heart from kicking like a mule when she exited the elevator on the third floor. Thanks to placards posted conveniently throughout the hallway, she was able to navigate from the Avery Building to the Clark Building within thirty seconds.

She ignored the twisting in her gut as she approached the double-doors that separated the towers. There wasn't much traffic at the intersection, but Naomi spotted a security camera overhead. She knew it was there to stop people like her from doing exactly what she was considering. But the camera wouldn't stop her. Once she got her baby, Naomi didn't plan on leaving through the same door. She'd take the stairs down to the ground floor and make her escape.

To the right of the double-doors, she saw a proxy card reader with a red light glowing. When she waved her badge over it, Naomi knew the light would turn green, and the reader would beep. She would hear a metallic click as the double-doors unlocked, and she'd be allowed to pursue her destiny.

As she stared through the windows on the doors, she was excited to see everything was as she hoped. There were nurses obliviously going about their tasks and PCT's doing the same. More importantly there were *babies*! The infants were all very small; in the hands of caregivers, rather than mothers – so Naomi knew this was the right unit.

But the PCTs' scrubs gave her pause. When it came to employees at the hospital, everyone's color scheme was set in stone, as far as Naomi knew. Female nurses wore pink, males wore maroon. Housekeepers wore gray, transporters wore black, and PCT's wore blue. But all of the PCT's on this unit had *purple* scrubs. Naomi stepped closer to the window. She rubbed her eyes, but they were not deceiving her. The nurses outnumbered the girls in purple, so they were definitely techs. But *purple*?

Naomi couldn't believe she was just now becoming aware of this. If the techs in Labor and Delivery wore *purple*, that's something she should've factored into the equation long before she made it this far. This was not a minor detail. It was crucial! Naomi would stand out even more than she already did, if she tried to infiltrate the unit wearing *blue*, when no one else on the floor sported that color.

She didn't realize how long she'd been staring through the window until her hot breath created a plume of fog on the glass. She backed away and noticed one of the nurses on the other side of the door was staring right at her. The sight of her large, questioning eyes caused Naomi's heart to rattle all the way up her throat. She swallowed hard but couldn't force it back down.

The nurse approached the door with an obvious frown. Her eyebrows were bunched in an expression Naomi read clearly: *"What the hell are you standing there for, weirdo?"*

Before the nurse reached the double-doors, Naomi shook her hand and waved her off. She turned and took a deep breath as she returned to the elevators down the hall. It took several attempts to press the DOWN button. Her fingers were trembling, and the buttons seemed a lot smaller than usual. A fresh batch of tears made her vision blurry.

In her peripheral, she noticed another employee approaching on her left. Rather than wait for them to get closer and inquire about her trembling, sweating and overall *up-to-no-good* aura, Naomi turned away from them and made a B-line to the stairway.

She ducked inside and was grateful to find herself alone. She cried aloud, briefly. The sound of her forlorn wail reverberating up the walls of the stairway was appalling, even to her.

She managed to get her tears under control as she descended the steps. When she reached the bottom, the physical exertion was a good excuse for the sweat that continued to pour down her face.

● ● ● ● ● ●

Naomi clocked out at 6:53 pm. She knew this because she'd been staring at the time clock for five minutes. Six-fifty-three was the soonest possible minute she was allowed to leave for the day.

On the way home, she stopped by her neighborhood Goodwill. They didn't have what she wanted, but she found it at a thrift store closer to her apartments: A pair of purple scrubs. They were a little small on her, but they fit well enough to make her look like she belonged when she visited the Labor and Delivery unit again.

The tears returned when she got back into her car. Naomi brushed them off her cheeks with her shoulders, until they became so overpowering she had to find something to blow her nose on. A frustrated scan of the front seat and glove compartment revealed she didn't have one fucking napkin in the car.

She continued to bawl as she yanked her scrub top up and blew her nose on it. She felt disgusting, and she knew she looked even worse. If she had any luck at all, she would make it home before her husband did. If not, she wondered if Bryan would even notice how repulsive she was.

She wished she could back out of all of her plans, but things had already gone too far. If it was only Bryan she had to contend with, *maybe* she could come clean. But after the baby shower, there was no way to ask for a mulligan. If she couldn't produce a baby, her life would be ruined. She might as well put a bullet in her brain to spare herself the grief and embarrassment.

She left the thrift store a determined woman. She may have looked like a blubbering mess, but her resolve was intact.

Four minutes later she cringed when she parked near her apartment building and saw her husband's truck was already there. But, as expected, he didn't even look her way when she entered their home. He slumped in his loveseat; his eyes glued to the television.

"What's for dinner?" he asked over his shoulder.

Naomi would've complained that she hadn't even put her purse down yet, and a *"Welcome home,"* would've been nice. But she didn't want to say anything that might make him look up at her.

"Gimme a second," she breathed and headed straight for the bedroom.

● ● ● ● ● ●

Eight hours later, on third shift, Central Supply employee Jalen Creel was finally able to put his master plan into action. The talk with his supervisor last week didn't go his way, but it revealed important bits of information. Jalen realized that in order for him to be successful, he had to work within the system that was currently in place.

When he requested the move to night shift, it was to help out with his daughter's school schedule. At the time, Jalen wasn't aware that the change was equally beneficial to his department. They wanted to provide Milton a *runner*, so he could hang back in the office all night. To Jalen, that sounded like a waste of resources. But if his department had the budget to pull it off, who was he to complain? His supervisor was correct on all accounts: Jalen enjoyed walking the hospital and mingling with his friends, whereas Milton preferred to remain in the cave like a hobbit.

Fine.

Jalen was cool with that, because there was one thing he knew to be true for all humans and hobbits: At some point, they had to go to the bathroom. When he got to work that evening, he was happy to find that Milton hadn't made their coffee yet. He volunteered, making sure to use five scoops rather than the four everyone was used to.

To his surprise, Milton complimented his brew. "Mmmm. This is good coffee," the older man hummed as he sipped from his personal mug.

"I made it a little stronger," Jalen admitted, "'cause I been getting a little sleepy."

"Taste good to me," Milton said before disappearing down one of the long aisles of supplies. "I like a little extra kick."

In the past week, this was the most amicable conversation he and Milton had had. Jalen hated for the good times to come to an end, but he was sure they would hate each other again come morning.

It took three hours before the hobbit had to go to the restroom. Jalen almost missed it, because his iPad was blowing up with runs he needed to do. He was determined not to leave the department until he got what he needed.

The moment Milton stepped out, he went to work. He snatched the duffle bag from beneath his chair and hurried to the back wall; where a lot of the more expensive equipment was stored. He snagged a fetal monitor, a surgical headlight and filled the rest of his bag with oral surgery equipment.

Jalen left the department and strolled casually out of the hospital. He dropped his bag off in his car and returned to do the jobs that had been piling up. The first run required a urology cart. Milton was back in the department when Jalen went to pick it up.

"Why are there so many jobs in the system?" the older man asked as he stared at his own iPad.

"Damn," Jalen commented as he loaded the necessary items onto the cart. "I didn't know you had one of those. You never use it."

Milton ignored him and waited for an answer. Jalen left again without responding to the question.

Thirty minutes later he returned for a set of disposable leads. Jalen was perturbed but not surprised to see Milton studying his clipboard again. Jalen knew he'd already done inventory earlier that night. There was no need for Milton to count the same items twice in one shift, yet there he was. Jalen sighed as he grabbed the leads.

"Are you putting that in the system?" Milton asked before he could take off. "We need to keep track of everything that goes out of here."

"I know how to do my job," Jalen snapped. "I been working here for a long time. It ain't no different on night shift."

Milton started to say something else, but he thought better of it. His mouth snapped closed, and he walked away; once again becoming one with the equipment.

The tension finally reached a boiling point at four am. Fatigue started to set in, and Jalen wanted to get off his feet. There were plenty of empty waiting rooms throughout the hospital, but there were cameras pointed at all of them.

Jalen hated to admit it, but his department was the best place for peace. There were no cameras inside, and his supervisor had virtually given him permission to take a nap.

When he entered the office, Jalen noticed the look of befuddlement on his coworker's face. Milton approached him slowly, as Jalen took a seat in the front of the room.

"What's wrong?" Jalen asked. "Man, you look like you're stressed out."

Milton didn't speak right away. Jalen could almost see the man's inner turmoil as he weighed his options and tried to decide how to broach the topic.

"You – we're, um…" The older man looked down as his papers. "It's not adding up," he revealed. "I looked at the runs, everything we've done tonight. Have you been to surgery? Something – maybe something they didn't put in the system?"

Jalen knew the question shouldn't bother him so much, but it did. Milton's never-ending inventory count was not only annoying, but it was deadly accurate. He could probably pinpoint the exact items Jalen had in his duffle bag.

It was too much! All Jalen wanted was a nap – not a goddamned inquisition.

"Man, what the hell is wrong with you?" he complained. "Why don't you put that damn clip board down and take it easy for a minute? Shit, man… Watching you run around this room is starting to drive me crazy."

"I, I don't see how it's affecting you," Milton said defensively. "I'm just—"

"Yeah, I know what you're doing!" Jalen said. "You counting everything in this department three, four times a night! I'm sick of seeing that shit!"

Milton recoiled, drawing his clipboard to his chest like a shield that might protect him from the onslaught. "It, it's not my fault if, if the numbers, the numbers aren't adding up," he stammered. "I just, I just need to know if you—"

"Say, get off my back!" Jalen shouted and rose to his feet. He made sure not to approach the old man or make any gestures that might be considered threatening. But if the two of them were going to work together, it was important to establish boundaries.

"If you wanna count equipment all night – *every night*, that's your business," Jalen told him. "But what you not gon' do is get me caught up in that mess. I don't care if your numbers aren't coming out right. Figure it out on your own! Don't ask me about *nothing* on your clipboard. And I don't need you keeping track of my jobs either. You crazy, and I don't want nothing to do with it!"

Milton continued to retreat from the verbal barbs, but he wasn't as intimidated as Jalen expected. As with most of life's uncomfortable situations, when you have *right* on your side, whom shall you fear?

"Two mouth mirrors," Milton said, reading from his clipboard. "A magnifying mouth mirror. Six dental probes. Two dental tweezers…"

Jalen's heart started to race. He fought to keep his expression hard and indignant. "What the hell are you talking about?"

"*Missing*," Milton said. "Three bone files. Two root tip picks. All here when we started. Now they're gone."

Jalen's mouth went dry. No way was this asshole so efficient! If Milton was upset about those nickel and dime items, Jalen could only imagine the fuse he'd blow when he realized they also lost a surgical headlight. Milton would shit his drawers when he made it to the fetal monitors!

None of this was funny, but Jalen cracked a smile as he watched his coworker lose his cool. Milton's beady eyes were bugging behind his thick glasses. His lips were trembling. He had dry spittle in the corner of his mouth.

It suddenly occurred to Jalen that Milton might be his winning ticket after all. Everyone knew he was a little off – but if Jalen could prove he was *stone cold crazy*, the hospital would have to let him go. If not, at least Jalen would find amusement in ripping his sanity apart shred by shred.

"I'm sorry I yelled at you," he said, returning to his seat. "But for real, I'm not answering any questions about your inventory, so don't even ask. Don't ask me about my runs either. You're not my boss. I don't have to answer to you, Milton. You can go be crazy all by yourself. Leave me out of it."

Jalen swiveled his chair away from him and pulled his cellphone from his pocket. He wasn't sleepy anymore. That left time for Facebook and Instagram.

An hour later he heard what might have been hyperventilating coming from the back of the room. Either that or Milton had turned into a werewolf.

*Sounds like **somebody** decided to count the fetal monitors*, he thought and laughed inwardly.

CHAPTER ELEVEN
EXPOSED

Towards the end of third shift, patient transporter Bobby Grant hit the jackpot. He had all but given up on his hopes of scoring another portable ultrasound in the ER. But, as luck would have it, he found that sometimes in life, working harder is not the answer. Sometime it's better to take a step back and wait for the things you need to come to you.

At 5:45 am his iPad notified him to take a patient from ER to surgery. When Bobby arrived in the exam room, he found a young, Hispanic woman surrounded by her family. They all looked distressed. Bobby would've felt bad for them, but he spotted a small case next to the patient's stretcher. He knew what it was immediately, but he wouldn't get his hopes up until he checked inside.

"Hi," he told the family. "I'm taking Ms...." He stared at his iPad but couldn't figure out how to pronounce her name. If not for everyone's forlorn expressions, he would've made a comical attempt. "I'm taking her to surgery," he said.

The family said a few words in Spanish before nodding and backing away from the stretcher. Bobby approached the patient and checked her wristband to confirm he had the right woman. When he let go of her hand, she immediately wrapped her arms around her midsection. She looked up at him with tears in her eyes.

Bobby had been working in the ER for so long, he was pretty sure he knew what her ailment was. *Miscarriage.* She was on her way to the OR, so they could remove the dead baby matter. Rather than compassion, Bobby's heart was filled with glee as he moved closer to the case the doctor left behind. If he was right about the girl's ailment, then this had to be a portable ultrasound.

He moved to the back of the stretcher and disengaged the brakes.

One of the family members asked, "Can we go with you?"

"Yeah, but not into surgery," he replied. "I'll show you where the waiting room is."

"Thank you."

As the family gathered their things, Bobby snatched the plastic case and stored it under the stretcher. He was so smooth, no one gave him a second glance. But then again, why would they? Hospital visitors had no idea who was allowed to handle certain equipment. Bobby didn't worry about them in the slightest.

He dropped the family off first and then wheeled the patient to surgery prep. He knew they would want to keep the stretcher, so he transferred his case to another empty stretcher before a nurse stepped out to greet them.

"Hi, Ms. Jaramillo," she said to the patient. She approached the stretcher and reached to hold her hands. "I'm so sorry for your loss. We're gonna take you back and get you cleaned up."

The patient started to cry again. Bobby's mood was quite the opposite. Adrenaline had his pulse racing. He was more alert and excited than he had been all night. He rolled his empty stretcher out of the unit, barely stopping to reply when the nurse told him, "Thank you."

The new stretcher should've gone to the ER, but Bobby took it all the way to his department instead. There were cameras in every hallway he strolled through, but he was free from their watchful eyes when he entered Patient Transport. At that hour, there were only three other transporters on duty. None of them were in the front of the department.

Bobby finally popped the case open and was rewarded with a beautiful sight. The portable ultrasound looked brand new. Dollar signs danced in his eyes as he rushed to his locker and deposited the case in his backpack. Before returning to the ER, he checked the schedule to see if Carl worked that day. Bobby waited until six am before he texted him to let him know he had the package.

That's what's up, Carl replied.

Don't forget my money, Bobby typed back.

• • • • • •

The two men met in Carl's favorite bathroom and sat in adjacent stalls. Bobby slid the case across the floor and listened as Carl propped it on his lap and popped it open.

"Hell yeah. That's what I'm talking about, baby. See, I knew you could pull it off!"

"I got lucky," Bobby said through the stall wall. "I barely got it; right at the end of the shift."

"I never lost faith in you."

Bobby frowned at that comment. Carl sounded like he wanted to come across as a mentor or father figure. But after their last little argument, Bobby wasn't sure if he even liked him anymore. They may have been friends in the beginning, but as far as he was concerned, it was all business between them now.

"Here, I got these too," Bobby said. He kicked his whole backpack under the stall, so his coworker could retrieve the items himself.

"Aw, hell yeah!" Carl commented. He scooped the instruments and transferred them to his bag. "How you get all this?"

"I came up on it yesterday," Bobby replied. "I was thinking that was all I'd have for you today, but then I lucked up on that ultrasound."

"Man, you finna get *paid*," Carl said as he zipped up his bag. He returned Bobby's empty backpack with his foot.

"Yeah, I wanted to talk to you about that," Bobby said as they stepped out of the stalls. "I think it's time for some *renegotiating*."

Carl's smile didn't disappear, but his eyebrows bunched together. "What you talking about, Bobby boy?"

"That ultrasound... You said you'd give me five hundred for it, right?"

Carl knew they were in the restroom alone, but he couldn't help but check their surroundings again before he responded. "That's right." He reached into his pocket and produced a fold of bills. Bobby couldn't stop his eyes from widening as he looked down at it.

"I'ma need six for that," Bobby informed him. "And those ear thermometers, I think you been getting over on me. They worth way more than fifty."

Carl's smile did fade then. But his tone remained conversational when he replied. "Naw, baby. That ain't the way this works. I said I'd give you *five* for the case, and that's what I'm giving you." He counted out five bills as he spoke. "And them tympanic thermometers ain't that damn expensive. You'll get fifty apiece for those, just like we always do."

"What about that other one; the one with the light on it?"

"That's an *otoscope*," Carl informed him. "You get fifty for that motherfucker too."

Bobby shook his head. "Nah, man. That ain't right. I *know* they worth more than that."

"Yeah, maybe brand new in a catalogue," Carl said. "But they ain't brand new, and they ain't in no catalogue either. You just gave me that shit in a dirty-ass bathroom. Ain't nobody gon' pay retail for that. Ain't no telling how long it's gon' take for me to move it. You get what we agreed on."

"Alright. I'll take fifty for those ear things, but that case... It's got to be six hundred."

Carl stopped counting money and stared at him for a few seconds. He tolerated Bobby because of what he could do for him, but he wouldn't say he liked him on a personal level. He weighed his options before deciding there was but one response. When you're a boss, you don't cave to your minions. Period. He hoped Bobby would accept that, but he had a contingency plan in case he didn't.

"If we was on the streets, you'd get fucked up for trying some shit like this," he informed him. "A man ask you to do something, you tell him your price, and then you do it. That's the end of the story. You don't do it and then tell the man you want more money."

Bobby's comeback was quick and cocky. "But we ain't on the streets, though."

Carl smirked and looked away for a second. He took a deep breath and bit his tongue on his next response. He finished counting the money and held it out to his coworker.

"Here, man."

Bobby took it. Rather than count it himself, he asked, "How much is this?"

"Six-fifty. Five for the case, fifty apiece for the thermometers and fifty for that otoscope."

Bobby's nostrils flared. "But I said—"

"Don't burn your bridges, baby. If you wanna renegotiate our prices, we can have that conversation *before* you bring me anything else. But this deal right here," he said as he hefted his backpack over his shoulder, "is *done*."

Carl stood tall for a moment, waiting to see if his nappy-headed associate would try the unthinkable. But Bobby knew better than to attempt to retrieve the equipment. He stuffed the money in his pocket and grinned.

"If I get another one, it's six hundred. And those ear scopes are a hundred apiece from now on."

Carl grinned at him.

"I hope that means you agree," Bobby said. He stepped past him on his way out of the restroom. "If not, I guess that means I'm through working for you."

Carl's lips remained sealed. He turned slowly and followed the boy out. The moment they exited the restroom, there was at least two cameras pointed in their direction. That wasn't the *only* reason Carl restrained from punching Bobby boy in the back of the head. But it was a good reason.

● ● ● ● ● ●

By noon that day, the sun was bright above the hospital complex. Overbrook Meadows was treated to baby blue skies and pleasant 75 degree breezes. Robert Stepp, a lifetime resident of the city and longtime employee of the Budweiser brewing plant off I-35, arrived fifteen minutes late for a follow-up appointment in the medical offices. Robert left the doctor's office twenty minutes later with a handful of pamphlets and the diagnosis he'd been dreading for over a week.

Despite his newfound ailment, his fear of chemotherapy and his unshakable belief that in the long run, nothing would cure him, Robert's eyes were dry when he returned to his vehicle in the hospital's parking garage. He started his car and drove slowly, up one level and then another. Higher and higher he went, until eventually there was nowhere left to go.

Robert parked his car on the roof of the garage and didn't bother to turn off the engine. He exited the vehicle and inhaled the pleasant late-winter, pre-spring breeze as he walked to the edge of the garage and looked over the side. He felt like he drove higher, but looking down, he didn't feel like he was very high up at all. The garage was only eight stories. He didn't believe he'd survive the fall, but he wasn't willing to take any chances. It had to be headfirst.

Robert said a prayer as he climbed the rim of the roof. It was only five feet tall. Surely they would've made it taller, if they cared about preventing semi-spontaneous acts like this.

Unlike the rumors he'd heard, Robert did not pass out on his way down. Also unexpected was a metal awning that protruded from the building more than he'd calculated. The awning snagged his left arm for a souvenir, but in the end, the suicide attempt was successful.

The coroner was not able to scrape his remains from the sidewalk (and his arm from the awning) before word of Robert's grisly demise spread throughout the hospital.

● ● ● ● ● ●

Three hours after one of their patients took the ultimate stand against cancer, patient transporter Carl Redding strolled onto the Continued Care Unit in the Avery Building. Despite the friction he'd experienced with Bobby earlier that morning, his shift turned out rather nice.

Most of his associates who were working that day texted him to let him know they had acquired the equipment he requested. Each pick up was as smooth as butter. As the stack of money in his pocket decreased, the amount of loot in Carl's lockers and car increased. He couldn't wait to put everything on the market and recoup his spending by twenty, fifty and in some cases more than two hundred percent.

In the Avery Building, he had to wait on the PCT he was visiting while she tended to one of the patients. Carl hadn't seen Danielle since last week. He was taken aback when she emerged from the room with a huge knot on her forehead.

"*Damn!*" He recoiled comically. "Shorty, what the hell happened to you?"

She frowned and rolled her eyes. Carl realized this was not the first time she'd been asked about the contusion, and she found no humor in it.

"I'm sorry," he said. He followed her to the hallway computer and watched as she inputted the patient's vitals. "You alright, though?" he asked.

"Yeah, I'm alright," Danielle said. "It don't look that bad, does it?"

Considering the knot was almost evenly centered on her forehead, Carl thought it looked *very* bad. She looked like a ghetto unicorn. He leaned against the wall and smiled. "Nah. It ain't even that noticeable."

She looked over at him with a grin. "Yeah, right. That's not what you said when you first saw me."

"I was shocked when I first saw you," he admitted. "But now that I look at it for a minute, it's not that bad. Least you not white – or light-skinned. It would probably be blue or purple."

Danielle smiled. Carl saw that despite the knot on her head, she was still attractive, in a hoochie kind of way.

"You right," she said. "Fuck them light-skin bitches."

Carl didn't think he said anything to warrant that response, but if it put her in a better mood, he'd take it. "So what happened?" he asked.

"I fell."

He shook his head. "Yeah, right. Who hit you? What's his name?"

She didn't look away from the computer. "I said I fell, Carl."

"I know you gotta tell these white folks that, but you ain't gotta lie to me," he told her. "Who was it? Was it your boyfriend, that Crook nigga?"

"Fuck him," she muttered. "I ain't with that nigga no more."

"I told you that nigga was *garbage.* His music's garbage too."

She smiled.

"Want me to whoop his ass for you?"

She shook her head. "He in jail."

"Good. They need to keep him in there for the rest of the year, for doing that shit to you."

"I didn't say he did it."

"You don't have to. Just know that you way too fine to let some nigga thump you upside the head like that. You can do better. Know that."

Danielle looked away from the computer. She turned to face him. "You always so nice to me."

Carl did not like the new look in her eyes. Danielle was a fine woman; any man could see that. But Carl preferred his women with a certain degree of sophistication. Plus life at the hospital was better for him as a single man.

"You deserve it," he said. "I know some good dudes up here – you should hook up with one of them. Fuck them hood niggas. Get a nigga with a *job*."

If Danielle noticed the deflection, she didn't mention it. "Yeah right," she said, her attention on the computer again. "Can't nobody making eight-fifty an hour do nothing for me."

"Hey, what's up with that tech on your floor?" Carl asked. "She was really giving one of these nasty-ass patients some head?"

"Yeah," Danielle said with a chuckle.

"Wasn't that the one who was acting all indignant a couple of weeks ago?" Carl recalled.

"Yeah, that was her. Then she ended up getting caught with a dick in her mouth." She laughed. "That's why I don't let these bitches act like they better than me. No matter how sweet and innocent they look, in the end, they some ho's too."

Carl laughed at that. He wondered if Danielle was aware that she just called herself a ho.

"Did you hear about that man who killed hisself?" she asked.

"'Course I heard about it. Fool's arm got tore off."

"I heard he came up here to confront a nurse his wife is having an affair with," Danielle reported. "She told him she wasn't gon' stop, and he decided to off hisself."

Carl smacked his lips. "That's not what happened! Damn. It don't take long for y'all to get the story twisted."

Danielle propped a hand on her hip. "Well what happened then, since you know so much?"

"Dude came up here with his wife," Carl explained. "She ended up dying in surgery, and he decided he didn't want to live without her. He went up to the parking garage and jumped."

"Dang," Danielle mused. "That's romantic."

"The hell it is. Bet you won't never see me kill myself over no broad."

"That's 'cause you prolly never been in love."

Carl was not happy to see the dreamy look was back in her eyes. He was grateful when the floor's charge nurse rounded the corner and interrupted them.

"Danielle, what's going on? You on break?"

She looked back at the woman and sighed. "No, I'm not on break."

"I can't tell," the nurse retorted.

Danielle's nostrils flared when she turned back to Carl. She cocked her head and asked him, "Is she still standing there?"

He looked over her shoulder and said, "She walking off."

"She get on my nerves," Danielle breathed.

Carl thought that was a typical response from a lazy thot who didn't deserve a job. He had plenty illegalities going on at work, but one thing he never did was clock-in just to be lazy. Of course that didn't make up for the thefts, but it made him feel a little better about it.

"Carl, can I borrow a hundred dollars?"

"What the hell?" He was not moved by Danielle's big, doe eyes. "Girl, I ain't got no money to be loaning you like that."

"I'll pay you back. I swear," she said. She touched his arm and let her hand linger there. "I can get you something off the floor. Maybe not today, but I'll get it, and you won't have to pay me nothing."

Danielle hated that she was in a position to beg a man for *anything*. She knew it was her own fault for falling for Crook. She never should've trusted that bastard with her money. She gave him nearly every dollar she made at the club for the past four months. Now here she was; wondering if she'd have enough gas in her car to make it through the week.

Come Friday night, she would be a *savage*. Every sucker in the club who even *looked* her way would get teased for every dime in his pocket. But making it to Friday wouldn't be easy. Danielle didn't have enough money to buy dinner, let alone pay for her motel room. On top of that, the stress from the whole ordeal had her fiending for a little nose candy. She wasn't a dopefiend, but Carl would be shocked to know the things she'd do for a baggie of brown.

He continued to frown as he reached into his pocket. He produced two twenties and handed them to her. "This all I got. But I don't be loaning money, Danielle. Shit ain't cool."

"I know Carl. I'm sorry. I hate that I even had to ask you."

She clutched the money in her fist and walked away.

Damn, that thing is swole. Carl couldn't stop staring at her ass every time he got a good look at it. He didn't fault himself for being a man. Even though Danielle appeared as primed as she would ever be, he was proud that he had enough sense and willpower to turn and walk away.

There were beautiful women at the hospital with a car and house in their name. A lot of them wanted to seduce him and make a meatloaf dinner afterwards. What the hell did a big booty hoodrat have to offer?

Absolutely nothing.

Carl chuckled as he got on the elevator.

● ● ● ● ● ●

Fortunately for Danielle, not every man at the hospital shared Carl's opinion. Many of them would actually prefer a big booty hoodrat over a middle-age successful woman – as was the case with Virgil Bason from patient transport. He showed up on Danielle's floor ten minutes before the end of her shift.

The sight of him made her stomach turn. Their encounter at the club was fresh on her mind. Now that she was fully clothed, she felt like a fool for allowing Virgil to fondle her goodies during their lap dance. She could imagine what he must think of her now.

But then again, *fuck him.* If she was a ho, then he was a bigger one. He was also a pervert and a loser who couldn't get his hands on anyone's cookie unless he paid for it.

She noticed Virgil was walking with another transporter who was pushing a patient in a wheelchair. As the second transporter rolled the patient into his new room, Virgil stepped to Danielle with a stupid grin that made her skin crawl.

"Damn, girl," he said. "What happened to your head?"

Danielle was so sick of that question, she could've screamed. This had to be the twentieth time she was asked today.

"I fell," she said and folded her arms over her chest.

""You must have fell on your ass too," Virgil joked, "'cause you got two big-ass lumps back there!"

"Man, that shit was corny as hell," she told him. "Have you ever gone more than five minutes without annoying someone? Is that even possible?"

"Why you being so cold?" he asked. "You wasn't acting like that at the club."

"Yes, I was acting *exactly like this*. You know I don't like you, Virgil."

"But why though? What I do to you?"

"You *immature*. I'm surprised you just now showing up to mess with me. Haven't you been here all day?"

"I did come earlier," he informed her. "A nurse told me you weren't here today."

"What nurse?" Danielle asked with a frown.

"I don't know. I think it was the charge. It was around twelve-thirty."

As much as Danielle hated Virgil, she hated her charge nurse even more. She had a good idea why Maria wanted to run her visitors off. During her shifts, Danielle had a constant trail of admires who stopped by to say hi. But her visitors weren't Maria's business! As long as they didn't interfere with Danielle's work, *which they didn't* (for the most part), then her charge needed to shut the fuck up. Maria was just upset because no guy ever came to say hi to her.

"I was here," she told Virgil. "I had just went to the cafeteria. I don't know why that bitch lied."

The transporter Virgil had accompanied to the floor pushed his now-empty wheelchair in their direction. Danielle didn't know him personally, but she thought he was kinda-cute. His ID badge identified him as Terrence.

"Say," Virgil told him, "this the girl I was telling you about; the one from the club."

"Really?" Danielle said. "You gon' do that shit right in front of me?"

Virgil laughed.

Terrence said, "You have to excuse my friend. He stupid."

Danielle couldn't have agreed more. She focused her attention on Terrence, who was getting cuter by the second. He was short with a crew cut that had serious waves. She thought he had a baby face – not only because he was clean-shaven. His skin was so fair, she knew he was mixed with something.

"Hey, you think you can hook us up with a lap dance?" Virgil asked her.

Danielle stared at him like the fool he was. "Why don't you get off my floor? I'm trying to get ready to clock-out. I ain't got time for this."

"Why you being such a bitch?"

"*What?*"

Virgil backed up, expecting a slap. "I was just kidding."

"*Man, I swear,*" Danielle grumbled, shaking her head.

"But you is acting different," Virgil said. "You wasn't acting like this at the club."

"Fool, we ain't at the club!" she snapped.

"We ain't gotta be at the club to get a lap dance," he countered.

Danielle thought Terrence was the more mature of the two, but he clearly enjoyed their banter. He stood quietly, smiling at the back and forth.

"Alright, gimme thirty dollars," she said, calling Virgil's bluff. "I'll give yo dumb-ass a lap dance."

His eyes widened. "For real?"

"Yeah," she said. "Where the money?"

Virgil looked over at his friend and grinned. "Shit, I wish I had it."

"That's what I thought," she said. "Now would you please get yo broke ass out my face?"

"What about me?" Terrence asked. "Can I get a dance?"

Danielle sighed as her eyes rolled to him. "And I thought you was all sweet and innocent."

"Not really," the boy admitted. "Me and Virgil both like fat asses."

Danielle laughed. She had to respect his honesty. "If you ain't got thirty dollars, then you can take yo broke-ass on too."

"I can get it," Terrence said right away.

"Bye, broke niggas." Danielle turned her back on them.

As she walked away, she considered the strange and unprofessional door she may have just opened. She didn't need to review her employee handbook to know this type of behavior could get her fired.

Fuck it, she decided. Her job at the hospital wasn't nearly as rewarding as she thought it would be. Her charge nurse was out to get her, and her checks looked like crumbs, compared to the money she made stripping.

Ever since Crook knocked her out and took off with her money, Danielle decided men would be a means to an end, nothing more. Thirty bucks from Virgil would buy dinner for the night and provide gas money. Thirty more bucks from Terrence would be enough to get her nose fixed. In return, all she had to do was grind on their laps for three minutes apiece. Anyone who thought that wasn't worth it was a damned fool.

When she approached the hallway computer to clock out, Danielle had to wait on her coworker Kelly, who had just logged into the system. Kelly gave her a disappointed look and couldn't keep quiet about what she had just witnessed.

"You work at a strip club?"

"Damn, ain't you nosey?" Danielle said. She didn't have a problem with Kelly, in general. But if this bitch wanted to look down on her, she could get snapped on too.

"I just, I'm sorry," Kelly said. Her face flushed with heat. "I wasn't trying to be nosey. But y'all weren't being that quiet..."

Danielle shrugged. "What about it?"

"You shouldn't have let them find out," Kelly warned. "You know they gon' start messing with you."

"Virgil came to the club all by hisself this weekend," Danielle told her. "Wasn't nothing I could do to stop him. I knew he was gonna mess with me when we got back to work."

"Maybe it's the way you responded to them," Kelly offered. "If you make them feel like it's okay to talk to you like that, they won't never stop."

"I don't give a damn what two broke niggas got to say," Danielle told her. "Everybody up here can kiss my ass."

Kelly assumed that applied to her too, so she didn't offer any more advice. She hurried to clock-out and get out of Danielle's way. If her coworker wanted to join the ranks of Jackson Memorial's ho's, that was her choice to make. Kelly would be a fool to stand in her way and try to swat dicks out of her face.

"See you tomorrow," she said and walked away from the computer.

CHAPTER TWELVE
BABY BLUES

What a beautiful baby!
Can I touch her?
Can I hug her?
Can I take her home with me and love her?
Blonde hair
Blue eyes
She looks just like her sister and brother
Are you sure you can handle another?
Don't be greedy
Hasn't anyone ever told you to
Give to the needy?
Hey, what's that over there?
*No, no, over **there**!*
What? Me?
Oh, no
I was just going to...
See if she was asleep
I wasn't gonna take her
That's silly
Why would I do that?
You're leaving?
Oh, okay
When will you be back?
I just...
Wanna see your baby again
Can I touch her?
Can I hug her?
May I please take her home with me
And love her?

At the same moment Danielle decided she might actually perform a lap dance at the hospital, PCT Naomi Gilcrease clocked-out after a long shift on the third floor of the Cardiac Tower. Rather than head straight to the parking garage, she went to the ground floor and reentered the hospital through the Jackson Building. She quickly passed through the tower and headed for the elevators in the Avery Building. She exited on the third floor and took a right; down the hallway that led to the Clark Building.

She made sure not to look up at the cameras as she casually approached the double-doors that led to Labor and Delivery. For her, the doors had taken on the feel of the Pearly Gates. They even seemed to glow as she stepped closer and dared to peek through the windows.

She was mindful not to linger too long. If the same nurse that spotted her last week saw her standing there again, Naomi might be forced to offer an explanation for her visits. But she didn't see the nurse today. She didn't stay long enough for anyone else to become suspicious. She only needed a few seconds to map out where a couple of things were.

She saw the unit's nurses' station in the distance. She saw a dozen patient rooms on either side of the hallway. She saw two PCT's; both females and both wearing purple scrubs. One of the techs was walking away from Naomi with a bundle in her arms. Although she didn't see anything but the swaddling blanket, Naomi's heart clenched.

Before her anxiety could set in, she made a right and continued down the hallway.

● ● ● ● ● ●

When she got home, Naomi found her apartment in its usual disarray. All of the gifts she received from the baby shower were still on the dining table where she had left them. They were now joined by a few dirty dishes, more unopened mail and Mr. Tucker. The ornery cat had officially claimed one of the baby's stuffed animals as his own. Since he was a stinky cat, Naomi suspected the toy was now stinky too. She had given up trying to shoo him off the table, but Mr. Tucker remained wary. He watched her with his good eye as she passed through the room.

Naomi entered the kitchen with three of her other cats on her heels. They mewed angrily as she entered the pantry and hoisted an enormous bag of Meow Mix. There were five cat bowls between her washer and dryer. She poured food randomly in the four that didn't have water in them.

Naomi headed to the bedroom next to change out of her scrubs. She didn't want to look, but as she passed the baby's room, she couldn't stop herself from pushing the door open. The smell hit her before the miserable sight. She didn't think it was possible, but the room smelled *worse* than it did before she removed the rotten kittens on Valentine's Day. The few boxes of junk she'd removed didn't put a dent in the work that was needed to get the room ready for her child.

Her heart shuddered. Her knees buckled as well. Sensing she was about to collapse in the hallway, she quickly closed the door.

● ● ● ● ● ●

For dinner, she and her husband had Totino's Pizza Rolls with French fries. Bryan complained about the meal, but he inhaled his first twenty rolls in less than five minutes, so Naomi considered her culinary skills a success.

Towards the end of supper, she decided watching her husband eat was kind of gross. He had pizza sauce in the corners of his mouth, ketchup on his fingers. There was always a half-eaten roll on his tongue when he opened wide to pop another one in. Naomi didn't say anything, because she figured she was just as disgusting. But she couldn't hold her tongue when it came to their child.

"Bryan, when are you gonna help me clean the baby's room?"

She watched his mood change right before her eyes. Naomi had been paying close attention to his reactions whenever she mentioned the baby. She hoped she was imagining it, but there was no mistaking the darkness that came over him.

He sighed and dropped what would've been his 31st pizza roll back onto the plate.

"I'm tired," he said. "I just got off work."

Naomi sighed as well. "I know you just got off. I'm not asking you to do it now. I just want to know *when* you'll do it."

"I don't know," he muttered. "We can talk about it this weekend."

"I don't wanna *talk* about it, Bryan. I wanna finally get something done. You said you'd help me last Sunday, but you didn't do nothing but play games all day."

"It helps me relax," he grumbled. "I work hard, come home stressed out. The game helps get my mind off things."

"What stress?" Naomi wondered. "Your job ain't that hard. You don't do nothing but drive around all day. Where is all your stress coming from?"

"Well, there's *you*," he said, looking her in the eyes. "Every day you're nagging me about something. Nothing I do is ever good enough."

"*Nagging*?" Naomi didn't realize her voice had become more shrill. "What am I nagging you about, Bryan? I only asked you to do *one thing* – clean the baby's room!"

"It's all *your stuff*!" he said, matching her volume. "Why do I gotta clean your stuff?"

"*It's not all my stuff*! And even if it was, I clean your stuff all the time! You think those shit stains in your drawers disappear by magic? I washed dishes tonight. When was the last time you helped with that? You didn't say one thing about the kitchen when you got home."

His eyes widened. "You want me to congratulate you for washing dishes? Hell, let's get the mayor on the phone. Maybe we can throw you a fucking parade!"

Naomi's eyes filled with tears that immediately spilled down her cheeks. "Well, what do you want me to do, Bryan? You want me to go in there, drag those big boxes out of that room all by myself? You know I could hurt myself, don't you? Do you even care what happens to the baby?"

He muttered his next comment, but Naomi was pretty sure she heard him.

"*Say it again*!" she blurted. When he wouldn't repeat it, she asked, "You don't want me to have the baby?"

He looked up at her angrily. "What difference does it make now, Naomi? You're pregnant, right? There's nothing I can do about it, right?"

He had never questioned her pregnancy before. The way he added *right* to the end of those statements made her wonder if he knew or at least suspected the truth. Her tears flowed even heavier.

"You wish I wasn't pregnant, don't you? You wish I wasn't, so you could leave and, and – go find that *bitch* Mallory, and–"

"*Goddamit, Naomi*! Seriously? This shit again?"

"*You fucked her*! I know you wanna be with her!"

"*That was two years ago*! She been done moved out of these apartments! I haven't seen her since the last time *you* saw her!"

"*But you still wanna be with her*!" Naomi blubbered. *"That's why you don't wanna have a baby with me, 'cause you still want her*!"

"Fuck this!"

Bryan shot from his seat and stormed out of the kitchen.

Naomi dropped her face into her pudgy hands and bawled. She cried hard and loudly, but her distress was not enough to lure Bryan back to the kitchen.

Ten minutes later, when she was good and cried out, Naomi left the room and discovered why Bryan was so good at ignoring her. He was planted on the loveseat with the Playstation controller in his lap. He had an expensive pair of headphones clamped over his ears.

The headphones were meant to get him closer to the action in his games, but their nagging-cancellation qualities were just as appreciated. Bryan did not look up at her when Naomi sulked past him on her way to the bedroom.

● ● ● ● ● ●

At the same moment Naomi and Bryan were stuffing their faces with pizza rolls, patient transporter Bobby Grant and his girlfriend Rochelle were having dinner in her east side apartment. She had made him baked chicken with a baked potato and steamed vegetables. Bobby didn't like to eat his vegetables – never had – but he ate them for Rochelle without complaint.

He always felt she brought out the best in him. Rochelle was in her second year at Overbrook Meadows Community College, working on her business degree. She was short and

151

skinny, with big, frizzy hair and coffee-colored skin. At times Bobby felt intimidated by her intelligence. He hadn't been to school since graduating from Finley High, and he didn't plan on pursuing a higher education. He worried that Rochelle would one day decide he was a waste of time. He couldn't say he'd blame her if she decided to pursue a relationship with one of her classmates who could hold a conversation about something they'd seen on CNN.

Until then, Bobby relished what they had. He cleaned his plate and asked for another serving. Rochelle brought him more vegetables along with the meat and potatoes. Bobby ate the veggies first, to hurry and get them out of the way.

"Did you decide if you're going to cut your hair?" Rochelle asked as she looked up at his afro.

"I'm not cutting my hair," Bobby said defiantly. "If they wanna kick me out the ER because of that, I guess it is what it is."

"Good." Rochelle was a natural-'do-black-power-princess to the fullest. "If they kick you out, do you think you could sue?"

Bobby shook his head. "I doubt it – not unless they fire me from the whole hospital."

"If they try to, you should let them," she suggested.

Bobby nodded. "The only thing is, if I get kicked out the ER, I can't get anything else for Carl."

Rochelle frowned and shook her head. "Baby, you need to let that go anyway. I told you that's not cool."

"But you saw how much I got from him this week. It's like I'm getting *two* paychecks."

"It's not worth it, though. You don't wanna be a *thief*. If you get caught, and they fire you for that, you won't be able to get another hospital job. It'll be hard for you to get *any* job with that on your record."

"I don't know about that. You remember that girl I told you about who got fired for fighting a patient?"

Rochelle continued to shake her head. "Yeah."

"I heard she just got a job at Baylor," Bobby told her. "That's right around the corner from Jackson. They said she was gon' get banned from working at another hospital, but she didn't."

"So, what are you saying? You're willing to take that chance because some random bitch got lucky? You're okay with stealing?"

Bobby realized this was one of those questions that might make him look like a bad investment in her eyes. Rochelle was okay with his lack of ambition and his $9 an hour job, but how much more would she tolerate?

"I'm gonna stop," he assured her. "But I wanna see if I can make some more money first. I been thinking about another angle I can play," he confided.

"What's that?"

"You remember I told you how Carl kept jumping up the price of that ultrasound, when I told him I wanted to quit?"

She nodded.

"That got me thinking," Bobby said. "How much is he selling those things for – and where? He went from giving me three hundred to five hundred with no problem. I told him I wanted *six* next time, and he said we could talk about it. If it's worth so much to him, it's got to be pretty valuable, right?"

Rochelle leaned forward with her forearms on the table. "You already know it's valuable, baby. It's a damn ultrasound."

"But where is he selling it?" Bobby repeated. "And all the other equipment I been getting him... That's not the kind of stuff you can sell to one of your homeboys."

"No, it's not," she agreed.

"I know he's not selling it back to the hospital," Bobby deduced. "And I heard he got at least two more people getting stuff for him every day."

"But – what difference does it make where he's selling it?" Rochelle wondered. "If you find out, how does it help you?"

"*Knowledge is power,*" Bobby said with a grin. "If I can find out what he's doing, I can make him pay me more. I wanna get five thousand real quick – then I won't have to fuck with him no more. I can walk away and be cool. If he don't go for that, I got something else in mind: I might be able to get him to pay me just to keep my mouth shut."

Rochelle's frown deepened. "You talking about *blackmail*?"

"You make it sound all *sinister,*" he said with a chuckle.

"But that's what you're saying," she insisted. "*Give me some money, or I'ma tell.*"

The way she said it, made Bobby feel like a snitch, even though he hadn't done anything yet. "You think it's a bad idea?"

She surprised him by saying, "Nope. Fuck that nigga. He been getting over on you for a long time. He needs to give you some more money, so you can hurry up and get out from under his thumb."

Bobby's eyes brightened. Just when he thought his woman might leave him if he didn't straighten up and fly right, he realized she was still his ride-or-die.

He nodded. "Yeah, baby. That's what I'm talking about."

● ● ● ● ● ●

After dinner, they went to the living room and got cozy on the sofa while they brainstormed. If Carl was only interested in small items, like gauze and catheters, then maybe he was selling them directly to patients. But it wouldn't make sense for a patient to buy a portable ultrasound – a nurse either, for that matter. If an RN needed equipment like that, it would be provided by whatever facility she worked for. Plus Carl's knowledge of medical supplies was unusually extensive.

"He knew the real name for those ear thermometers," Bobby told his girlfriend. "He know the real name for everything."

"What about medical students?" she said. "They might need stuff like that."

"The ones I see at the hospital don't bring anything with them," Bobby told her. "They use whatever's at the nurses' station."

"None of the hospitals would buy from someone like Carl," Rochelle guessed. "Even little clinics get their equipment from medical supply stores – unless Carl *is* a medical supply store, or he represents himself as such."

Bobby's smile widened. He loved when his woman talked *smart*.

"Okay," Rochelle said. She pulled her legs under her and sat Indian-style on the couch. "Let's try to think like him: If I had an ear thermometer, and I wanted to sell it to a stranger, what would I do?"

"The newspaper?" Bobby suggested. "Or the Green Sheet?"

Rochelle's eyes narrowed. She shook her head. "The newspaper maybe, but I don't think he'd use the Green Sheet.

Most people only pick that up if they're looking for a used car or a free kitten."

"What about Amazon?"

She nodded. "Maybe. But you have to create an account if you sell with them. You have to give them your bank info, your real name... Everything he has is stolen, so he's not gonna do that. Where's a good place to sell *stolen* stuff?"

Bobby thought for a second and said, "Craigslist?"

Rochelle smiled. "I think that's probably it."

She left the couch to retrieve her tablet. When she returned, Bobby sat closer, so he could look over her shoulder while she browsed the internet. Rochelle pulled up Craigslist's website and typed "medical supplies." There were a lot of entries, a lot of pictures to choose from. She narrowed her search to "Overbrook Meadows," and many of the options went away.

"Type in 'ultrasound,'" Bobby suggested. "*Portable ultrasound.*"

Rochelle did, and all but one picture disappeared. Bobby's eyes widened.

"That's it!" he told her. "That's the one I got him."

She looked over at him. "You don't know that."

"Yes, I do. I'm the one that got it. That's it right there!" He jabbed his finger at the screen. "*He selling that thing for $4,000*! See, baby! I told you he was getting over! He gave me five hundred for it!"

Watching him made Rochelle's pulse quicken. She clicked on the picture and pulled up the seller's information. The contact was listed as "Robert." There was a phone number provided.

"Call him," Bobby said anxiously. "Call and see if it's him."

"And then what?" his girlfriend asked. "If it is, what am I gonna do, just hang up?"

"Naw, you right," Bobby said. He thought for a second and said, "You need to set up a buy."

"I'm not buying that thing."

"Naw, baby. Just play like you wanna buy it. I'll show up at the meet spot and surprise him. Once he sees that I know what he's doing and how much he's making, then I can tell him I want *two thousand* next time I get one for him. Shit, really I should get *three*. He'll still make a thousand for doing *nothing*."

Rochelle considered his plan and said, "Okay. But let's make sure it's him before we call. We need to find out what else he's selling; see if it's any of the other stuff you took."

"Look up those ear thermometers," Bobby suggested, "or the one with the light on it. I forget what he said it was called..."

It took a little research to get the correct names for the equipment. Bobby was grateful that Rochelle was book-smart and good with the internet. She returned to Craigslist and typed "otoscope" and "tympanic thermometer." When she found them, she went through the same process of narrowing the search.

Each time, Bobby swore, *"That's it! That's what I gave him!"*

Rochelle wasn't convinced until she looked up the seller for both of those items, and they came back to the same "Robert," with the same phone number.

"I knew that nigga was getting paid!" Bobby told her. "That thing with the light – what you say it was?"

"An *otoscope*."

"He gave me *fifty* for that. Now his bitch-ass over here selling it for *four hundred*! Call that nigga. Set up a buy for the ultrasound."

"From *my* phone?" In addition to adrenaline, there was a trace of dread in Rochelle's bloodstream. But she couldn't deny this was exciting.

"I can't call him from *my* phone," Bobby said. "He know my number."

That made sense. Rochelle grabbed her cellphone and called "Robert." She put the call on speaker. Someone answered after a couple of rings.

"Hello?"

"Hi," she said. "Is this *Robert*?"

"Yes it is, how may I help you?"

Rochelle mouthed, *Is this him?* to her boyfriend.

Bobby was holding his breath in the background. He frowned and shrugged. It sounded like it *might* be Carl. But the man was speaking properly, and it was hard to tell.

"I was calling about the portable ultrasound I found on Craigslist," Rochelle said, continuing her role. "Do you still have it?"

"Yes ma'am," Robert said right away. "It's in excellent condition."

Rochelle looked to Bobby. He shrugged again and rolled his hand in a *Keep him talking* motion. Rochelle grimaced and sighed silently.

"Great," she said. "I was wondering if you would take thirty-five hundred for it, instead of four thousand…"

"No way. My prices are set in stone. If you wanna haggle, I suggest you keep looking around. Call me back when you see that this is the best price out there."

Bobby's eyes lit up. He could barely sit still. *That's him!* he mouthed. *That's that nigga!*

Rochelle nodded and motioned for him to calm down.

"Okay," she said. "Sorry – I was hoping to get a better deal, but I'll take it for four thousand."

"Great," Carl said. "When would you like to meet?"

They set up a meeting for tomorrow at a nearby Starbucks. When Rochelle hung up, she and Bobby laughed excitedly. He couldn't wait to see the look on Carl's face when he showed up at Starbucks and realized a huge portion of his criminal enterprise had been compromised.

When they were done laughing, Bobby took his girlfriend to the bedroom and peeled her leggings off. He buried his face between her thighs until she went cross-eyed. Before she came, he rolled her onto her stomach and slipped in from behind. After a few strokes, he grabbed a fistful of her 'fro and pulled her head back. Rochelle pushed up on her knees and cried out in appreciation.

Oh how Bobby loved his natural woman! He never got any of that *Don't pull my hair!* or *I can't go swimming* shit from Rochelle.

As the blood rushed from his brain down to his manhood, Bobby decided he would do whatever it took to keep her – even if that meant going back to school. He hated books more than he hated vegetables, but some women are simply worth it. Rochelle was worth much more than he currently had to offer.

CHAPTER THIRTEEN
FIGHTING NEVER SOLVED... EH, NEVER MIND

Later that night, Central Supply employee Jalen Creel was hard at work on phase two of *Crank up the Crazy*. He hadn't planned on giving his coworker Milton a hard time that day. The fetal monitor and surgical supplies he secured would hold him for a month. But when he got to work, Jalen saw a few dozen boxes lined against the wall in his department.

"Shipment came in today?" he asked his supervisor Corey.

"Yeah, we left it for you guys to stock tonight."

"You mean *Milton*?" Jalen joked. "You know he wants to do that all by himself."

"And, as we discussed, you should let him," Corey said. "Keeps him busy, keeps him happy, and you know you don't want to do it."

"True," Jalen said. "But if I get *super-bored*, I can help stock some of this, can't I?"

"Yeah, but you know you don't want to. You'd have to be *really* bored."

"Stranger things have happened," Jalen said with a grin.

By nine pm, first shift was gone, and Jalen's iPad was buzzing nonstop. He enjoyed delivering supplies throughout the hospital, but it was impossible to get under Milton's skin if he was away from the office all night. At ten o'clock he walked in and took a seat in his favorite chair. Milton had a lot of the boxes open by then. He was hard at work stocking their inventory and keeping track of everything; first on his clipboard and later in the computer.

Jalen yawned loudly and demonstratively. "Man, I'm tired."

He had his eyes glued on his coworker. Milton did not look his way.

"Hey," Jalen called. "How you doing over there? Prolly a lot better than I'm doing with these runs…"

Milton looked his way, briefly. He grunted or hmphed. Either way it wasn't a proper response. Jalen left his seat and walked up to him.

"Hey, you hear me, man?"

"Yes," Milton said, his eyes on his clipboard. "It's as busy in here as it is out there. You see all of the work I have to do."

"Yeah, but you're working in one spot," Jalen pointed out. "I'm walking around the whole hospital."

"That's your preference," Milton said knowingly.

"Most of the time it is," Jalen agreed. "But a nigga need a break sometimes."

Milton looked his way uncomfortably. Jalen could tell he didn't like the N-word used around him.

"You, you should take a break," Milton suggested. "I can let dispatch know you're running a little behind, so the floors won't get upset."

The little booger had a rational response to everything. Jalen was undeterred.

"Why don't you do a few of these runs," he suggested, "while I take my break. That way we won't have to call dispatch."

Milton frowned and pushed his glasses further up his nose. "I – I don't think that's–"

"C'mon," Jalen said. His smile was nice and neighborly. "You used to do *all* the runs before I came to this shift. Now you can't even do two or three?"

"But, but they sent you–"

"I know I came to this shift to help you out," Jalen said, "so you won't have to do runs anymore. But if we're gonna work together, you should help me sometimes too. If you needed help with anything in here, I'd be willing, if you asked. We're teammates, right?"

Milton continued to stare at him with uncertainty fogging his glasses. Jalen had not been a cooperative *teammate* thus far, but he was using buzzwords that were hard to ignore. Not only did their department want them to work together and get along. The hospital's board of directors wanted that too. Milton had been at Jackson Memorial for decades. He knew full well what was expected of him.

"Okay," he said. His shoulders slumped as he placed his clipboard on the shelf in front of him. "I'll do a few runs while you take a break."

"Thanks!" Jalen said.

He patted him on his back as the two headed to the front of the department. The slight contact made Milton jump and pull away, as if he'd been shocked.

"Sorry," Jalen said, laughing. "Didn't mean to hurt you, man. You okay?"

"I'm fine," Milton said gruffly. "I'm – I'm fine."

● ● ● ● ● ●

The moment he left the room, Jalen initiated his mischief. His actions reminded him of how he used to behave at Christmastime when he was little. Every year he found the gifts his mother hid around the house. Even if she had only run across the street to borrow a stick of butter, Jalen would find one of his toys, admire it, put it back and sit innocently on the couch by the time his mother returned.

He grinned delightfully as he ran around his department; opening boxes, stashing supplies, stocking things incorrectly and writing nonsense on Milton's clipboard. By the time his coworker returned, Jalen had not only wrecked everything Milton had done since the beginning of the shift, but he sabotaged everything Milton hoped to accomplish for the rest of the night.

Milton knew something was up the moment he entered the department. Boxes he hadn't opened were now open. Some were still full, while others were missing half of their contents. Jalen left some boxes in the middle of the aisles, while others were moved to the other side of the room for no apparent reason. Milton's eyes widened as he staggered to the shelf where he left his clipboard. Even that wasn't there anymore! Jalen sat in his favorite chair, watching nonchalantly as Milton marched his way again.

"Wh, what did you do?" he breathed.

Jalen found all of this hilarious, though a part of him felt sorry for the old man. Milton looked like he was going to cry.

"I tried to help you," Jalen said. "I started to stock some of that stuff, but after awhile I realized I don't understand your system. I thought it would be best if I stopped and let you handle it. Here." He held out his clipboard, which had been sitting on his lap.

He noticed Milton's fingers were trembling as he reached for it. His hands began to shake even more when he brought it close enough to read the numbers Jalen had scribbled. He flipped a few pages, his breathing becoming more unstable.

"Wha, wha – *why*?" he pleaded. "Why did you do this?"

"I told you: I was trying to help."

"No, you weren't." Milton's forehead glistened with sweat. Crimson flashed in his watery eyes. "You're not helping! This isn't helping! *You know it isn't!*"

"Yo, stop yelling at me, man. You–"

"Are – are you *stealing*? Is that what this is about?"

Jalen's smile fell away. "What?"

"*Stealing*! Is that what's going on? Why else would you do this?"

For Jalen, the accusation was infuriating; possibly because he'd been caught dead to rights. He stood suddenly and took an aggressive step towards his coworker.

"Why you say I'm stealing? Is it 'cause I'm *black*? Just because I'm black, I got to be stealing?"

He looked meaner than a Rottweiler off its chain, but Milton didn't back away.

"It has nothing to do with what color you are!"

"Then what is it? You trying to get me fired? I got a wife and daughter to take care of!"

Jalen continued stomping forward until he and Milton were chest to chest. Jalen outweighed him by thirty pounds. He also had the height and youth advantage. He looked down at his coworker with his fists balled, his eyebrows bunched together. A deep sneer distorted the side of his face.

"*Back up, nigga!*"

Whether Milton was in the right or not didn't matter at that point. His fight or flight mechanisms kicked in, and he wisely chose to back up.

"You say you like stocking this shit?" Jalen growled. *"Then shut the fuck up and stock it!"*

All of the air left Milton's lungs. He couldn't have responded if he wanted to. He stood shivering like a wet puppy, while Jalen stared him down for several more seconds.

The younger man eventually turned and stormed out of the office, leaving Milton to make sense of the chaos he'd created. Jalen had to return to the department dozens of times throughout the night to retrieve equipment for the floors, but he and Milton did not speak again. They went as far as avoiding eye contact.

By morning, both men were eager to clock-out and get the hell out of there. Despite Milton's meticulous bookkeeping, he was not able to prove that Jalen had actually stolen anything, so he didn't report the incident to their supervisor.

Jalen had a wife and daughter to take care of. Milton didn't want to get him fired for something he might not have done.

● ● ● ● ● ●

At two am, while Jalen and Milton were in the midst of ignoring and avoiding one another, RN William Harkins sat in the hospital cafeteria with his favorite girl. Sherry wore her tight scrub bottoms that night – at his request. William had been staring at her ass all night as they tended to their duties on the unit. He had wanted to skip lunch and head to their special elevator for some private time, but they were both ravenous. Plus there was plenty of time for both.

That night the hospital special was baked tilapia with a bunch of crap dumped on top of it. William and Sherry opted for the grill instead. They ordered chicken tenders and fries with a side of gravy. They sat across from each other and ate from the same tray.

"Would you kill yourself like that if I died?" Sherry asked him.

"Like what, that guy who jumped off the garage?"
"Yeah."

"Hell no," William said. "I heard he lost his leg on the way down."

"Lost it how?"

"It got stuck on an awning or something."

"I didn't hear that," Sherry said. She dunked a French fry in their gravy. "But why'd you say, '*Hell no*' like that?"

"'Cause I could never kill myself," he said. "I got kids and stuff."

"You don't think that's romantic, what he did?"

"A big, nasty splatter on the sidewalk?" He chuckled. "Sorry. I don't think that's very romantic. Are you saying you would do that for me?"

She shrugged and ate the fry. "Maybe."

"What about your kids?" he asked. "And your *husband*?"

"I'd feel bad about leaving my kids," she conceded. "But why'd you bring up my husband? You think I'd want to stick around for him if you died?"

"I don't know. Why not? If I was gone, you might as well give your heart back to him."

"Is that what you'd do, give your heart back to your wife?"

He frowned as he considered that. Sherry waited, but he didn't answer the question.

"Asshole." She threw a fry at him.

"Hey!" He jumped back as it bounced off his chest. He relaxed when he realized it didn't have any ketchup or gravy on it.

"You love her, don't you?" Sherry asked seriously.

"Of course I love my wife," he replied. "But I'm *in love* with you. Don't act like you don't love your husband."

She shook her head. "I don't know. Every time I see him, I wish he was you. Then my life would be perfect."

"I know what you mean," William said. "But since that can't happen, don't you ever try to find perfection in the way things are now?"

"Really?" she said sarcastically.

"I'm serious. You have a beautiful family at home, and you have me here at work. A lot of people wish they could have their cake and eat it too."

"I guess. But I feel like I'm constantly fighting the fact that it won't last."

"Why do you say that?"

"William, you can't be that optimistic. I know you know this could all go away at any second. We could get found out. One of us could lose our job."

"No, you could lose *your* job," he joked. "Everyone loves me. You're the biggest slacker on the floor."

She sighed with a roll of her eyes. "Can't you ever be serious?"

"You want me to be serious about our relationship's impending doom? I don't want to think about that. Why would you want to?"

"Because it scares me." She wrapped her arms around her body to ward off a sudden chill.

The fear and sincerity in her eyes broke William's heart. "I would die if I lost you," he told her. "That's the truth. Maybe I won't jump off a building, but inside I'll feel like I have nothing to live for. That's why I don't want to talk about it. I also don't want to talk about what I'd do if I got cancer. What's the point?"

She watched him for a while and then smiled, despite the dark turn their conversation took. "Okay. Can I ask one more question before we stop talking about it?"

"Shoot."

"Whatever happened to that lady who saw us together the other day – your wife's friend who came up here? Jennifer never asked you about her."

William shook his head. "Nope. I went home waiting for it. I had a great excuse planned out, but she never brought it up. I went to sleep, and Jennifer went to work. When she got off that day, she still didn't ask me. At this point, I don't think the question's coming."

"How can that be?" Sherry wondered, frowning again. "That lady looked like she wanted to slap me in the face, like she couldn't wait to go back and tell your wife what she saw."

"We were just eating lunch together," William said. "And we didn't overreact when we saw her. If we looked nervous, things may have gone differently."

"Speak for yourself. I was really nervous. I don't know how you were able to play it off so easily."

"No one pays you any attention unless you look guilty," he informed her. Then, "Hey, are you done eating? We'd better get a move on, if we're gonna pick up a bed..."

Sherry didn't respond. William noticed her eyes were as big as doorknobs.

"*Oh my fucking God*," she breathed, barely moving her lips.

"What?"

"Don't look!"

She kicked him under the table, when he started to follow her gaze.

"Ow! What the hell?"

"*Don't look*," she hissed through clenched teeth.

"What is it?" he asked. He wanted to reach down and rub his sore shin, but she made him feel like he shouldn't move at all.

"I think it's your *wife*," Sherry whispered. She'd never met the woman in person, but she and William were friends on Facebook. Over the years, she had "liked" plenty of his family pictures.

William's eyes widened too. "No shit?"

"Yes," Sherry whispered, daring a glance over his shoulder. "She just walked in. *Oh, God, she's looking right at us.*"

William looked down at her hands and saw that her fingers were trembling.

"Well, I guess that answers the question," he said.

"What question?"

"Why she didn't ask me about what her friend saw. Apparently she wanted to see it for herself."

Sherry's jaw dropped. "How can you be so calm about this?" Her eyes darted again, and then she squeezed them closed. "*Oh God.*"

"Calm down," William coached her. "Remember, we're only guilty if we look guilty. Open your eyes."

She did, reluctantly.

"How far away is she?" he asked.

Sherry took a deep breath and said, "Twenty feet."

"Does she look mad?"

"Yes, William. She came to the hospital at two in the morning to catch you cheating. She looks very upset."

"Let me do the talking," he said.

Sherry wouldn't have had it any other way. When she looked again, William's wife was almost within clawing distance. William looked back at that moment and feigned surprise.

"Jennifer? Wha – babe, what are you doing here?" His expression quickly morphed from confusion to worry. He shot to his feet and asked, "Oh my God, is everything alright? The kids – are they okay?"

His wife watched him, in a zombie-like trance. Jennifer was tall and slim. She was in her late thirties, like her husband. And, like William, she was physically beautiful. Even now, while Jennifer struggled to hold it together, Sherry felt like a mud duck compared to her. Jennifer's figure was modelesque, whereas Sherry was short and lumpy. Jennifer had a flat tummy and surprisingly perky boobs. She wore jeans and a tee shirt with an oversized jacket Sherry assumed belonged to her husband.

Of course Jennifer's most obvious features (and the most perplexing, as far as Sherry was concerned) was her long, blonde hair and creamy white skin. Sherry never drilled William about why he married a white woman, because after knowing him for so long, she'd accepted that he was one of those rare Americans who was truly colorblind.

But still, she couldn't help but wonder.

Regardless of Jennifer's race, Sherry couldn't deny that she was gorgeous. After seeing her pictures on Facebook, Sherry often wondered why William slept around. What could he possibly want that he didn't already have at home. Seeing his wife in person brought those feelings back tenfold. Sherry felt so inadequate, she wanted to find a troll cave to crawl into. She didn't deserve to breathe the same air as Jennifer.

The wife looked past her husband and stared at the mistress. Jennifer appeared weak up until that moment. But when she and Sherry locked eyes, a fire ignited in Jennifer's soul. She suddenly appeared strong, threatening even. She looked down at the troll, shooting lightning from her eyes. Finally she spoke through clenched teeth.

"Could I please speak with *my husband* – alone?"

Sherry's jaw dropped. Her tongue became lodged in the back of her throat. She couldn't get her mouth working, but her legs moved just fine. She stood hastily and nearly tripped over her feet as she fled the scene. She was a few steps away before she realized she hadn't responded to the question.

"Yuh, yeah," she said to Jennifer, without looking her in the eyes. "Sorry, uh..."

The cafeteria suddenly felt like a furnace. Sherry's whole body was on fire. As she fled the scene, she looked around and felt like everyone was watching her. Regardless of how this played out, the people she worked with would never let her live this down. They had memories like elephants.

"Babe, tell me what's wrong," William said, forcing the attention back to himself.

He took hold of his wife's hands, and gradually her eyes returned to his. As they did, so did her grief. Jennifer's baby blue orbs glistened in a pool of sorrow.

"Is that her?" she asked.

William's eyebrows meshed together in confusion. "What? What are you talking about?"

"Is that the one Claudia said you were with? She saw you having lunch with her."

William was pissed that a snitch was trying to ruin his marriage. He suppressed his anger.

"Oh – *wait a minute.*" His eyes registered understanding. "I saw your friend a few nights ago. The way..." He shook his head. "The way she looked at me when she saw us having lunch – I felt like something was up. But Sherry and I are just friends. Did Claudia – babe, did she tell you something crazy – is that why you're here?"

Jennifer didn't look like she believed him. In fact, her countenance continued to deteriorate as they stood there.

"Baby, please... Tell me what's wrong," William said.

He reached and placed a hand on her cheek, just as her whole face crumpled. His only goal at that point was to get her out of the cafeteria, before she had a complete breakdown in front of his coworkers.

"Come on," he told her. "Let's go outside and talk."

He put an arm around her waist and turned her towards the exit. Jennifer lowered her face into her hands and cried audibly as they walked. William's look of concern was genuine now. His only saving grace was the fact that this was a hospital. Anyone who spent enough time there would eventually happen upon someone in mourning. Usually it was a whole family in tears. Hopefully people would think William was comforting one of the bereaved.

One person who did not believe that was Sarge, a security guard who worked the night shift. He knew about the affair and didn't try to hide a smirk as William and Jennifer approached him on their way out of the cafeteria. His smug expression was infuriating. William wanted to punch the flashlight cop right in the choppers. But not only would that get him fired, it would reveal to Jennifer that she was right about everything she suspected. Instead William sneered at him and held his wife closer.

Sarge was polite enough to step aside and hold the door open for them.

●　●　●　●　●　●

In the basement of the Jackson Building, dispatch employees Rosa and Tamara grinned giddily as they watched the scene unfold on five security cameras that monitored the cafeteria. The two am lunch hour always provided great entertainment when William and Sherry were working. Tamara even made popcorn for the girls to snack on during the show.

Tonight they were thrilled to see their soap opera introduce a new character – *The Wife*! Even more captivating was *The Wife* was *White*! The girls couldn't hear what she said when she approached the table, but *The Mistress* took off like a bat out of hell. *The Husband* seemed to be having a hard time explaining himself.

"Did you know his wife was *white*?" Tamara asked her friend.

"No!" Rosa stared wide-eyed at the monitor. "How the hell would I know?"

"Why the hell is he married to a *white woman*?"

"Aw hell. Don't tell me that pisses you off."

Tamara couldn't hide her disgust. "Yeah, it does. Every time a brother get out the hood and make something of himself, he wanna strut around with a white bitch on his arm."

Rosa laughed. "You don't know if he made it *out the hood*. You don't know nothing about him."

"I know he like *sisters*," Tamara countered, "or else he wouldn't be fucking that chick he work with. If he want some dark meat that bad, he shouldn't have married pinkie. I wish these cameras had audio…" She reached into the Pop Secret bag in Rosa's lap and grabbed a handful of buttery goodness.

"I know, right?" Rosa said. "But you already know what they're saying."

Both ladies were completely enthralled in the drama. One hundred percent of their attention was focused on the cafeteria monitors. A baby thief could've ran past ten cameras in their peripheral, with a screaming newborn in her arms and eight nurses chasing her, and dispatch wouldn't have sounded one alarm.

"I know his wife is like, *'Bitch, what you doing with my man?!'*" Tamara didn't bother to cover her mouth as she spoke. "And that bitch is like, *'Oh my God, I didn't know he was married!'*"

Rosa laughed. She said, "Girl, they not even talking that much. And ol' boy's wife don't have that kind of energy. Look at her; she's the one crying."

"Yeah, she is," Tamara noticed. "White women don't never do nothing right. Bitch, what the fuck you crying about?" she asked the screen. "That nigga sleeping with his coworker. No tears! You need to be yanking that bitch hair out!"

Rosa laughed. "I bet they would be fighting, if she was black."

"You already know," Tamara agreed. "Look! She's taking off," she said as Sherry made her escape.

"Don't let her get away!" Rosa yelled at the screen. "Get that ho!"

"Man, she not doing *nothing!*" Tamara said, growing impatient. "Just standing there, looking stupid." She shook her head. "If I have to go to my husband's job at two in the morning to confront some bitch he's fucking, best believe I'm snatching that ho's hair out – especially if I find out she's black."

Rosa frowned, still grinning. "*What?*"

"I mean if I was white."

"Does that make it worse, if the wife's white and the mistress is black?"

"I don't know," Tamara said. "But she gotta be feeling some type of way. I mean, she can give her husband everything he wants – except *one thing.*"

Rosa didn't think she wanted the answer, but she asked anyway: "And what's that?"

"Some *black pussy*," Tamara said with a smile.

Rosa rolled her eyes. "Whatever. All I know is that lady's making herself look like a fool by not doing nothing."

"Well, we don't know what they're saying," Tamara commented.

"I know it's not enough. She's not even moving her arms. Who curses a bitch out with their arms by their sides?"

"Oh, now look at this fool," Tamara said. "What do you think he's telling her?"

"'*Aw, baby.* I'm sorry,'" Rosa guessed. "'*I didn't mean to let her suck my dick. I just fell down, and her mouth was open like that.*'"

That cracked Tamara up even more. She laughed so hard, she spilled most of the popcorn in her hand. By the time she got hold of herself, William had walked his wife to the cafeteria's exit. A security guard held the door open for him and his wife.

"Where they going?" Rosa wondered.

"How the hell should I know?"

They munched on popcorn as William and Jennifer walked into the range of another camera and then another. Neither of the women in dispatch were happy to see the nurse lead his wife to the hospital's main exit and leave the building.

"*No!* The bitch is the *other way!*" Rosa yelled at them. "*Why is she walking with him?* He's playing her!"

"Damn." Tamara was disappointed as well. "That nigga must got a big-ass dick. He got both them ho's in line. '*Come on, baby. I know I'm fucking other women, but you need to go home and let me do my job.*'"

Rosa laughed. "I wouldn't be surprised if he *did* tell her that."

"I don't get it," Tamara said. "If he like black women, why he marry her?"

"It's not all about race," Rosa offered. "Maybe he fell in love with one woman, and then he fell in love with another one. Just because everything's black and white with you doesn't mean everybody sees it that way."

Tamara narrowed her eyes. "I would've believed that shit, if y'all didn't put Trump's bitch-ass in The White House. This country is as black and white as it gets."

"*Y'all*? You think I voted for him? Hell naw! I got too many illegals in my family!"

The ladies continued to laugh as the bearded nurse walked his wife to the parking garage and finally out of view of their cameras.

● ● ● ● ● ●

When they got to Jennifer's car (and away from the prying eyes in the hospital), William stood before his wife and sighed. He forced himself to look her in the eyes.

He denied everything wholeheartedly during their walk from the cafeteria to the garage —only because he didn't want her to do anything outrageous in the hospital. Now that they were alone, he could no longer keep the truth from her, not while looking into her wet, woeful eyes. William loved his wife dearly. Ironically, honesty had always been a major component of their relationship.

"Babe, I'm sorry. I did sleep with that woman."

As expected, Jennifer's sorrow was a tragic, all consuming experience.

"*You lied to me!*"

She charged forward and beat his chest with soft hands that had never been in a real fight. William accepted it. She hit him a dozen times before succumbing to weariness and heartbreak. When she was spent, he reached out to her. She pushed him away.

"*Get off me! Get away!*"

Her cries were heart wrenching, magnified by their solitude and the echoes in the parking garage. William was sure her grief was audible several levels above and below them. He also knew there was no one around to hear her at that hour. Even still, he'd never felt so low. He had told Sherry that without her, he'd be dead inside. He now realized it was Jennifer that he couldn't live without.

"*Why?*" she cried. "*Why would you do this?*"

"I don't know. I'm stupid. I don't know why it happened."

"I loved you! I gave you everything!"

"I know, baby. I love you too."

"No you don't! You're a liar! I hate you! I hate you! I swear to God I hate you!"

"Baby, please don't say that. I'm sorry. I'm so sorry."

"Is it because she's black?" Jennifer wailed.

The question caught William off guard. "Wha, what? No, baby, it's–"

"If you wanted a black woman, why didn't you marry one?" she cried.

"It – babe, I promise you it has nothing to do with–"

His wife's tears flowed even harder. *"Then what is it, William?* **Why'd you do this to me***?"*

William wasn't completely colorblind, but for the life of him, he never considered Jennifer would be even more upset about the affair because Sherry was black. He now understood how inadequate she must feel.

As he watched his wife in the throes of the worst strife their marriage had ever experienced, the last fifteen years of William's life flashed before him. He saw their wedding, their parents, their honeymoon. The birth of all three of their children. He saw laughter, smiles, birthday cakes and Christmas trees. He saw their children grow from snaggletooth to pimply and finally their current stage. He saw Jennifer wearing Victoria's Secret on their anniversary.

At the end of it all, he saw Sherry going down on him in the elevator.

He felt like a fool. He had to be the most ignorant man in the world. Jennifer was everything he ever needed. He loved Sherry too, but she wasn't his life. She was not his wife. She could never mean more to him than Jennifer did.

When he reached for her again, she allowed it. She might have been too exhausted to continue fighting. But William hoped she accepted his touch because she recognized their union could never be destroyed. As long as he loved her and she loved him, there was hope. He pulled her to his chest, and he began to cry too. Her tears stained his scrub top. His dampened her hair.

"I'm sorry, baby. I don't know what the hell I was thinking. I love you and only you. We'll get through this. I promise."

Jennifer didn't respond. William felt her arms shift. He thought she would push him away, but she surprised him by reciprocating the embrace. The gesture made him cry even harder.

"I promise I will never hurt you again," he vowed. *"Baby, I am so sorry..."*

CHAPTER FOURTEEN
ENTERPRISE

How could you?
After all we've been through
Mind, body and soul
After all I've given you
You stood before God and accepted this union
Don't give me that shit
About how you're only human!
You're not a man at all!
You're a liar! A cheat!
A low-down dirty dog!
You're a coward!
A freak!
Get away from me!
Don't touch me!
I hate you!
You disgust me!
Go be with that troll
Who made you forget about your wife
And your home and your children
Have a wonderful life!

On Monday morning, patient transporter Carl Redding woke up at four am. His shift at the hospital didn't start until six-thirty, but he had a few stops to make before he got there. He felt alert and refreshed when he pulled the sheets aside and sat up on the side of the bed. Unlike most bachelors, he took the time to make his bed properly, before he headed to the bathroom to shower. Forty minutes later, he was dressed and ready for the world.

At the hospital, Carl had worked himself up to eleven dollars an hour. That wasn't enough to afford the home he lived in; a four bedroom flat on the west side. But he had an accountant friend who had made his illegitimate income appear legit, as far as the IRS was concerned. The year before he bought his home, Carl's tax return put his income at $62,000. He had made more than that in the years that followed, but Carl no longer bothered to inflate his income. He already had a house and a few Visa's with extensive credit lines. As far as he was concerned, he no longer needed the white man's financial approval.

He stopped at a 7-11 for gas and breakfast. Carl enjoyed living alone, though at times he longed for a nice, home cooked meal. Eating on the road made him feel like a lonely trucker. But living alone was his preference. In the past year, Carl only allowed three women to spend the night at his house. They all got evicted by sunrise.

On the way to work, he stopped first at Regency Hospital for kitchen supplies and then headed to Baylor Downtown, where a cute nurse named Rebecca brought a bag of goodies to his car. Carl didn't inspect the bag before giving her $200, nor did he exit his vehicle.

He unlocked his doors and instructed Rebecca to, "Put it in the back seat, baby."

The nurse complied, knowing Carl wouldn't expose himself to the cameras mounted around her hospital unless it was necessary. After depositing the merchandise, she leaned on Carl's doorframe, grinning broadly. The move gave him a nice view of her cleavage, which he assumed was the point.

"Where you finna take your dark, chocolate self to?" Rebecca asked him.

Carl did not take offense to a white woman calling him that. Rebecca had a hood accent, so he knew she grew up around blacks.

"Gotta work today," he told her. "On my way now. How was your night?"

"Same as always," she said. "Long and stressful."

"Patients getting on your nerves?"

"No, it's the staff. I told you I'm charging now. I don't have to take patients, unless we're short."

"Oh yeah, I forgot. Congrats on that."

"Thanks," she said. Then, "When we gon' hook up, Carl? You got you a woman yet?"

"Nah," he said chuckling. "And you know I don't like to mix business with pleasure."

"Why? What you think gon' happen?"

"I think you gon' get sprung and then get jealous. Then you gon' get mad at me, and we won't do anymore business," he said honestly.

"I am not gon' get sprung on you," she promised. "You must think you all that."

"Shit, I'd be a fool not to think that," Carl said. "I gotta go, baby."

"Why you always rushing me?"

At that moment her pager beeped loudly. She checked the display and told him, "Yeah, I guess I gotta go too."

He nodded. "I'll holler at you later."

Carl allowed himself a few seconds to stare at the nurse's backside as she walked away. He considered Rebecca slim-thick; small boobs and waist with thick thighs, hips and ass. Carl never let on, but he certainly had a thing for her. She was one of his associates he planned to smash after he retired. But that list was growing longer every month. Carl thought it might take him a whole year to bed them all.

● ● ● ● ● ●

He arrived at Jackson Memorial twenty minutes before his shift started. He entered through the Jackson Building and greeted the ladies at the registration desks.

"Morning, Carl," Miss Beverly said. "I see you're early for work again. Your supervisor must love you."

"She does appreciate it," he acknowledged. "How your feet doing?"

The woman smiled and grimaced at the same time. "They're a little better today. Thanks for asking."

"Make sure you drink plenty of water," Carl suggested. "And stay off your feet as much as possible. Did you try to soak them in ice?"

She smiled sheepishly. "I told you I don't like the cold too much. I don't think I could stand it."

"Give it a try, Miss Beverly. One of my aunties got gout. She says it helps a lot. It'll be uncomfortable at first, but it's worth it."

"I'll give it a try. Thanks, Carl. You always got a good word."

He unzipped his backpack as he continued walking. Carl produced a squeaky-clean Rubbermaid container and handed it to the woman at the third desk.

"Here you go, Flora. Those tacos tasted like you got 'em from a restaurant. I ate 'em all and passed out like a fat pig!"

Flora smiled and blushed. "Thanks, Carl. You don't look like you gained any weight, though. Still as slim as ever."

"Is that what this is?" he joked. "You trying to fatten me up?"

"No," she said giggling. "You know you look just fine." She caught herself flirting too directly and blushed again. "You didn't have to clean this," she said, admiring her container. "You could've kept it."

"Nah. I figured if I gave it back to you, you might put something else in it."

Her eyes lit up. "I will. Whatever you want. I was thinking about making fettuccini tonight. You back tomorrow?"

"No. I got a couple of days off."

Flora would've been ashamed of herself, if she saw the way her face suddenly drooped. "I can make you something else when you get back," she offered.

"Bet," Carl said. "Thanks, baby. You the best."

Flora knew Carl was from New Orleans, and "baby" was part of his dialect, rather than a term of endearment. But her heart shuddered just the same.

"You're welcome, Carl."

He continued down the hallway and hopped on the staff elevators. He descended to the basement and met up with Jalen from Central Supply. Jalen filled his backpack with more goodies.

"How's the nightshift going?" Carl asked him.

"Fine – except I had to go off on my coworker," Jalen informed him. "If that nigga wasn't so old, I woulda whooped his ass."

"Don't do that," Carl said. "I need you, baby. We can't make no money, if yo ass get fired."

"I know," Jalen said. "I ain't gon' do it. I'm just saying..."

Carl took his backpack to the fitness center and exchanged it for an identical one he had in his locker. He checked the time before visiting a nurse on the dialysis unit. Luther was tending to a patient when Carl tracked him down.

"Check the bathroom by the elevator," Luther called from the bedside. "Leave mine in the TP."

"Good looking out," Carl responded.

He went to the restroom and found a box waiting on him. He emptied the contents into his bag and left the nurse's money in the toilet paper dispenser.

With his backpack full again, Carl headed to his department to clock-in. So far, he'd invested $500 in his business this morning. That put his profit margin at around thirty-five hundred. And people wondered why he was always in a good mood!

• • • • • •

At lunchtime Carl retrieved his first bag from the gym. He took it to his car and drove merrily off the hospital's property. He had a few more errands to run during his 45 minute break.

He returned to all three of the neighboring hospitals and collected supplies from a few more associates. He then stopped at a carwash to meet a coworker from Jackson Memorial. He relieved the man of three heavy boxes. Carl did not ask the janitor how he got the boxes out of the building without arousing suspicion, just as the janitor didn't ask why Carl wanted the cleaning supplies.

Carl's final lunchtime appointment took him to a Starbucks on the outskirts of the hospital district. When he arrived, he was upset to find that the woman he was meeting with had not arrived. He was even more upset when he saw a familiar face pull into the parking lot a few minutes later.

Carl remained seated at a table for two, hoping it was a coincidence. He watched through the front window as Bobby found a parking spot close to the entrance. The nappy-headed transporter exited his vehicle and chuckled when he spotted Carl through the window.

Carl felt an uncomfortable sense of foreboding settle over him. He considered stepping outside to initiate the confrontation, but there was a chance this was still a coincidence. Maybe Bobby just happened to be in the neighborhood. Maybe he *looked* uncouth, but Bobby had a thing for expensive cafés and pastries.

It could happen.

Carl knew it wasn't a coincidence when his coworker walked directly to his table and took a seat, his shit-eating grin growing wider by the second.

"Yo, what's up, Carl. You got my case?"

Carl had the portable ultrasound on the floor between his sneakers. He was fuming so hard, his nostrils flared. Bobby became more giddy as he watched his frenemy struggle to comprehend what was happening.

The boy lowered his voice and said, "My *ultrasound.* You got it?"

Carl's expression was deadpan, but the muscles in his face clenched and remained frozen that way. He looked around to make sure no one was close enough to eavesdrop on them before saying, "What the fuck is this?"

"What you mean?" Bobby said. "Didn't you tell somebody you was gon' bring that case here today? You said you wanted four G's for it, right? Where it's at?"

Bobby ducked his head under the table. It took every bit of strength Carl had to keep his hands to himself, rather than punch the punk on the side of the head. When Bobby came back up, his smile had somehow gotten bigger. He was all teeth at that point.

"Hey, you brought it!" he announced. "That's what's up, Carl. You a real businessman."

"What the fuck you doing?" Carl asked again.

"Ooh." Bobby's eyes widened. "Dang, it's like that? I thought we was boys."

Carl shook his head. He looked around again. No one in the restaurant had noticed the tension on their side of the room — not yet anyway. Carl told himself to play it cool. This was bad, no doubt, but he had been through worse.

"What you want?" he said. "You out of line, dog. Big time."

"Oh, *I'm* the one who out of line? Really? You gave me five hundred for that thing, and now you selling it for four thousand."

"That's *business*," Carl told him. "Ain't personal. But this shit you doing, this here ain't business. I don't know what the hell this is."

"This *is* business," Bobby countered. *"I'm all up in yo business.* I know where you selling yo shit, and I know how much you charging for it. You making a *killing* off us. And, yeah, I know it's more than just me getting stuff for you. I checked your profile on Craigslist. You selling stuff from all over the hospital. How many thieves you got under your belt, Carl? Five? Ten? *Twenty*? I bet if I start asking around, half the transporters prolly working for you."

Carl realized the punk was threatening his whole livelihood. He hadn't thought about his late uncle in a while, but Curley's warning came back to him at that moment.

It won't be you that mess it up. It'll be a hating-ass nigga. Watch out for him, and you'll be fine.

Carl didn't believe Bobby would really start asking around, but then again, he never expected him to figure out how he was fencing some of the supplies.

He doubted if Bobby was smart enough to do this on his own. Carl suspected the woman who had called him was the real brains behind this sting – but that didn't matter now. Carl made $30,000 last year from the hospital and $80,000 more from his illegal enterprise. He wasn't about to let this goofball screw that up.

He asked him, "What you want, nigga?"

"What you mean?" Bobby said, laughing again.

Carl rolled his eyes. "Either you came here to buy this case, or you came for something else. I gotta get back to work. Hurry up and tell me what you want."

"Oh, okay," Bobby said. He rubbed his hands together and then rested his forearms on the table. "First off, I want a bigger cut off everything I get for you; starting with the case between your legs. If you getting four for it, I want two thousand. You ain't finna bullshit me no more, thinking I don't know how much that stuff costs. That tympanic thermometer – *yeah, nigga, I know the name now* – is worth $400. You ain't finna pay me fifty for it and think everything is gravy."

Carl barely considered his proposal before shaking his head. "Nope. That ain't gon' happen."

Bobby expected that but asked, "Why not, Carl? That's a fair deal."

"Not for me. That ain't enough money for the risks I'm taking. Just like you showed up for this thing today, the laws might show up tomorrow. What I gotta go through ain't worth it, unless I'm making what I'm making."

"What about the risks *I'm* taking?" Bobby asked.

"Ain't nobody forced you to do nothing. I asked you to get me something. I told you how much I'd pay. You decided to do it. *That's business*. If you decide the risks ain't worth it, then don't do it. I ain't tripping."

"That's 'cause you got more people working for you."

The way Bobby kept bringing up the others made Carl's blood boil. He knew this wouldn't end amicably. There was no way it could.

"Alright, so I'm not paying you half," Carl said. "What's next? What you gon' do, bail or start snitching?"

"Nah, I ain't no snitch," Bobby said. "At least I wasn't one when I woke up this morning. But now, I don't know. This meeting going kinda bad. Ain't no telling what might happen."

Be cool, Carl told himself. *White people watching*.

He managed to keep his hands on the table, but they were balled into fists now.

"I'll give you two G's to get the hell on," Carl proposed. "You don't know me, and I don't know you. Lose my number. We don't work the same shift, so we ain't never gotta speak again."

"Two G's?" Bobby said skeptically.

"You heard me."

"Make it *five*."

"What? Nigga, why would I give you five?"

"'Cause you want me to keep quiet. You want me to act like I don't know shit..."

"Ol' ugly-ass snake in the grass," Carl growled. "I knew you wasn't no good from the day I met you."

Bobby smirked. "You the one put me on the payroll."

"*Four thousand*," Carl said with a grimace. "I'll give you *four stacks. That's it!*"

Bobby pretended not to be excited about the offer. "Fine. Give it here."

"I don't got it on me," Carl said, frowning. "Maybe if you hadn't set me up for this big-ass waste of time, I would've had it today."

"What time you get off?" Bobby asked him. "I know you got it in the bank."

"*You don't know what the fuck I got in the bank!*" Carl caught himself and lowered his voice. "What difference do it make if you get it today, tomorrow or two days from now? You not doing nothing for it. You best count your blessings and give me a minute. I'll pay you as soon as I sell this case."

The money was already starting to burn a hole in Bobby's pocket. But Carl was right. He hadn't done anything to earn it, so why not show a little patience? He knew Carl would pay. He had too much to lose, if he tried to be stingy.

"Alright," Bobby said. "Call me when you get it."

Carl snatched his case and rose to his feet. Before he left the table, he asked him, "Have you told anybody at work about this; about what's going on with us?"

Bobby shook his head. "Naw. I ain't trying to lose my job. I don't trust nobody up there that much."

"Good," Carl told him. "Keep it that way."

"I'ma keep my mouth shut," Bobby promised him, "as long as you do what you say you gon' do."

"I keep my word," Carl assured him. "I ain't no shady-ass nigga, like you. Don't call me. Wait for me to call you."

"Don't take too long," Bobby said, smiling.

The muscles in Carl's face remained rigid again as he exited the coffee shop.

● ● ● ● ● ●

At the same moment Bobby was shaking Carl down for four G's, PCT Danielle Boyd was midway through a miserable shift on the Continued Care Unit. This was only the first day of her workweek. After a phenomenal weekend at Club Paradise, coming back to the hospital felt like torture. Her patients were all half dead. They were constantly vomiting and shitting on themselves. Whenever messes like that occurred, the nurses were quick to send Danielle to do the dirty work.

Most of the nurses had forgotten that they were once techs themselves. The moment they got their degree, they put their ass-wiping days behind them. Danielle couldn't stand them, and she didn't need any of this. Between her purse and her motel room, she had $800 stashed. If she didn't have a baggie of white in the pocket of her scrub pants, she would've quit hours ago.

But the 'caine made everything tolerable – even some old bastard's diarrhea.

When she spotted Virgil and his cute friend Terrence stroll onto her floor without a patient, she knew trouble was coming her way. Danielle was ready to curse them out when they walked up to her, grinning like Dumb and Dumber.

"Hey, what's up," Virgil said.

"How you doing," Terrence added.

Their eyes and smiles were devilish. Danielle sneered at them.

"What the hell y'all want?"

"Damn, girl. Why you being so mean?" Virgil asked her.

"You having a bad day?" Terrence chipped in.

"My charge don't want y'all visiting me on the floor no more," Danielle informed them.

"Well, how we supposed to get in contact with you?" Virgil wondered.

"You ain't got no reason to get in contact with me."

"What about that lap dance?" Terrence asked. "You said you would hook us up, if we had the money."

Danielle didn't remember agreeing to anything like that. She couldn't believe baby-face Terrence was the one propositioning her. "I didn't say that shit. I ain't no ho!"

"Hey, calm down," Virgil said. He couldn't wipe the smile off his face. "You told us that last week."

"You did," Terrence cosigned.

Danielle's mind was nearly mush, but she remembered parts of that conversation. She was broke at the time – and desperate. But now she was balling. She didn't need anything from these assholes.

Virgil told her, "You said if we bring twenty dollars–"

"Lap dances are *thirty*!" Danielle snapped.

"I got thirty," Terrence said right away.

"I do too," Virgil said.

Danielle felt a rush of adrenaline. It was such a strong sensation, she got goose bumps. Common sense told her this was a horrible thing to do. But ho-sense told her, *Bitch, is you stupid? You better get paid!* Employees at the hospital did worse things on a daily basis – *for free.* And it wasn't like her job there was secure. Her charge nurse was out to get her, which meant her days were surely numbered.

"Y'all got thirty dollars *apiece*?" she clarified.

The boys' eyes lit up. "Yeah." They nodded in unison.

"Alright, come on." She walked past them, towards the elevators. As an afterthought, she looked back and told the nearest employee, "Tell Maria I'm going to lunch."

Kelly, another tech on the unit, heard her just fine. But she couldn't respond. Her jaw was unhinged. In the back of her mind, she heard one of her grandfather's favorite sayings: *Close your mouth, girl, or you gon' let some flies in.*

Kelly closed her mouth and turned away, pretending she did not see the transporters follow Danielle off the floor with their dicks already stiffening their scrubs. She went to the nurses' station and told Maria that Danielle had taken a break.

"What?" the nurse snapped. "Why didn't she tell me herself? Better yet, why didn't she *ask*?"

Kelly kept her lips sealed. She shrugged, gave her an *I don't know* hum and walked away.

● ● ● ● ● ●

"Where we going?" Danielle asked when she and the men were alone in the elevator.

Virgil reached past her and pushed *B* for basement. "To our storage room," he said.

"How you know ain't nobody coming in there?" Danielle wanted to know.

"We keep extra beds down there," Virgil told her. "We got about twenty beds in the office already. They'll get 'em from there, before they come to the basement for more."

With two horny men standing so close to her, Danielle felt like she was at the club again. It felt like home.

"Where the money?" she asked as the elevator lowered them to a makeshift Champagne Room.

Terrence reached for his pocket, but Virgil said, "Hold up. What if we give you the money, and you don't do nothing. Ain't like we can run and tell nobody."

Terrence thought that made sense. He removed his hand from his pocket.

Danielle reached with two hands and grabbed both of their dicks. The transporters seemed bold, but all men had the same response when it came to an unexpected dick grab: They jerked away, butt first, with surprised, embarrassed expressions.

"Whoa!" Terrence said. But then he grinned and thrust his hips forward. "Do it again."

Danielle shook her head and left only one hand extended, palm up. "I'ma give you your lap dances, but you gotta pay me first; just like at the club."

Neither of them had a problem parting with their money this time.

● ● ● ● ● ●

The basement of the Jackson Building was unfamiliar to Danielle, but the transporters knew every corridor of the hospital. They didn't talk much as they led her to the storage room. Danielle caught them exchanging glances as they walked, but she didn't comment on it. This too was something she experienced at Club Paradise.

When they got to the storage area, she was amazed by how big the room was. It was as large as a high school gym, if not as tall. The room was filled with hospital beds and stretchers. There was other random equipment lined against the walls.

Virgil told Terrence, "Look out for us," as he led Danielle deeper into the maze of beds. She started to feel apprehensive about performing in such an open space.

"Ain't no cameras in here?" she asked, looking around.

"Nope," Virgil said knowingly.

After another fifty steps, she asked him, "Where we going?"

"There's an office over here," he said.

Sure enough, he stepped into a much smaller room that had a desk with a computer and not much more. Danielle felt a lot more comfortable there, especially when Virgil closed the door behind them.

There were two chairs in the office. One was a comfortable executive chair with wheels. The other was wooden, with no padding. She told Virgil, "Sit over there," because the wooden chair didn't have arms. It was difficult to straddle a man's lap in a chair with arms.

Virgil didn't mind either way. When he took a seat, Danielle saw his erection poking up in his pants.

"You get *one song*," she told him as she removed her cellphone from her pocket. She went to the media player and scrolled through the albums she had stored, looking for the shortest tune.

"You gon' play it on your phone?" Virgil asked.

She nodded.

"Don't pick a short one," he warned.

She sighed inwardly and selected *Desperado* by Rihanna. Three minutes and eight seconds. When she pushed PLAY, Virgil spoke up again.

"Naw. You said it was gon' be *just like at the club*."

"It is," she promised.

"You ain't *naked*," he noticed. "At the club, you get *naked*."

"I ain't finna get naked at work," she said with a sneer.

"Why the hell I want a lap dance then? That's the only reason we came."

Danielle couldn't believe his audacity. "I'll get *topless*," she bargained.

He shook his head. "If you still got pants on, that ain't no lap dance. If you only wanna get topless, that's worth *twenty dollars*. That's how much they charge at the topless clubs. And you gotta have a *G-string* on. I don't want no lap dance with no granny panties."

Ain't this a bitch, Danielle thought. The $60 was in her pocket, and they weren't getting it back. They weren't even getting *a portion* of it back. She didn't remember what kind of panties she put on that morning, but she didn't think they were a G-string.

Danielle weighed her options and decided on a resounding *Fuck it*. If this made her a whore, then what she did at the club also made her a whore. If she was going to be viewed as a ho either way, what difference did it make? Virgil and Terrence were the fools paying money to see a naked woman. She was a *boss* for capitalizing on their horniness.

"Fine," she said and quickly disrobed, all the way down to her pubic hair.

Virgil's breathing became audible as he watched her.

Without taking the time to prep, after working half a shift of manual labor, Danielle wondered if she smelled a little ripe downstairs. If so, it would serve him right. She hoped Virgil's scrubs smelled like coochie for the rest of the day, and his girlfriend slapped the black off him when he got home.

She started the music and commenced her dance. Virgil's hands were all over her from the moment she sat on his lap. Danielle didn't mind, until he tried to reach between her legs.

She blocked his hand and told him, "If you wanna do that, you gotta come with some more money; *just like at the club*."

"I ain't got no more money," he whined. "You know we don't get paid till Friday."

"Then keep your hands out from between my legs."

"You ain't got no security in here," he noticed.

Danielle looked him dead in the eyes. She didn't stop grinding her hips as she told him, "Try something, if you want to, nigga. I'll break yo motherfucking nose."

Virgil fully believed her. His dick got even harder.

He walked stiffly out of the office a couple of minutes later, starry-eyed and still in shock. Terrence could hardly wait for his turn. As they switched places, with Virgil now looking out for him, Terrence asked, "Was it worth it?"

Virgil nodded vigorously. "Hell yeah, dog. Hell yeah."

CHAPTER FIFTEEN
NOT SO SIMPLE

Release me!
So dreadful
Deceitful
Sick demons
These legions are screaming
My soul trapped between them
I'm sane
And I know it
You can't take that from me
No schemes or foul nightmares
Can take that from me
I'm righteous!
Though doom clouds hover above me
Showering me with despair
As I reach for glory
This fire in my lungs
As I breathe the foulest air
Will not break me
Satan's minions will never take me!
Victory is within reach
Peace and love intertwined
Will free me
From the demons
Trapped inside my mind

By Friday, PCT Naomi Gilcrease was eager to leave work after a boring shift in the Cardiac Tower. One of the nurses held her up with a string of questions Naomi wasn't prepared to answer.

"When's your due date?"

"Could be any day now," Naomi said. She walked to one of the hallway computers and pulled up the time clock.

"I can tell," Tabitha said as she followed her. "Looks like you're about to pop."

Naomi knew the barb shouldn't hurt. It shouldn't even be considered an insult. The problem was Naomi wasn't with child, she was just overweight. Apparently she was fat enough to appear nine months pregnant. She wondered what people would say after she acquired a baby. If she didn't lose any weight, would she look like she was about to pop for the rest of her life?

"When are you going on leave?" Tabitha asked.

Naomi shrugged. "I don't know – when I have him, or her."

"You're gonna work till the day you deliver?"

Naomi wasn't sure how to respond. The way Tabitha asked made her feel like that was something she shouldn't do.

"Yeah, I think so."

"Did you make sure to get your long-term disability?" Tabitha asked. "When June had her baby, she didn't have a chance to do that. She didn't plan to get pregnant, and she had to use all of her PTO. But you got pregnant last year, so you had time to update your insurance."

Naomi had no idea what she was talking about. Her eyes remained glued to the computer screen. "I was, um, I was just gonna take two months maternity leave."

Tabitha chuckled. "*Yeah right.* You know they don't offer that here."

Naomi's silence made the nurse's smile go away.

"Wait, you *did* know that, didn't you? Haven't you talked to the benefits department?"

Naomi took a deep breath. She shook her head, still avoiding eye contact.

Tabitha's eyes widened. "You're due *any day now*, and you haven't talked to anyone about going on leave? Naomi, *what are you doing*? There's no 'maternity leave' at this hospital. You have to go on long-term disability. If you don't have that on your insurance, you have to use short-term. If you don't have *that*, they make you use your PTO. And if you don't have enough PTO, then you just take off without pay. That's what happened with June, except she had enough PTO to cover her for most of her leave. She only went a week with no pay. Can you afford to do that?"

Naomi felt like she was trying to help, but she also thought Tabitha was making fun of her. Of course she couldn't afford to take time off with no pay – not for a week or even a couple of days. It was suddenly much too hot on the unit. Naomi felt the sweat glistening on her forehead. Her intestines twisted like a pile of serpents.

Noticing her discomfort, Tabitha said, "I didn't mean to freak you out. I was just wondering if you'd looked into that stuff yet. You know they only let you change your benefits in November. But if you forgot to sign up for disability, it's not the end of the world. The only thing that matters is you having a healthy baby. Everything else will work itself out. You'll see." She smiled.

Naomi forced a smile, but hers didn't come out quite right. Tabitha felt awkward as she backed away and left her at the computer.

● ● ● ● ● ●

Rather than head straight home, Naomi went to her locker in the break room and grabbed her duffle bag. She had never brought the bag to work before. It was mostly empty; just one outfit inside. Her anxiety began to eat away at her nerves the moment she closed her locker and left the unit with the bag in hand.

She didn't plan to secure a baby that afternoon. But she would if the opportunity presented itself. She'd stuff the little bundle of joy in her duffle bag lickety-split and use the stairway as a means of escape.

Instead of taking a baby, today was more of a test run. She planned to enter Labor & Delivery and at least find out where the babies were and map out a plan for getting her hands on one. She understood that if things went wrong, this could be the day she got fired from the hospital. She might even end up in jail. She was terrified of both those scenarios, but if that was her fate, then so be it.

There was no longer time to pussyfoot around the inevitable. Her marriage was in shambles, and her coworkers were starting to get suspicious. If Naomi didn't produce a baby soon, she would lose everything – so she might as well *try* to carry out her plan. For all she knew, it might not be half as daunting as she imagined.

She took the elevator to the basement and ducked inside one of the single-toilet bathrooms that had a lock on the door. She tried to still her heart as she unzipped her bag, but it was no use. Her chest was on steady drum mode. She wondered how much more stress her heart could take before it threw in the towel. It wasn't like she was healthy to begin with.

The restroom was a bit chilly, but she broke out in a sweat as she stripped down to her underwear. When she bent to pull on the new scrub pants, her belly rumbled and contracted with a sense of urgency. Naomi couldn't make it to the toilet before she felt vomit rushing up her esophagus. She rushed to the sink instead and regurgitated what felt like everything she'd eaten all week.

When she finally spit out the last of it, the reflection in the mirror above the sink revealed what Naomi knew all along. She was a mad woman. She was disgusting. Sweat dripped from her face and matted her hair to her forehead. Her breathing was ragged. Saliva dripped from her mouth in discolored, ropy streams.

Her vision blurred as tears joined the mess on her face. She didn't bother wiping them. She turned the water on and used her fingers to smush her vomit down the drain. When she was done, Naomi washed her face and dried it with a paper towel. She stared at the mirror again. She thought she still looked disgusting, but at least she was her *normal* disgusting self.

She left the sink and changed into the purple scrubs.

● ● ● ● ● ●

Five minutes later, Naomi exited the elevator on the third floor and made her way to the Clark Building. When the magical doorway to Baby Wonderland came into view, a voice in her head offered unhelpful advice.

Don't go over there, you idiot!
There's a camera right above you! They'll see you!
They keep track of your badge swipes.

If you go in there, they'll know.
You're never gonna make it out of there with a baby.
You don't deserve a baby, you freak!
You don't deserve your job.
You don't deserve Bryan either.
He's fat too, but you're **fucking disgusting**.
I hate you!
Why don't you kill yourself?
Naomi squeezed her eyes closed and responded to the voice, which was surely a demon parading as her conscious.
Shut up! I hate you too!
Every part of her body trembled as she stepped closer to the doorway. Naomi felt like she was going to throw up again as she reached for her badge. She wondered how that was possible. Her stomach had to be completely depleted. But there was no mistaking it. Her eyes watered, and the bitter taste of gastric acid burned her throat. The rotten cantaloupe in her womb flipped over, sending tremors through her intestines. She—
"Naomi?"
She spun, half expecting to find no one there. Her break from reality had become so complete, the demon that taunted her could be heard and felt in the real world.
Naomi was relieved to see a real person approaching her. It was Brooke; a nurse who used to work in the Cardiac Tower. She transferred to Labor & Delivery a few years ago. Brooke smiled brightly when she and Naomi locked eyes. That was surprising. Naomi assumed she looked as deranged and disheveled as she felt.
"Hi," she managed.
"Look at you!" Brooke said. She stepped closer and threw her arms around her. When she backed away, her smile was bright and cheerful. "I haven't seen you in *forever*," Brooke stated. "I miss you guys! How's everything on C3?"
"The same," Naomi said. She fought to keep her features normal. Thankfully the nausea began to subside. "Nothing ever changes over there. What about you? How you liking your new job?"
Brooke's smile intensified. "It's great! Best move I ever made. I don't know why I didn't start working with babies from

the beginning. I don't know if I told you, but I was getting burned out on our floor."

"I know what you mean," Naomi replied.

Brooke looked past her and asked, "What are you – were you going to my floor?"

Naomi's heart stopped beating completely. She didn't think it would be wise to deny that she was headed to L&D, but admitting it could be just as risky. Luckily, Brooke had been away from the Cardiac Tower for so long, she didn't know about Naomi's supposed pregnancy. She probably wouldn't assume her coworker had come there to steal a baby.

"I came to visit someone," she said vaguely.

"Really? Who?"

Naomi was not prepared for a follow up question. Her heart and tongue stammered simultaneously. "It's, um... I just..." She shook her head. "Wow. I just forgot her name."

Brooke's eyes narrowed, but then she laughed. "Don't worry. I get brain farts all the time!"

Naomi forced a chuckle. "Yeah."

"Well, you know you can't get in through this door, don't you?" Brooke asked.

Naomi felt her eyes widen. She tried her best to get them to go back to normal size. "Really? No, I didn't know that."

"Yeah," Brooke said. "Your badge will only work on this door if you work in L&D."

"Wh, why is that?" Naomi asked. "I thought the unit was, you know, open to the public. I remember when I was little, my grandma had to stay in the hospital for a few days. One morning while she was sleep, me and my mom went to look at the babies; the newborns. They were all in the nursery..."

Brooke got a laugh out of that. "That must have been over twenty years ago! Things have changed a lot since then. You know people try to steal babies, right?"

Naomi's legs weakened. She bit down on her tongue, hoping to maintain a grip on consciousness. The pus-filled cantaloupe in her womb swelled and throbbed, making her feel like she had to pee, fart and vomit, all at the same time. She swallowed hard. She thought she tasted blood but didn't think she had bitten her tongue that hard.

"Ye, yeah, I knew that," she said. "Do they, what do they do to stop it?"

Despite her panic, Naomi realized her question was genius. This was a perfect opportunity to get intel from someone on the inside.

"Well," Brooke said, "the first step is keeping weirdos off the unit. That's why most badges don't work on this door. And all of the newborns have wristbands. They can only come off when the baby gets discharged with mama – and only the charge nurse can take them off. If they come off at any other time, the alarms will go off."

Naomi felt more blood seep into her mouth. She swallowed it and managed to ask, "Wha, what happens when the alarms go off?"

"All hell breaks loose," Brooke told her. "They announce a Code Pink overhead. Security rushes over here. They lock down the elevators and stairwell. If there was ever a fire and a Code Pink at the same time, I think we'd all die." She chuckled. "No one's getting out of the building while a baby's missing."

Brooke's mood was jovial, while Naomi's whole world turned upside down. Wristbands? Lockdowns? Even the stairway? Brooke had unwittingly sent Naomi's plans all the way back to square one. Getting a baby off the unit was impossible. Her purple scrubs wouldn't help at all.

Thinking of scrubs, Naomi wondered how long it would take for Brooke to realize she was wearing a color that was exclusive to PCT's in L&D. There was nothing Naomi could say to explain that.

But, possibly because she was used to seeing techs in purple, Brooke didn't mention it. She sidestepped Naomi and said, "Anyway, I gotta get going."

She swiped her badge, and the card reader beeped once. The light turned green, and Brooke pushed the door open. She looked back at Naomi with a thoughtful expression.

"I would let you in, but I could get fired. You have to go to the ground floor and take the elevators up to three again. Then go through the lobby, like a regular visitor – once you remember who you're here to see, that is." She chuckled. "It was good seeing you, Naomi!"

"You too," Naomi said. "Thanks. Bye."

She turned away from the entrance to Baby Wonderland –
which might as well have been the entrance to the oval office – and
hurriedly left the hospital.

• • • • • •

Down in dispatch, Rosa and Tamara had yet to arrive for
their night shift. Instead Josh and David were tasked to keep an
eye on the hospital's security monitors. Josh stared at one of the
screens, wondering if he'd just seen something that might earn
him praise from as high up as the president of the hospital, if it
had played out fully.
"That bitch was trying to steal a baby."
David looked over at the monitor he was staring at. All he
saw was a large woman walking away from Labor and Delivery.
He said, "Nuh-uhn."
"Uh-huh!" Josh said, laughing.
"Doesn't she work here?"
"Yeah, but not on that unit."
"Why is she wearing purple then?"
"*Exactly!*" Josh replied.
David chuckled. "What do you mean '*Exactly*'?"
"I think she got those purple scrubs so she could get on the
unit."
David frowned. They both watched as Naomi stood
waiting for an elevator.
"Did she try to swipe in?"
Josh shook his head. "No. Someone came and started
talking to her, and then she walked away."
"If she tried to swipe in, I'd probably agree with you."
"Why can't you agree with me *now*? All of the evidence
fits."
"What evidence?" David asked, smiling again.
"She's white. She's fat and ugly."
"Wow. That's cold. And you're fat too, by the way."
"Yeah, but at least I'm not ugly," Josh said.
David contradicted him. "You got a face only a mother
could love."

"She stole those purple scrubs. She's probably been going around telling people she's pregnant," Josh guessed as they watched Naomi step onto an elevator.

"Now you're back to speculating," David said. "But if you're so sure, why don't you call it in?"

Josh didn't have an answer for that.

"Could it be because of the time you got the bomb squad to come and look at that backpack?"

"We got an alert that said ISIS might be planning something," Josh said defensively.

"All you had to do was go back and look at the footage to see who left it," David reminded him. "And what about that time you called in a possible rape?"

"At first glance they—"

"*Upon closer inspection,* the guy grabbed his girlfriend's butt, and then he chased her around laughing. Women usually don't laugh while a rapist is chasing them."

"Fine," Josh said. "I won't call. But if she comes back later and steals a baby, you owe me a beer."

"Deal."

"You know, you hurt my feelings when you called me fat," Josh revealed.

David looked over and was relieved to see his friend smiling. "Sorry. I meant to say you were... What's the word that comedian uses? *Squishy?*"

"*Fluffy,* you asshole."

"Yeah. You're *fluffy,*" David said. "And very handsome."

Josh knew he was only saying that to make him feel better, but it worked. He leaned back in his seat and smiled and scanned the monitors for his next moment of vigilance.

• • • • • •

By the time she got to her car, Naomi was on the verge of another breakdown. She sat behind the wheel afraid to drive with the stream of tears blurring her vision. She wracked her brain for her next move but could come up with nothing. It wasn't like babies simply fell out of the sky. She thought working so close to Labor & Delivery was a godsend. Instead it was a nightmare; a tease from the devil!

In her peripheral, she noticed employees heading to their vehicles. She hastily wiped her tears and got her car started. She avoided eye contact with everyone as she rolled out of the parking lot.

She knew it was time to come clean. There was no way around it, nothing else left for her. She would start tonight with Bryan. He'd been acting like he didn't believe she was pregnant in the first place, so the news might not be a shock to him. Either way, he would use it as an excuse to leave her. As far as excuses go, Naomi couldn't deny it was a good one.

When he moved out, Bryan would probably reignite his love affair with *Mallory*. Naomi had no proof that he was still in contact with that bitch, but she knew he was. The devastation their affair caused had never stopped hurting.

When she confessed to the people at work, her career would be over. Even if the ruse wasn't enough to fire her, there was no way she could look her coworkers in the face again. Everyone would know she was crazy. A sociopath. She would be the laughing stock of the whole hospital.

A few blocks away from the garage, Naomi found her vision impaired again. The pain she felt in her chest was all-consuming. She felt sick in her head, even in her fingers and toes. She prayed this heartache was mortal, but she knew it wasn't. God wouldn't let her off the hook that easily. He wanted her to take her own life, so she would be guaranteed a spot in hell.

But when she wiped the tears from her eyes, Naomi realized death was not her only option. And God was still in the blessing business.

She slowed to stop at a crosswalk, and there it was – *a baby* – just as clear as day. It wasn't a readymade baby, like the ones at the hospital. Getting her hands on this one would be an ugly, messy affair. But Naomi did not believe in coincidences. This was a gift from God! She rubbed her eyes again and stared at the woman walking across the street; no more than ten feet away from her car.

The mother was short and blonde. She didn't appear stressed, but Naomi could tell she was uncomfortable. She was so big, she looked to be *twelve months* pregnant. Naomi recalled there was an OB/GYN clinic near the hospital; in one of the adjacent medical buildings. The clinic had to be closed at that hour, but the pregnant woman might still be one of their patients.

*That's not a gift from God, you evil bitch! What you're thinking about is called **MURDER**! You can't get a baby from a pregnant woman, unless you deliver it yourself. And she's not gonna let you do that, unless she's **DEAD**! Are you really considering that? Is that where your depraved mind has taken you?*

"Shut up! Shut up! Shut up!" Naomi didn't realize she had responded to the demon in her head aloud. She barely noticed that she was knocking herself upside the head with the heel of her hand.

THUM!

THUM!

THUM!

"Ouch."

That didn't seem like a sane course of action, but it worked. The condescending voice piped down, and she could concentrate on her next move. In retrospect, her new plan might have been even easier than the first one:

Step one – Acquire pregnant woman

Step two – Acquire baby

Easy peasy, lemon squeezy.

Naomi continued to cry as she drove past the intersection, but the corner of her mouth was twisted in what might have been a smile. The rotten cantaloupe bounced excitedly in her womb, like a grasshopper trapped in a jar.

CHAPTER SIXTEEN
BLOODY MESS

That night on the sixth floor of the Meredith Building, RN William Harkins was back from a full week off work. No one brought up his absence, although it was a huge elephant in the room. Everyone knew what happened last week with him, Sherry and his wife. Surprisingly most were sympathetic – towards William. It broke their hearts to hear that he had cried that night. Despite his flaws, the consensus was he was a great nurse who had a good rapport with his patients. He was a pleasure to work with.

For Sherry, life on the unit had been nearly unbearable. Her colleagues saw her as a home wrecker. She was a succubus who had seduced William and caused great harm to his family. None of her coworkers had actually seen William's wife when she showed up in the cafeteria, but they heard that Jennifer was devastated. It was rumored that she looked Sherry right in the eyes and told her, *"Get away from my husband, you whore!"* before she broke down in tears.

The vibes Sherry had been receiving from her colleagues made her wish she had taken a week off too, or maybe even a leave of absence, until things cooled down. But, like the winds of time, the hospital kept right on trucking, no matter what was going on. Even the nurses who hated Sherry would show up in her patients' rooms dutifully if she asked for help with anything. And there was no hospital policy against having an affair, so Sherry knew there was no disciplinary action coming her way.

The hardest part was going a week without seeing William – the waiting and wondering. What happened between him and his wife when he got home that day? Was he brutally honest? Did he tell her about the *special* elevator? Did Jennifer leave him? Did she *kill* him?

That last option seemed farfetched, but Sherry found that she had no peace until she got an answer to all of her questions. She didn't attempt to contact William by phone while he was away, because even a text message might get him in trouble if his wife was around to hear the notification. She stalked his Facebook page furiously, but he didn't post anything all week. His wife didn't either. Sherry didn't expect either of them to be childish enough to vent their marital troubles to strangers, but a vague, cryptic post on his timeline would've been nice.

When Sherry learned that William was back on the schedule that Friday, she doubted if he'd really come. But he did. He clocked-in that night and got his patient assignments as usual. Sherry hoped he'd come to her, first and foremost, and tell her what was going on. She needed to know that he was alright, and they would be alright.

But, like everyone else on the unit, William barely looked her way that night. She gave him time and space, but after the first hour rolled into three, she realized he really was avoiding her. This was more nerve-racking than not having him there at all. Sherry hadn't experienced anything like it since high school; when she and one of her boyfriends broke up and tried to pretend the other didn't exist, even though they had several classes together.

By midnight, Sherry decided she had to take the initiative. She made a couple attempts to get his attention. Staring at him from down the hallway didn't work. William didn't respond when she walked into one his patients' rooms and evaluated them for no reason.

As lunchtime neared, Sherry felt she had no choice but to force his hand. William had been chilling in the nurses' station most of the night, while she spent her time in one of the hallway nooks. When she saw him go to the restroom, Sherry went to the nurses' station and took a seat near the computer William had been using. The staff began to watch her surreptitiously.

When William returned, his smile slipped away when he saw that Sherry had changed positions. He looked her in the eyes for a brief moment and then continued down the hallway, as if he never meant to stop at the station. Sherry looked back at her colleagues and caught a couple of nurses grinning before they had time to look away.

It was too much. Sherry didn't know what was worse; missing William, feeling heartbroken over their aborted affair or enduring the subtle ridicule from her peers. She was near tears when she stood suddenly and told the charge nurse, "I'm gonna take my lunch."

The charge was so used to her and William going together, she looked around the station for a second, prepared to tell both of them she'd see them later. Her face reddened when she caught herself.

She said, "Okay, Sherry," and looked down at the papers on her desk.

Sherry waited until she exited the unit, before she allowed the first tear to spill from her watery eyes. When she heard the doors open again, she quickly wiped her face before turning to see who it was.

To her surprise, it was William. Sherry took in a deep, cool breath as he walked towards her. She had never felt so anxious and confused and relieved at the same time. He hadn't said two words to her all night, so Sherry didn't speak first. He was the one who followed her off the unit.

"I'm, uh..." He put his hands in his pockets and looked around uneasily. He stood a safe ten feet away from her. "Sorry I haven't tried to contact you. You, um, you know how upset Jennifer was. I thought she was going to leave me, but she didn't. She's willing to try to work it out – under a few circumstances."

Sherry took another deep breath. She blew it out audibly. Her tears started to leak again. She didn't wipe them. He needed to know what he was doing to her – to *them*.

"I can't go to the cafeteria anymore," William stated. "Jennifer, she, um... She made my lunch tonight. She planned on making it from now on, but, um... Well, that's the second part. I'm moving to dayshift. I talked to Ray already. I start next week."

Sherry was floored by everything he said. But at the same time, it all made sense. Normally it would take an employee weeks to move to a different shift, if there was even an opening. She knew William must have told their manager about the affair to get the wheels moving so quickly.

"I'm sorry," he said. "I think we both knew this would come to an end sooner or later. I mean, neither of us was going to leave our marriage, right?"

Sherry shook her head. He sounded like he was over them already. What happened to, *I would die if I lost you*? William had told her, *Maybe I won't jump off a building, but inside I'll feel like I have nothing to live for*. What happened to all of that?

"I'm sorry," he said again. "I see you're hurting. I wanna comfort you. I want that so bad. But I know if I hug you, it'll bring back everything I feel for you. So it's best if I don't." He started to back away. "This is my last night shift. I'll always care about you. I'm sorry."

He hesitated for a moment, as if waiting for a response. Sherry never gave him one.

Rather than head for the cafeteria when she got downstairs, she left the building and went to the parking garage. When she got to her car, she realized she'd left her keys in her purse, which was still on the unit. Her cheeks were wet with tears again when she took the stairs back down to street level.

It was chilly outside, but the cool air felt good to her. The moon was bright. There were plenty of stars in the sky. Sherry left the garage and continued to walk, past the hospital's entrance and past the adjacent towers, until she reached the main thoroughfare. She looked right and left before settling on a destination; a brightly lit 7-11 down the road.

Walking alone at that time of night could be dangerous, but Sherry didn't give a damn about rapists or muggers. She needed a cigarette. She hadn't smoked in fifteen years, hadn't had a craving in ten. But that night she needed a drag more than she needed food or water.

She entered the convenience store and was disgusted to find that not only did she not have her purse, but she didn't have a dime in any of her pockets. She began to cry again, intensely, much to the surprise of the night clerk.

"Are you okay?" he asked.

Sherry wasn't sure what she told him. From her perspective, it all made sense. But from his point of view, it was a lot of nonsensical babbling about how wretched her life was, how nothing made sense anymore and how all she wanted was *one fucking cigarette*, and she couldn't even have that.

The clerk reached into his pocket and produced a pack of Marlboros. "Here." He opened it and offered her one. "Take it. Please, don't cry. Do you need a lighter?"

Sherry was bawling so hard, she barely managed to tell him, "Ye, ye, yes."

She exited the store and stood on the side of the building to smoke her heartbreak cigarette. It was the best Marlboro she had ever had.

• • • • • •

An hour after Sherry returned from her smoke break, Central Supply employee Jalen Creel reclined in his favorite chair in his department, while his co-worker did the majority of the jobs in their system.

If someone had predicted this scene a month ago, Jalen would've told them they were crazy. On the nightshift, Milton virtually ran the department. Everyone knew he didn't like to do the runs. Even the supervisors were okay with him hanging back and tending to their inventory.

That all changed three days ago. Jalen threw everything into a tailspin when he tricked Milton into leaving the office and wreaked havoc on his inventory while he was gone. Jalen compounded the friction between them by appearing threatening when Milton tried to confront him.

In retrospect, Jalen felt guilty about the way he had handled things. Milton knew he was stealing. Rather than acknowledge it – or better yet, not steal in the first place – Jalen defended himself by becoming aggressive and playing the race card.

Like most irresponsible people who acted first and considered the consequences later, Jalen had spent the next couple of days wondering if he should even bother returning to work. Surely Milton would report the incident and have him hauled off to Human Resources for one of those *special meetings*; the ones that ended with his ID badge being confiscated and security escorting him off the premises.

But Jalen didn't get any calls from his supervisor on his days off, so he bit the bullet and showed up for work. Surprisingly, no one said anything to him about the altercation on his first or second day back. It was now day three, and he was fairly confident that he'd gotten away with it.

Even better, it was obvious that Jalen had broken Milton's spirits. No longer could the old man choose to hang back in the department, while Jalen dropped off all of the supplies. Now Jalen did the runs *only when he felt like it.* If he didn't, he'd walk up to his coworker and tell him, "Hey, it's some jobs in the system. I'm finna chill, so you need to do them."

Milton wouldn't respond, but he'd abandon whatever task he was working on and leave the department immediately. Of course that left Jalen plenty of time to fill his backpack with whatever Carl desired. When Milton returned, he wouldn't mention any of the missing items, even though Jalen could tell he noticed things were out of place.

The scenario reminded Jalen of stories his brother told him about prison: The first time you take an inmate's manhood, they'll put up a hell of a fight. But they won't fight so much the second time. It's even easier the third. After that, they'll pretty much roll over for you whenever you please. Jalen wasn't only fucking his department; he was fucking Milton too. He wasn't gentle about it, either.

That night, as Friday transitioned into Saturday, Jalen decided he now had the best job in the hospital. He did a little work, sure. But for the most part he was either stealing or slacking for forty minutes out of every hour. He loafed so much, he was starting to get bored of it. That was something he never thought was possible.

When Milton returned to the department at 4:12 am, Jalen stood tall and stretched his arms and back. He wasn't standing very close to his coworker, but he noticed Milton cower away from him.

Jalen found his behavior amusing, but he wasn't the type of guy who could delight in this on a daily basis. Jalen considered himself a family man. He had a wife and daughter whom he loved dearly. Contrary to his actions in the department, he was not a violent or aggressive individual. He only had two physical altercations in high school. He didn't initiate either one, and he hadn't had a fight since then.

Ideally, he wanted Milton to give him the leeway he needed for mischief *without* making him feel like a bully. Jalen wasn't sure if it was possible to reach this middle ground, but he was willing to try.

He approached his coworker as Milton headed to the back of the department, where he'd left his trusty clipboard. As usual, Milton avoided eye contact, even when Jalen stepped directly in front of him.

"Hey, man. You alright?" Jalen asked him.

Milton tried to sidestep him. Jalen reached and placed a hand on the shelf to his right. He leaned on it, effectively cutting off his coworker's path. It was hard to watch Milton's physical reaction to this move. Not only did he began to tremble, but his beady eyes darted right and left, as he sought an avenue of escape.

"I'm, I'm fine," Milton replied. He tried to move forward on the left. "Excuse me."

Jalen stretched his other arm in that direction. "What's your problem? Why you acting all scary?"

The irony of the question struck him, and Jalen couldn't help but chuckle. He was like the wolf asking the sheep, "What's the problem, my tasty friend? I thought we were going out for lunch..."

Milton finally looked him in the eyes. He hadn't reacted to much of Jalen's antics, but it was hard to ignore his smile. Milton's eyes narrowed, and the trembling in his hands became more pronounced.

"Sorry," Jalen said, "I'm not laughing at you." At that moment, he was overcome by a fit of giggles, so the validity of his statement was debatable. "For real," Jalen insisted, trying to subdue his humor. "I'm laughing at you, but not *at* you. You know what I'm saying? I don't mean no harm. It's just..."

Milton continued to stare at him, while Jalen covered his bullshit with potpourri.

"Never mind," he said. "I just wanted to make sure everything's okay with you. You been acting weird lately."

Milton didn't respond. Gradually Jalen found his gaze unnerving. His smile slipped away.

"You ain't gotta stand there without talking."

"Then let me go by."

Although Jalen had been begging him to speak, he was surprised when he actually did. Milton's appearance exuded weakness. His voice did too. But his words were strong. Jalen realized he was wrong about this man being completely broken.

"So that's it?" he said. "We gotta work together damn near every night, but you don't wanna talk? That's gon' make it awkward, ain't it?"

His coworker continued to stare without speaking. Jalen knew he brought this upon himself, but he didn't like it at all. He felt Milton was trying to assert his position as a man, but he wasn't a man. He was a freaking *hobbit*. He lived alone in an apartment that was probably filled with cats.

Based on Milton's eagerness to pick up extra shifts on the weekends and holidays, Jalen knew he didn't have a life outside of work. He doubted if there was one person, other than their supervisor, who gave a damn about him.

"So that's how it's gon' be?"

Jalen didn't intend for their conversation take this turn, but he felt powerless to stop it. No one got under his skin more than Milton did.

"I try to be cool with you," he continued. "I know we had our shit, but I thought everything was gon' be okay. I wanted us to work together and get along. Not you, though. You wanna hold on to that funky attitude, just 'cause we had one, little argument."

Milton remained mute, but he couldn't stop his body from responding. His breathing was unsteady. The shakiness in his arms reached his face and was now joined by a twitch under his eye. He squeezed his hands together, hoping to stop his fingers from trembling. But when Jalen looked down, all he saw was two balled fists.

"Oh, you gon' hit me?" He took a step back to avoid a sucker punch. Jalen didn't raise his fists, but he was prepared for whatever Milton might try. "Come on then. You wanna take it there? If you take *one* swing, I'll..."

Jalen caught himself. Milton realized the part he might have played in this, and he unclenched his fists.

"I just, just let me by," he pleaded. "I don't want this. I don't want *any* of this."

Jalen's face heated. His heart sank to the pit of his stomach. Jesus, what the hell was wrong with him? His wife would kill him if she knew he was behaving this way at work. His mother would make him take off his belt, so she could whoop him with it. This wasn't the Jalen they knew. This Jalen was nearly unrecognizable.

Caught up in a moment of clarity, Jalen didn't bother to apologize before he turned and headed for the exit.

The hospital had a serenity garden, where patients and family members could go to find peace and contemplate their circumstances. Jalen thought he should go there to cool down. It was time for some serious soul-searching. Jackson Memorial also had a beautiful chapel that was open 24 hours a day. Jalen wasn't a church-going man, but he was open to prayer when life was kicking his ass or when he knew he had done wrong.

Was he treating Milton this way because of the things he needed to get for Carl? Jalen didn't think so, but he couldn't come up with a better explanation. If that was it, he was a bigger fool than–

THUNKE!

The first strike sounded off like an aluminum bat smashing a fastball. Jalen vaguely felt the blow to the back of his head before he dropped to his knees. His eyes swam in opposite directions. The rest of his features registered confusion. His right hand instinctively moved to the location of the injury. Before his fingers encountered an immense amount of blood that was squirting from his newly fractured skull, he heard the sound again.

THUNKE!

This time everything went limp; his face, eyes, arms and legs. Jalen grunted before his body fell forward lifelessly. He did not react when his face impacted the hard, cold tiles – nor did he react when Milton continued the assault with what turned out to be a orthopedic mallet.

THUNKE!
THUNKE!
THWAP!
THWAP!

The sound of his blows took on a wet quality. Milton didn't know a human head could bleed like that; with the spraying effect of a sliced throat – not that he really noticed then. Even as he followed Jalen down, and the bright crimson coated his hands, face and chest, he was only vaguely aware that someone was bleeding.

All he knew for certain was there was a body between his legs, and the more he hit it with the hammer, the less threatening it became. The body had been completely limp for the past ten blows. After the fifteenth, Milton could no longer see what he was hitting. Tears impaired his vision. Blood stained the lenses of his glasses. Blood ran down his face, in his mouth and dripped off his chin.

The mallet was so slippery. He tightened his grip and continued to swing. He didn't stop when the mallet got stuck in the boy's skull, and he had to use both hands to pry it out.

THWAP!
THWAP!
SPLAP!

Milton didn't stop until he was physically exhausted, and he could no longer raise the weapon above his head for another strike. By then it was hard to tell Jalen ever had a normal head sitting atop his thin neck. Milton would've vomited if he saw the mess he created. But he didn't bother to wipe his glasses before he rose to his feet.

With his first step, he slipped and fell forward. An enormous puddle of blood, originating from what was once Jalen's head, spread four feet in all directions. Milton reached to catch his fall, but his hand slipped as well. He fell flat, stretched spread-eagle on his coworker. His scrub top was already soaked. He didn't notice the additional gore it collected when his chest came to a rest in the center of the carnage.

Rather than attempt to rise immediately, Milton crawled forward, until he made it past the worst of the mess. He then rose to his feet in a jerky, stumbling fashion. He had to remove his glasses to get a vague sense of where the department's exit was. The beady eyes behind those lenses were *clearly deranged* – according to the first security guard to spot him.

Milton staggered to his desk three minutes after leaving his department. A trail of blood made it easy to track his journey. There were bloody handprints on every surface he had touched along the way.

The guard, a military vet and current police officer, had taken part in peacekeeping missions in Iraq and Afghanistan. Despite all he'd experienced, the sight of Milton in the hospital's lobby, covered in blood and mumbling unintelligibly, would forever remain the most ghastly thing he had ever seen.

He rushed Milton to the ER to assess his injuries.

It took nearly thirty minutes to determine he was the assailant rather than the victim.

CHAPTER SEVENTEEN
COCKLEBURS

I told him
But he wouldn't listen
So I showed him
I didn't want any of this
I'm *the victim*
He thought he could treat me like shit
Now look at him
So bloody
His blood runs in streams
It's on me
It's on him
*It's on **everything***
All I see
*Is **blood***
Is he breathing?
Impossible to tell
If he isn't
I suppose I will see him in hell

Murder.
At Jackson Memorial.

The hospital experienced its fair share of deaths. With a facility that big, it was an inevitable, daily occurrence. But this wasn't a cancer patient or an accident victim who arrived in the ER with no pulse. This was one of their own. The hospital mourned Jalen's death the same as the police department did when one of their brothers was taken down in the line of duty.

The grieving was complicated because of the bizarre circumstances surrounding Jalen and Milton's incident. The hospital usually sent out flowery emails to celebrate the life of elderly employees when they succumbed. But what would they do with Jalen's story? The combination of sorrow and morbid curiosity created a sense of gloom that permeated every department at Jackson Memorial. Smiles were few and far between.

Carl heard about the murder over the weekend. The reports were sketchy at first, but gradually more details were released. It broke his heart when he learned the victim was Jalen. The boy was only 25 years old. He had a wife and a young daughter. If not for the love of his family, Jalen never would've transferred to third shift. He wouldn't have exposed himself to an apparent psycho who had been working at the hospital – totally undetected – for over thirty years.

Jalen was one of Carl's top associates, but their business relationship came second to the anguish he felt that day. He wasn't alone. On Monday morning, Carl felt the despair-laden tension the moment he arrived at the hospital. Jalen had worked the dayshift for most of his time there. He had always been a welcome face on the units. Nurses and techs appreciated that he was prompt and friendly when he delivered their supplies. They respected him because he never allowed the whores at the hospital to corrupt him.

Carl went on a fact-finding mission after he clocked in. Most of the information he collected was either a rumor or no more detailed than the reports he had seen on the news. When he ran into a Central Supply employee at ten o'clock, Carl was sure he'd finally get the full scoop. Misty was distraught; with no makeup and red, puffy eyes that were threatening to leak again at any moment. Carl approached her with concern and compassion.

"Hey, I'm sorry about what happened to Jalen..."

As expected, Misty shed more tears for her fallen coworker. She wiped her eyes and sniffled. "Thank you, Carl."

He didn't want to become part of the rubberneckers who had no doubt been hounding her with questions, but Jalen was his friend too. Carl wanted to know the specifics surrounding his death, just as he would if one of his relatives was murdered.

"What happened?" he asked Misty. "Have they told you anything?"

She shook her head woefully. "They told us not to talk about it, Carl. I could get in trouble."

He nodded. He knew the hospital had strict rules when it came to sharing certain types of information.

"I understand." He stepped closer and gave her a hug. "That was my nigga, though. I can't believe that shit happened."

"Me neither," Misty said, her voice muffled against his chest. "Everybody loved Jalen."

Carl struck out with the next six people he questioned, but a friend in security had answers.

"You can't tell nobody I told you," Justin warned him.

"I won't," Carl said. "Man, you know me better than that."

"This is different," Justin said. He sat at an information desk, looking around for anyone close enough to eavesdrop. "The police are still investigating, so it's not just the hospital that will be on my ass."

"I won't say nothing," Carl assured him. "*I promise.* I just wanna know what happened to my homey."

Justin looked around one more time before he met Carl's eyes and told him, "That white man said Jalen was threatening him. Said it had been going on for weeks; ever since Jalen went to third shift. He say the boy was stealing stuff and messing up his notes, so he couldn't keep track."

All of the heat left Carl's body. He felt like his soul departed as well. He exhaled roughly and couldn't immediately take in another breath.

"I don't know why he didn't report it," Justin said. "He coulda got the boy fired, and that would've been the end of it. Instead he let all that tension build up, until he just – *snapped.* He hit that boy in the head over twenty times and left him to bleed out. He didn't tell nobody what happened when he went to the ER. But they couldn't have saved Jalen, even if he did. The boy was prolly dead after the fourth or fifth hit. Police say it's the worst case of overkill they ever seen."

Carl barely pulled it together enough to tell the guard, "That's messed up. Thanks, man."

He turned and concentrated on every step as he left the information desk. His legs were so weak, he feared he'd pass out.

Carl got on the nearest elevator and took it down to the basement. A tech from the Avery Building rode down with him.

The woman was not accustomed to seeing him so quiet. She said something, but Carl couldn't get his stunned eyes to focus on her.

When the elevator doors opened, he asked her, "Sorry, did you say something?" as they stepped out.

"Yeah. I was gonna ask if you heard about Jalen, but it looks like you did."

"Yeah," Carl said. He continued to one of the one-person bathrooms near ultrasound.

When he got inside, Carl locked the door and went to the sink. He turned the water on and gave up trying to control his breathing. The running water didn't mask his ragged breaths as much as he'd hoped. Anyone who approached the door would know someone was in distress.

Everything Carl knew about good and bad, right and wrong, told him this was his fault. He might as well have smashed Jalen's head himself.

But Carl refused to accept that – *he couldn't*. He was no more at fault than Ford was when a drunk driver plowed into someone's kid. He never forced Jalen to steal. He even warned him about getting into it with his coworker. If Jalen had been clear about the severity of their friction, Carl would've told him to stop. Lifting equipment wasn't worth losing his job. It definitely wasn't worth his life.

The matter settled, Carl allowed himself a few more moments to grieve his fallen comrade. When he was done, he washed his face and dried his eyes. He had to accept what everyone else in the hospital already understood: Despite the tragedies life throws at you, the show must go on.

● ● ● ● ● ●

Carl wasn't feeling any better by noon, but he had business to attend to. He couldn't put it off any longer. He transported a patient from the Cardiac Tower to MRI and called Bobby before he accepted another assignment.

"Hello?"

"What's up?"

"Who dis?"

"It's Carl."

"What number is this you calling me from?"

"It's my new cellphone. Dropped my other one in the toilet."

Bobby chuckled. "Ol' clumsy ass."

Carl bristled, but he kept his tone even. "You ready to get this money or what?"

"Yeah," Bobby said. "You got it?"

"Yup."

"Alright. I'm on my way."

"Not at the hospital," Carl said. "I ain't doing this kind of business here. I don't want nobody to see me with yo bitch ass. They gon' think I'm a snitch too."

Bobby laughed again. "Man, I ain't never snitched on nobody."

"That's prolly 'cause they paid you off, like I'm doing. Can you meet me in twenty minutes?"

"Yeah. Where?"

Carl gave him an address in one of the neighborhoods surrounding the hospital.

"What's over there?" Bobby asked him.

"My girl's house. That's where I left the money."

"Bet."

• • • • • •

When Bobby arrived at the address, he found the street quiet. His coworker sat on the porch of his girlfriend's house. Carl wore the black scrubs required by patient transporters at the hospital. He stood and walked to the curb as his former associate pulled to a stop. Bobby rolled down the window on the passenger side and grinned at him.

"What's up?" Carl greeted him. He pulled the door handle and found it locked. "You gon' let me in?"

Bobby pushed a button to unlock it. Carl took a seat on the passenger side and sighed audibly. Bobby grinned and rubbed his hands together.

"Where my money at?"

"I got it," Carl said. "Just need to ask you a few questions first, to make sure this arrangement is gonna work out."

"It's gon' work out," Bobby assured him. "Soon as I get paid, we ain't got nothing to do with each other."

"Yeah, you say that," Carl replied. "But how I know you haven't told somebody already?"

"I haven't. I told you I haven't told nobody."

"What about that girl who called me?"

"What girl?"

"The one who set up the meet at Starbucks, said she wanted to buy that ultrasound."

"Oh." He laughed.

"Nigga, this shit ain't funny. Who was that ho?"

"That was my girl," Bobby said. "And she ain't no ho."

"I don't give a fuck about you sticking up for her. I wanna know what she knows about me."

"Damn, nigga. Calm down. She don't know nothing about you."

"You had to tell her *something*... She know my name?"

"Naw," Bobby said, frowning. "I told her it was some dude I work with, but I never said your name."

"Don't bullshit me, nigga. What if y'all break up, and she decide to snitch on you? She could call the hospital and tell them you be stealing for somebody. Can she give them my name? Tell the truth."

"Bruh, I ain't never told her your name. I only said it was some dude at work."

"You told her I was gon' pay you?"

Bobby hesitated. Carl's eyes narrowed, and the younger man said, "Yeah, I did tell her that. But she still don't know who you are."

"You told her where you was going right now?" Carl asked.

"Naw. She at school."

Carl didn't know if he believed all of that, but he had no choice but to accept it. It wasn't like he could contact Bobby's girlfriend and ask her directly.

"Man, why you asking all these questions?" Bobby wondered. "You ain't never been scary."

"I ain't ever been *blackmailed*," Carl told him. "This a whole new ballgame for me. I gotta cover all my bases."

"Oh. Well, sorry about that."

"No, you ain't sorry, ol' snake-ass nigga. If you was sorry, you wouldn't have never done it."

"Alright, well, where my money?"

"I got it, nigga..."

Carl reached into his pocket – except he didn't reach into his pocket. Instead he reached under his scrub top. By the time Bobby realized the difference, it was too late. His coworker had pulled a gun on him. Bobby didn't know what kind it was. He wouldn't even be able to describe the color if he reported this incident to the police later. All he saw was a barrel pointed right at his chest. Beyond that, he saw the steely eyes of a man he didn't really know at all. His heart began to rev like a motorboat. Bobby's eyes were as big as half dollars when he looked up at Carl.

"*What the fuck*?!" he squealed.

He tried to back away, but there was nowhere to go. His door was closed. He knew that if he reached to open it, Carl would start squeezing the trigger. Bobby thrust his hands forward, as if they would protect him from bullets flying towards his face.

"*Man, what you doing? Don't point that shit at me!*"

"I'ma ask you again..." Carl said. Though his blood was racing as quickly as Bobby's, his voice was surprisingly calm. "Does that *bitch* know my name?"

"*No!*" Bobby screamed. "*I told you no!*" His arms were trembling. His fingers were shaking twice as much. Carl had never seen anyone so spooked.

"Did you tell her where you was going today?"

"*Please, man! Please don't do it!*"

"I ain't gon' shoot, you dumb ass boy! I just gotta protect myself."

His promise to let him live barely calmed Bobby. "*I didn't tell nobody, man. She at school. I told you.*"

"What about the hospital?" Carl asked. "Who'd you talk to about it up there?"

"*Nobody, man!*" Bobby was crying now. He couldn't help it. "*Please take that gun off me, man. I'll give you whatever you want.*"

"I ain't paying you no four thousand dollars," Carl told him.

"*Okay!*" Bobby cried. "I don't want it. I don't want nothing from you. Just leave me alone. *Please!*"

Carl stared him down for another second before he reached back and opened his door. He kept the gun trained on the boy's chest as he exited the vehicle. The street was still as quiet as it was when Bobby first arrived.

Carl did not close the door when he stepped out. Bobby's hands were up and away from the steering wheel. He probably could've made a getaway while Carl got out of the car, but he didn't try. Why would he? It wasn't like his coworker would murder him in broad daylight.

Carl's heart hammered as he pushed the safety down on his 9mm. It was a subtle move; just a quarter inch with his thumb. He didn't think Bobby noticed, but the boy started to scream.

"Wait! Don't do it, man! Please don't!"

"Sorry, nigga. I can't trust you."

"Noooo!"

BLAK!

BLAKBLAK!

BLAK!

Carl quieted him with three shots to the midsection and one to the head.

The blood splatter was immediate and all encompassing.

Carl had never shot anyone before.

It wasn't an exciting or fun experience, like some of the gangbangers from his old neighborhood made it seem. For Carl, it was horrifying. The sight of mortal wounds squirting blood made his bowels shudder.

Every fiber of his being wanted to run immediately. But he had a plan, and he had to remain disciplined. He took a few moments to remove a towel from his pocket and wipe the door handle on the car – both inside and out. He knew he hadn't touched anything else. The whole time he was in the vehicle, he made sure his hands remained in his lap.

When he was done wiping, Carl made the mistake of looking at the body one last time, before he gave into survival instincts that were urging him to flee the scene. That was a mistake. The sight of Bobby's bloody face would be forever ingrained on his psyche. He would see the slumped figure in his dreams and during his conscious hours.

He turned and sprinted towards his "girlfriend's" house. The back fence was open, as he'd left it. The ground seemed to shift beneath him as he ran past a "FOR SALE" sign that was lying face down in the backyard. Ten minutes ago, the sign was standing tall in front of the house.

Carl hopped the back fence, touching it only with his left hand, which was buffered by the towel. As he sprinted through the alley, he encountered a few barking dogs in adjacent backyards. The temperature was in the low-seventies, but he felt sweat pouring down his face when he hopped the fence into another backyard four houses down. This house was vacant as well.

Carl looked around frantically as he approached the back porch. He didn't spot any witnesses, but that didn't mean no one was watching through a kitchen window. If so, that was a variable he couldn't control.

What he *could* control was the area he picked for his crime. It was a working-class neighborhood – a *white* neighborhood, so he didn't expect to be spotted by any Section 8 moms chilling in the front yard at that hour. He was pretty sure there were no Hispanic families either; with the mothers at home raising children while the men worked.

Carl entered the carport, where he'd left his car. Once inside, he reached for a pair of latex gloves on the passenger seat. He put them on and swiftly wiped his prints off the murder weapon. He pulled his throwaway phone from his pocket and did the same with it. He leaned forward and placed the phone and gun on the floorboard on the passenger side. He already had a trash bag laid out to protect his mat and a bleach-based cleansing spray waiting. He sprayed the evidence profusely on both sides before he started the car and rolled out of the driveway.

When he made it to the street, he looked right and left. He didn't see any neighbors who had come outside in response to the gunshots. Three miles down the road, he pulled over and deposited the phone and gun in a gutter. He pulled his gloves off and stuffed them in his pocket.

Carl was still sweating profusely when he returned to the hospital. He stared at his reflection in the rearview mirror, barely recognizing the man looking back at him. He felt sick to the stomach and sick in the head.

When he left New Orleans after the hurricane, he vowed to break the cycle of criminality in his family. Three of his five brothers had committed murder. Two were still incarcerated. Carl's father died in prison while serving time for a double homicide. Even his disabled uncle Curley had fatally stabbed a man over a small debt.

Now Carl had joined their ranks.

He believed this killing was justified. Bobby was threatening his livelihood. If he had given him $4,000, there was a great chance Bobby would come back later asking for more – or he'd start bragging about how he got the loot. Carl had to silence him. There was no question about it.

He understood that Bobby was the first but probably not the last person to try to extort him. Even if Carl got away with this murder, it wasn't possible to kill everyone who threatened to expose him. The only thing that made sense was to shut down operations. Carl was okay with that, but he needed to stack up a little more paper first. If he could keep his business rolling for one more year, he'd be fine with that.

He wasn't a greedy man.

● ● ● ● ● ●

Within seconds of walking into the hospital, Carl ran into the very person he hoped to avoid for the next ten minutes. His supervisor frowned and looked down at her watch.

"*Carl*! Where the hell you been? You been on a run for *twenty minutes*."

He had left himself on a job when he went to meet with Bobby, rather than clock-out for lunch. Carl knew he'd get in trouble for taking too long, but he needed to remain in the system. Being at work was the perfect alibi.

He was not accustomed to Edna chastising him, but if this was the worst thing that happened to him today, he'd consider himself fortunate.

"Sorry. I was looking for a wheelchair," he told her.

"What? How are you looking for a wheelchair for twenty minutes, Carl? The office is full of them."

"I thought I saw some outside earlier," he explained. "I figured I might as well use one of those – to save us the trouble of bringing it in later. And I was in the bathroom for most of that time. Sorry," he said, gripping his stomach. "I got diarrhea."

Carl was astonished by his ability to speak clearly, while every part of his body felt like it was on fire. Sweat glistened on his forehead. His fingers were trembling, his breathing unsteady. He couldn't believe his supervisor didn't question his wide-eyed stare.

"You don't look good," Edna acknowledged. Her expression softened. "Do you need to go to the ER?"

"No," he said right away. *God no.* "I'm okay. I feel better now."

Edna watched him for a second before saying, "Alright, well hurry up. That lady's been waiting for you to take her down."

"Okay," Carl said. "I'm on my way..."

He hurried past her, on his way to the Clark Building. When he got on the elevator, he wiped the sweat off his face and dried his hands on his pants. That was when he noticed the grassburs. Carl's heart froze as he stared down at his legs. His shoelaces and the bottom portion of his scrub pants were sparsely covered with the spiny seeds.

Carl knew he collected the burs while running through the alley after concluding his business with Bobby. He thought he had everything planned perfectly. He didn't account for Mother Nature attempting to foil him in this manner. If his supervisor had seen the burs, she would've known he'd left the hospital.

He could not make these types of mistakes!

Rather than get off the elevator on the third floor, Carl redirected it to the basement. He found another single-person restroom and locked himself inside. He sat on the toilet and removed the grassburs as quickly as possible. It shouldn't have been a difficult task, but it was hard to remain focused. Bobby's bloody face was superimposed over everything. The burs were so pointy, Carl poked himself a number of times, despite the balled tissue paper he used to extract them.

He accepted the pain as a small punishment for his evil deeds.

After five minutes, he knew Edna would wonder why he still hadn't picked up his patient. She would probably clear the job and assign it to another transporter. When she questioned him again, Carl would tell her his diarrhea returned with a vengeance after they spoke. She would have to accept that. Everyone knows the runs are unpredictable.

CHAPTER EIGHTEEN
MONSTER

Towards the end of his shift, Carl began to feel confident that he'd gotten away with murder. Of course it was too soon to call it. It had only been five hours since he pulled the trigger. The homicide detectives were probably still on the scene collecting evidence.

But he knew it wasn't an open and shut case, or the police would've come to the hospital already. They would've hauled him off for questioning, even if he was in the middle of a run.

Carl had encountered several security guards since he returned to the hospital. Each time he saw them, his heart skipped a beat. The silver badge on their chests meant they were an extension of the law, even if they didn't have a firearm. But the guards never gave him a second glance, unless it was to greet him or spark up a conversation.

With two hours left in his workday, Carl picked up a patient from X-ray and dropped her off on the Continued Care Unit. When he got there, he was not happy to see Danielle was working that day. He was confused by his reaction, considering she used to be one of his favorite people at the hospital.

Carl realized his fondness for Danielle began to decline when she came to work with a knot on her forehead. The bump had gone away since then, but he thought about it every time he saw her. The contusion was confirmation that Danielle was a hoodrat living a hoodrat lifestyle. The latest rumors buzzing around the hospital was that she was a stripper. Carl didn't know if that was true. In any event, she wasn't the kind of woman he wanted on his team or in his life.

But distancing himself was easier said than done. He tried to hurry off the floor after leaving his patient. Danielle caught up with him at the elevators.

"Carl! Hey, wait up!"

She rushed to him and threw her arms around him for a hug. Carl couldn't hide his discomfort as he looked over her shoulder. He locked eyes with another PCT down the hall. He knew her name was Kelly, but they never spoke before.

"You trying to take off without speaking to me?" Danielle asked when she backed away.

"My bad, baby," Carl said. "I didn't know you was here. Why you hollering my name so loud? Got everybody looking at us."

Danielle looked back and saw a couple of employees watching them. "Fuck them," she said. "Say, did you hear about Jalen?"

Carl's mood took another hit. He didn't like that Danielle was smiling.

"Yeah, 'course I heard about him. That's all everybody's talking about."

"Do you know what happened, though?" she asked. "I heard that old man he works with beat him with a hammer. They say he hit him so many times, it looked like his face got ran over."

Danielle had the decency to lose her smile this time, but Carl didn't like her tone. This wasn't some random World Star video she was talking about. This was *Jalen*; a coworker and friend. Where was the reverence?

He sighed. "Yeah, that's what I heard."

"Do you know why it happened?" Danielle asked.

Carl shook his head.

"Me neither," she said. "Won't nobody talk about it."

"That's good," he told her. "Jalen was my friend. I don't like the way people are gossiping about him."

Danielle seemed dense, but she picked up on that. "Sorry. I liked him too."

He nodded. "I uh, I gotta go. It's a bunch of jobs in the system."

"Oh, it's like that? You don't come holler at me no more. When you do come, you ain't got time for me?"

"It ain't personal," he said. "I got in trouble earlier today for taking too long on a job. My sup's watching me now."

"What about the supplies?" she asked. "You haven't asked me to get you anything lately."

"I'm taking a little break from that," he said. "Sorry. Did you need some money?"

Danielle was happy to shake her head. She just enjoyed a very fruitful weekend at Club Paradise. She didn't need a man to give her anything. "Nah. I'm good, Carl."

He grinned. "Glad to hear that." He turned and pressed the down button on the elevator.

"Hey," she reached and touched his arm. "Since I'm not with my boyfriend anymore, and it sounds like I'm not working for you right now, I was wondering if you wanted to... You know... I ain't really down with dinner and movies, but we can pick up a box of chicken and watch Netflix or something..."

She couldn't have been more forward. And Carl still found her attractive. She had nice boobs, a fantastic ass. He loved her dark skin. But he shook his head.

"I'ma have to pass on that." He didn't have an explanation, so he didn't offer one.

"Okay," Danielle said. "That's cool."

She didn't seem upset, but Carl wasn't a mind reader. If he was, he would've heard her thinking: *Fuck you, nigga! You think you too good? You don't want this pussy? Fuck you! You ain't that damn fine. Fuck all y'all!*

When his elevator arrived, he pushed his wheelchair ahead of him.

"Alright. I'll holler at you..."

Danielle walked away without responding.

● ● ● ● ● ●

PCT Kelly Phillips had been employed at Jackson Memorial for nine years. She started in housekeeping and worked her way up with educational programs offered by the hospital. She knew the secret to longevity at work boiled down to two things; covering your ass and staying out of people's business.

The first part required a lot of attention to detail, but the second part was easy – at least it was until a hellcat named

Danielle started working on her floor. In the past few weeks, Kelly had seen things she never thought possible; things she assumed were only hospital rumors.

Kelly now understood that all of the wild stories she'd heard over the years might be true. If Danielle could be *Danielle* and still keep her job, then employees probably were having affairs all over the hospital. The rumors about how steamy the parking garage got on third shift – maybe there was something to that.

Despite the sleazy atmosphere, Kelly loved the hospital. She loved the role she played in healing people – because that's what it was all about. Who cares who gave who a blowjob? The patients were the only thing that mattered. With that in mind, she was willing to turn a blind eye to all of Danielle's bad behaviors.

But enough is enough.

When a transporter named Virgil paid them a visit a few minutes after the one named Carl left, Kelly paid close attention to his interactions with her coworker. She was floored when Danielle smiled at the boy, gave him a hug, and then looked back and told her, "Hey, I'll be back in a minute."

Kelly shook her head and did not respond. She watched Danielle and the transporter hop on an elevator together. Danielle didn't ask her to tell their charge she was leaving, so Kelly didn't feel obligated to do so.

● ● ● ● ● ●

When Danielle returned fifteen minutes later, their charge nurse Maria was ready and waiting.

"Where have you been?"

Danielle turned slowly and looked down at her. Maria was almost a foot shorter.

"What?" she asked with a frown.

Maria's eyes widened. "Wha, what do you mean *what*?"

"Why you running up on me?"

Every nurse and tech within earshot began to gravitate towards the argument. Kelly didn't want to join the gawkers, but it was impossible to look away from this train wreck.

"Who do you think you're talking to?" Maria asked her.
"You're the one who just left the floor – *again* – without telling

anyone! You are not on break. Even if you were, you can't leave without–"

"I had to go to the bathroom," Danielle snapped. "I told what's-her-face to tell you."

"The *bathroom*? There's four bathrooms on this floor!"

"Well, I wanted to go to a different one. You can't tell me what bathroom to go to."

"You been gone *fifteen minutes*."

"I got my *period*," Danielle said, matching her volume unabashedly. "Sometimes it take a little while to get everything cleaned up." She cocked her head, daring Maria to question that.

The men and women standing around them cringed in embarrassment. Kelly shook her head. She couldn't believe one of their team members was so foul.

Maria was red-faced and flustered. She knew Danielle was full of shit, but it was hard to catch her in a lie.

"Okay, so who did you tell you were leaving?" she asked her.

"Her," Danielle said, pointing. "Kelly."

Kelly closed her eyes and sighed. When she opened them, everyone was looking her way.

"She told you she was going to the restroom?" Maria asked her.

Kelly looked Danielle in the eyes and tried to telepathically convey how much she had grown to despise her. "She told me she'd be back," she said to Maria. "She didn't say where she was going."

"I ain't gotta tell you about my period and stuff," Danielle cut in.

Rather than ask Kelly why she didn't deliver the message, Maria turned back to their troubled tech. "Listen, I don't care how many times you bring up your *period*, I'm not letting this go. You've been coming and going as you please, bringing all these damn visitors up here. You barely do any work. We're gonna have a sit down with the manager."

"Fine," Danielle said. "Is that it? Are you finished embarrassing me in front of everybody?"

Maria's face turned another shade of red. She wanted to send Danielle home immediately, but the tech had said something that made Maria wonder if she was making the right moves. She confronted her in front of everyone, and Danielle's period came up in the conversation. Did Maria have the right to *embarrass* her like this? Honestly, she thought Danielle was doing more to embarrass herself. But Human Resources might see it differently.

"We'll be talking to the manager," Maria said before storming back to the nurses' station.

"Y'all know where to find me," Danielle shot back before she returned to her hallway.

Kelly became more upset when the charge nurse left. After covering her ass and minding her business for the past nine years, she realized Danielle might be the tipping point. She was worried their pitiful tech might find a way to weasel out of this – *again*. The thought of having to witness this catastrophe for another day, week or even a whole *year* was more than Kelly could stand.

Maybe Maria was restricted by *rules* and *hospital policies*, but Kelly wasn't. And if there was one thing Kelly knew about hoodrats, it was how easy it was to set them off. If she got under her skin, she was fairly confident Danielle would become belligerent and get herself fired – not tomorrow or next week, but *today*. Kelly knew she may have to take a slap to the face in the process, but that was a small price to pay. She didn't mind taking one for the team.

She walked to Danielle's hallway and found her seated near one of the computers. Kelly took a deep breath as she approached her. She looked her right in the eyes and told her, "You a ho."

Danielle looked up at her, a deep sneer growing on the side of her face. "What?"

Kelly's heart raced. She realized a lot worse could happen than just a slap. But she had already come this far. "I said you a ho."

"*I'm a ho*?" Somehow Danielle mustered the nerve to become irate. She shot to her feet. "Bitch, who the fuck you think you talking to?"

As predicted, Danielle was loud enough to bring a few staff members to the hallway. Now that she had witnesses, Kelly reverted to covering her ass. She couldn't let them know she initiated this.

"Nothing," she said, backing away.

"*Naw, bitch, say it again!*" Danielle shoved her hard in the chest, with both hands.

The push had plenty of force behind it, so Kelly didn't have to do too much acting. She flew backwards five feet and landed painfully on her butt.

"*Hey*!" she wailed.

Danielle advanced on her with her fists balled; her arms up in a boxing stance. Kelly's eyes bugged. It only took half a second to determine Danielle could fight. She looked like she could give a man a run for his money.

"What the hell?" Their charge nurse rounded the corner just as a PCT reached to restrain Danielle.

She pushed him away roughly. "Get the fuck off me!"

"*Stop!*" Maria belted. "*What the hell are you doing?*"

"*This bitch called me a ho!*"

"*No, I didn't!*" Kelly cried. "*I didn't do nothing!*"

"*That's it!*" It didn't take Maria long to pick a side. "*Danielle, go! Go home! Now!*"

"What?" Despite all she'd done to warrant termination, Danielle knew she didn't deserve to get fired over *this*. "Fuck you!" she told Maria. "And fuck that bitch too!"

She charged forward again. Maria didn't think twice before stepping in front of her.

Bad move.

Danielle caught her with a right hook no one saw coming. Maria's head snapped nearly all the way around. Her upper body followed, about a second later. Her legs wobbled and then collapsed, bringing the whole body down.

For a moment no one reacted. They couldn't believe what they'd just witnessed. Kelly was the most horrified. She was prepared to take one for the team, but she didn't want Maria to become a victim.

The good thing was Danielle would *definitely* get fired now. If pushing Kelly wasn't enough, knocking their charge unconscious sealed the deal. The bad news was Danielle was still on a rampage! No one who had seen what just happened wanted to intervene.

At that point, the only thing left on Danielle's to-do list was kill the bitch who had started this mess. Kelly screamed and cowered as the monster drew within a few feet.

"*Help! Stop! Somebody help!*"

"Naw, bitch! Don't try to get help now!" Danielle shouted. *"You gon' get this ass whooping!"*

Kelly thought she was a goner, but it turned out Maria wasn't the only person on the floor who was willing to take charge. From out of nowhere, a caped hero rushed to the scene.

"Get back!" he yelled and stepped between the two. *"What are y'all standing around for? Somebody call security! Get back!"* he shouted at Danielle. *"Get your ass back!"*

Upon closer inspection, Kelly realized her savior wasn't a super hero. It was Mr. Westbrook from room 408. His *cape* was actually the sheet from his bed. He had jumped up so quickly, it flowed behind him. As the sheet fell away, Kelly was greeted to a full moon: Mr. Westbrook was standing over her, facing Danielle. The back of his hospital gown was wide open.

Realizing a terminally ill patient had more balls than them, Kelly's coworkers finally sprang to action. Two nurses restrained Danielle, while another knelt to check on Maria.

"You going to jail!" a tech yelled as she ran to call security.

Danielle looked around angrily. She knew she'd lost her job, but she'd be damned if she went to jail that night. She broke away from the nurses and rushed to the break room. She snatched her purse from her locker and kicked the door open on her way out. She thought someone might try to lock her in the room, but her escape was unimpeded.

Maria was starting to come to her senses by then. Her eyes didn't focus in time to see her worst PCT make a mad dash to the stairway.

By the time security arrived, Danielle was long gone.

● ● ● ● ● ●

Kelly usually clocked out at 6:54pm. That night she didn't leave until eight. After Maria went to the ER for an evaluation, the unit manager showed up along with a couple of police officers. Kelly had to fill out separate reports for the hospital and the police. She told her side of the story so many times, she started to believe it. In each retelling, her version of events started the same:

"All I did was tell her she was wrong, and she went crazy."

"You told her she was wrong?" their manager asked, pen in hand.

"Yeah." Kelly nodded. "I told her, '*You know you wrong*,' and then she called me a bitch and started trying to fight. I don't know what her problem was."

"That's okay," the manager said. "She's gonna have a warrant out for her arrest. We'll take care of it."

When Kelly left the unit, she went to the ER to check on her charge. Maria was okay, about to be discharged. She sat up in a stretcher with her husband and several staff members in the exam room. The side of her face was swollen, but overall she didn't look too bad. She held a cold compress to the back of her head.

"I'm sorry," Kelly told her. She was near tears.

"Oh, come here," Maria said. She gave her a hug when Kelly stepped closer. "Why are you so upset. It wasn't your fault."

"I feel like it was. If I didn't say anything to her…"

"If you didn't say anything, we wouldn't have found out what an animal she is," Maria said. "She shouldn't have reacted that way, just because you told her she was wrong."

Kelly was never good at keeping secrets. She felt so guilty, she almost came clean.

You a ho.

What?

I said you a ho.

"It'll be alright," Maria assured her. She smiled. "I'm fine, and we'll never see Danielle again. It's a win-win."

But she was wrong about that.

When Kelly exited the hospital, she didn't make it to the parking garage before she saw something peculiar. There was a car parked in the valet area. Valet parking was closed for the day. After hours, the spot became a tow-away zone for anyone silly enough to leave their vehicle there.

But technically no one *left* the car there. It was still occupied. In fact, it was *very* occupied. As Kelly drew near, all four doors opened. Before she recognized any of the faces, she heard a familiar voice say, "Bitch, I told you you was gon' get this ass whooping."

Kelly stopped cold. She couldn't believe her eyes, though she wasn't sure why this was so surprising. Danielle had shown her true colors time and time again. But still, this was beyond ignorant. This was jailhouse *I'ma-stab-you-five-times-right-in-front-of-the-guards* dumb.

All four of the women who exited the vehicle were dark and menacing. Kelly didn't see any weapons, but that didn't mean much. She didn't have time to evaluate each one before they were within striking distance. The leader of the pack stepped forward. Danielle hadn't changed out of her scrubs, but she had time to smoke some green. The marijuana aroma was strong. The white of her eyes was perfectly pink.

At that point, Kelly knew her ass whooping was unavoidable, so what difference did it make if she spoke her mind?

"You really are stupid," she told her former coworker.

Danielle grinned. Behind her, one of the girls said, "*Ooh! She called you stupid!*"

The women let Danielle connect the first few blows before they piled on. Kelly was right; the stripper fought like a man. Kelly tried to protect her face above all else, but it was impossible. When the ghetto girls joined the fray, they yanked her hair and targeted her beauty, almost exclusively. The ones who couldn't get a shot to the head kicked her in the stomach and ribs. Kelly felt the contusions as they rose all over her body.

She felt almost every shred of clothing ripped from her body. She felt her forehead split when they stomped her head against the pavement. Towards the end, the feet rained down more than the fists. She felt the blood. *Her blood.* It was everywhere; in her eyes and mouth. Each time she rolled over, she saw it splattering onto the pavement, leaking freely.

The women berated her during the beat down. Kelly didn't understand much of what they were saying. She got the gist of it though: Apparently she was a *ho* and a *bitch*, she deserved this ass whooping. And although the hoodrats had complete control of her, they kept pointing out the need to *Get her! Get that bitch!*

The only voice Kelly was familiar with kept repeating, "*I told you, bitch! I told yo ass!*"

All told, the mauling only lasted a couple of minutes. But from Kelly's perspective, it felt like it went on for much longer. She didn't start crying until she heard the clomping of security guards' boots rushing towards them.

"*Hey! Hey! Get off her!*"

"*Get 'em!*"

"Grab her!"

From her defeated position, Kelly pushed up on her arms so she could watch her attackers flee. With one eye swollen closed and blood in the other, her vision was poor at best. She wiped her good eye and saw Danielle and her friends running in every direction. None of the girls tried to make it to their car, where they would've been easily apprehended.

Despite the pain she felt in virtually every part of her body, Kelly couldn't help but laugh at her tormentors. What kind of idiot commits a crime like this without planning their escape? One of the hoochies could've stayed in the car and left the engine running.

Kelly spit out a tooth and a mouthful of blood and called them, *"Dumb motherfuckers."* She knew it was crazy to laugh at a time like this, but she couldn't help it.

The first security guard to approach her didn't know what to make of her bloody smile. Kelly was so lumped up, she looked like the Elephant man.

"Don't try to move," he told her. "We'll bring you a stretcher."

CHAPTER NINETEEN
THE FINAL CHAPTER
NAOMI'S BABY

Hair pulled
Shirt ripped
Bra popped
Titties out
This is what yo dumb ass get
For running off at the mouth
Bitch slapped
Pimp slapped
Knee to the ribs
Foot to the mouth
You didn't think I was coming back
With some bitches from the south?
Pretty face
Not no more!
Two teeth loose
Blood gushing out
Bet you think about this shit
Next time you run off at the mouth

That Monday, Naomi called-in for her morning shift in the Cardiac Tower. It was the first time she'd done that in over a year, but some things couldn't be avoided. She could no longer face the questions from the nurses on her floor.

When is your baby due?
When are you going on leave?
Is everything alright?
You don't look well.

When was your last check up?

Don't you have any ultrasound pictures?

Even worse were the questions from Naomi's husband. She was pretty sure Bryan knew she wasn't pregnant. She didn't know why he didn't come right out and say it. Instead he said things like, *Shouldn't you be going to a doctor?* and *I know you don't want to know if it's a boy or a girl, but can't you still get an ultrasound?* or *You don't seem to be getting bigger – not in the stomach at least. Maybe you're not pregnant. It could just be gas.*

The worst was, *It's okay if you're not pregnant.* Bryan told her that often, especially in the past few weeks.

It's okay if you're not pregnant.

The last time Naomi heard it was Saturday night, when she accidently left a sanitary napkin in the bathroom wastebasket. Bryan was playing his games past one am. A six-pack of beer sent him to the bathroom multiple times. Naomi had been in bed since eleven, but he woke her up with that declaration. He exited the bathroom and didn't turn the lights off right away.

"You know, it's okay if you're not pregnant. It'll be alright."

Naomi lie with her back to him, the sheets pulled up to her shoulders. She pretended not to hear him, but when he returned to the front room, she went to the restroom and saw her pad. She flushed it, hoping it wouldn't clog up the apartment's cheap pipes. She returned to bed with tears in her eyes.

The thing about Bryan's comment was she knew it was a lie. She could see it in his eyes each time he told her. He was waiting for her to take the bait. The moment she came clean, he'd shout, *"Ah ha! I knew you were full of shit!"* He'd pack his things with glee, happy that he finally had a justifiable reason to leave her. No one would tell him he was wrong for divorcing a crazy lady.

Bryan said he hadn't spoken to Mallory since Naomi uncovered their affair, but she never believed that. That bitch was somewhere waiting for him. Naomi spent many a night imagining their conversations:

I miss you, baby. When can you come see me again?

I'll come after work. I love making love to you. You're not fat and ugly like Naomi.

I want you forever. Why can't you just leave the cow?

I will. Give me a few more weeks. Once she comes clean about the pregnancy, I'll tell her she's a lying cow, and then I'll leave.

Are you sure she's not pregnant?

I'm positive. She's a fat, ugly liar. I hate her so much.

I hate her too. I wish you would come make love to me now.

After work, baby. I'll be there.

Promise me you're not having sex with your wife.

Ewww. Gross. Never, baby!

Naomi replayed the conversations in her mind so often, she could hear their voices. They followed her to work, in the grocery store and especially while she slept. It was no wonder she was upset with Bryan every morning and every evening. He had either fucked Mallory that day, or he planned to fuck her when he got off work.

Naomi didn't think she was crazy for believing a baby would solve all of this. It would be *crazy* to give up on her marriage without a fight. Telling everyone at work that she had lied – *that* was crazy. Acquiring a baby would be the only sane thing she'd done in the past nine months.

She arrived at the OB/GYN clinic near the hospital at 6:45, the same time she would've clocked in if she had gone to work that morning. The clinic didn't start taking patients until nine, but she had nowhere else to go. Waiting there made as much sense as the rest of her plan.

She ate two sausage biscuits with cheese and downed two cans of Coke while she watched the sun rise over the hospital complex. It was March 6th, a beautiful day by anyone's standards. The morning temperature was 66 degrees. The high was expected to be a pleasant 78.

At 8am, Naomi realized she hadn't planned for her morning BM. She didn't want to be seen at the hospital, so she drove to 7-11 and handled her business in their bathroom. On the way out, she picked up two more breakfast sandwiches and another Coke. She had no idea how long she'd be waiting at the doctor's office. She didn't want to leave again if she got hungry at lunchtime.

Back at the clinic, she spotted two cars in the parking lot that weren't there when she left. She guessed these were employees arriving to get things ready for their workday. Naomi parked further away from the building to avoid suspicion from anyone else who got there early.

When she turned off her car, she checked the bag sitting on the passenger seat. Everything was as she'd left it. There were towels, plenty of gauze, a couple of scalpels, an umbilical cord clamp and scissors. She even packed a bulb syringe to clear her baby's mouth and nose.

In the glove compartment was her husband's snub nose .38. It had been in Bryan's nightstand for so long, he probably forgot he owned it. Naomi didn't want to use the pistol, but it was unlikely the host would lie back and say, "Go ahead, cut me open."

Once Naomi neutralized the donor, she knew she'd have less than ten minutes to complete the operation. She expected it to be very messy.

She wasn't sure how Bryan would react when she came home with a baby. She hoped he'd simply accept it, as he accepted that she was pregnant and later that she might not be pregnant. It would be awkward for a few days, sure, but they would get past it. He'd fall in love with his son or daughter and forget about Mallory. He'd forget that he ever wanted to leave Naomi.

If she was wrong, and he packed his things anyway, Naomi thought she'd be okay with that – because she wouldn't be alone anymore. She'd have her baby. The baby would call her *Mama* and love her unconditionally, because that's what babies do.

This was all good news, but Naomi couldn't stop crying as she peeled the plastic off her next breakfast sandwich. She'd been crying so much, it was a wonder her eyes still worked. They should have been completely dried out by now.

She knew the crying would come to an end soon. All of her suffering would.

Today was a beautiful day.

● ● ● ● ● ●

Best case scenario, Naomi wanted the pregnant woman she first saw near the clinic. That woman was beautiful, in great shape, and she looked to be a full nine months pregnant. If she couldn't get her, Naomi would settle for an unattractive or overweight woman, as long as she was close to her due date.

But as she sat in the parking lot and watched the office open and start to take patients, she realized her plan might not flow as smoothly as she hoped. The first ten patients who arrived were either not white or not showing. Some didn't look pregnant at all. Naomi wondered why they were even there.

It took three hours before a fully pregnant *white* woman arrived for a checkup – but she ruined things by bringing her husband along. Technically he brought her. He hopped out of the drivers' seat and hurried to open the passenger door. Naomi didn't think chivalrous guys like that still existed. Bryan never asked to accompany her to any of her doctor's appointments. Sure she didn't have any, but he never asked.

By noon Naomi's car felt hot and muggy. She began to doubt if she'd be successful at all. She'd forgotten that OB/GYN doctors didn't see pregnant women exclusively. They also took patients who needed physicals and pap smears. That would explain all of the skinny women she observed arriving and leaving the clinic. Naomi guessed only one out of ten was actually pregnant. Of those, only a few were showing.

She was reluctant to accept that her odds of finding a fully pregnant white woman (who was also alone) were very slim. Naomi began to cry again as she ate her last breakfast sandwich. If she didn't find the right woman today, could she pull off another stakeout tomorrow? Technically she could, but every hour she sat in her car, she felt her grip on sanity loosening.

God, why is this so hard?

There were approximately 70 babies born in Overbrook Meadows every day. Naomi only needed one! She wondered if she should try another clinic. She decided against it, because she didn't want to drive around all day and find the same results elsewhere. Even worse, she might end up in a poor neighborhood; where all of the patients were minorities.

At one o'clock she had to relieve her bowels again. She went to McDonalds this time and got lunch while she was there. When she returned to the doctor's office, she had everything she needed. She munched her burger and fries and sipped her soda, resolved to stay there until the office closed. Hopefully she'd find her host before then.

● ● ● ● ● ●

At four pm Danielle socked her charge nurse in the jaw, dropping her like a hot potato. Half a mile away, Naomi was still in the clinic's parking lot, waiting on her donor. She played Candy Crush on her cellphone to fight the boredom. Her phone hadn't rang the whole time she was there. She wasn't bothered by that, but it was a reminder of why she desperately needed a baby. Friends and spouses will disappoint you, but her son or daughter never would.

At a quarter after four, Naomi *finally* spotted her victim. The breeze blowing through her open windows was warm, but her body felt icy as she sat up with a start and stared at a woman who had just exited a late model Camry. The woman had long, dark hair. Her belly was big and swollen. She was so far along, she walked up the few steps to the clinic with a waddle. Even better, she was not accompanied by *anyone*!

Naomi brought her hands together in prayer as the woman disappeared inside the building. The moment she was out of sight, Naomi began to doubt herself. Was she really pregnant? Or did Naomi want it so badly, her mind was playing tricks on her?

"Please, God. Please. I need this. Let it be real. I need this so bad..."

Naomi barely blinked for the next thirty minutes, while the woman was inside the clinic. Her breaths were shallow. Her knee bounced uncontrollably. Her reflection in the rearview mirror revealed a sweaty woman, with short, unkempt hair and dark bags under her eyes.

All of the soda she'd consumed in the past few hours waited until that moment to wreak havoc on her bladder. Naomi crossed her legs and squeezed her thighs together, but the pressure didn't subside.

"Fuck!" she growled.

She knew this was the devil. He wanted her to leave and take a piss. When she returned, the red Camry would be gone. The clinic would close, and Naomi would go home empty-handed. She looked down at her McDonald's cup, wishing she had a penis. She had seen Bryan pee in a Gatorade bottle during a road trip. Maybe she could–

The first squirt of urine seeped out. Naomi's eyes widened. She sucked in a breath of air and held it.

Really, God? Really?

Naomi caught herself. No, this wasn't God. It was the devil! He wanted to embarrass her. He wanted her to fail. She gritted her teeth and started to breathe again. She uncrossed her legs and relaxed her muscles. The urine flowed freely. It was hot, and there was a lot of it. Peeing on yourself as an adult is a strange experience. Naomi felt like she was in one of those dreams where you think you're in the bathroom, but you're really still in bed.

But as creepy as it was, it was very relieving. Naomi didn't think she'd ever had a better urination. She didn't worry about the mess, because women did a lot of icky things when they had a baby. When Bryan asked about it – if he ever did – she would tell him the mess occurred when her water broke.

Easy peasy.

● ● ● ● ● ●

The woman reappeared at 4:45. Naomi was ready and waiting. She started her car as the dark-haired donor waddled back to her Camry. Naomi was pleased to see that she really was pregnant, at least seven months. She was also grateful that the woman was pretty. Even with a pudgy face and no makeup, her attractiveness shined through.

On the downside, the woman looked like she *might* be Hispanic. Naomi squinted and leaned closer to the windshield. It was hard to tell. Something about her features was not 100% Caucasian.

No, she is white. She looks like Angelina Jolie.

Naomi agreed with herself. She did look like Angelina. But still...

*Okay, maybe she's got just a **little** Mexican in her, a grandparent maybe. But one of her parents has to be white. If her husband is white too, no one will be able to tell the baby's not fully white. That lady's not dark-skinned. Plus it's impossible to tell a white baby from a Mexican baby.*

Naomi frowned. She didn't know if that was true. The muscles on the right side of her face began to contract rhythmically. She didn't notice.

What are you gonna do, come back tomorrow? God gave you this baby! He's not gonna give you another one.

The voice in her head wasn't always on her side, but Naomi knew it was right about that. Many people missed out on their blessings because they weren't paying attention to the miracles God worked in their lives. Naomi didn't want to be one of those people.

She put her car in gear as the woman drove out of the parking lot. They hit the street one right after another.

● ● ● ● ● ●

As she drove, Naomi was not aware that the tick on the side of her face grew steadily worse. She gripped the steering wheel so tightly her fingertips were cold. She focused her attention on the Camry ahead of her, almost oblivious to the rest of the traffic. Naomi did not hang back far enough for another car to get between them. She didn't want to risk losing sight of Angelina.

When they stopped at a light, she reached into the glove compartment and wrapped her trembling fingers around the pistol. She removed it and placed it on the passenger seat, next to her duffle bag. Her breath was hot and funky. She could taste it. The urine under her butt was cold now. She felt disgusting. The devil filled her mind with a million horrible scenarios. The many ways things could go wrong completely outweighed the one or two ways this might go right.

Naomi knew she had to ignore the negativity, if she wanted to be a mother. This wouldn't be easy, but it was worth it. It was worth everything; even her freedom or her life.

The further away they traveled from the hospital, the more Naomi was convinced Angelina was Hispanic. From Rosedale, they made a right on Hemphill; heading towards a predominantly Hispanic community. There were so few non-Hispanics in the area, all of the billboards advertised in Spanish.

That doesn't mean she's Mexican.

But didn't it, though? If she looked Hispanic and lived in a Hispanic neighborhood, why wasn't she Hispanic?

*She only looked a **little** Mexican,* the voice in her head reminded her. *If she's married to a white man, the baby won't look Mexican at all.*

Naomi appreciated that her inner voice was helping now, rather than berating her. But she doubted its wisdom. At least when it was saying mean things, it was being brutally honest.

Okay, if she's Mexican, so what? No one will be able to tell until the baby's three or four. By then, everyone will be okay with it. It'll be fine.

That made sense. Naomi was sure she could come up with a dozen reasons why her baby had Hispanic features if she had three years to think about it. No one at work knew anything about her parents. If she told them her mother was Mexican, they'd have no reason to doubt her.

The Camry turned off Hemphill onto a slower, quieter street. Naomi had enough sense to give her a little space then. If Angelina had noticed someone was following her, she didn't show it. She didn't drive to a police station, like Naomi would've done. And apparently she didn't call the police on her cellphone. They would've caught up with them and pulled Naomi over by now.

She followed the Camry for six more blocks, until it made a right at a stop sign. When Naomi approached the intersection, she waited twenty seconds before she made the turn. By then she saw the Camry pull into a driveway four houses down. Naomi followed slowly, creeping at only five miles per hour. She reached the house just as Angelina walked through the front door.

Naomi considered parking on the next block, but decided against it. She didn't want to walk too far with her baby. She certainly didn't want to run that far, if she happened to be fleeing with the bloody bundle of joy in her arms.

She pulled to a stop in front of Angelina's house. She put her car in park and decided to leave the engine running. She looked up the street and studied the opposite direction in the rearview mirror. There were a few people outside, but none close enough to pay her any mind.

A short, chain-link fence surrounded Angelina's front yard. It wasn't locked. Naomi noticed a few children's toys in the lawn. She wasn't surprised that Angelina had more children, but it did give her pause. If the children were young enough to play with these toys, Angelina wouldn't have left them home alone, would she? Did that mean there was another adult in the house? There was another car in the driveway, other than the Camry, but it didn't look like it was running.

Naomi's hair was damp. Sweat glistened on her face and rolled down her cheeks. Her heart thundered as she checked her supplies on the passenger seat. What the hell was she doing? A gun? Scalpels? Jesus, had it really come to this? Was she crazy? She didn't feel like she was. But if not, what the hell was she doing?

A glance in the rearview mirror told her all she needed to know. Her eyes were wild, certainly deranged. She didn't need her husband to tell her she looked like shit and smelled like piss. What she saw in the mirror was the lowest form of human depravity. Tears filled her eyes and thankfully clouded her view.

"Oh God!" she cried. *"God, help me. Please!"*

God helps those who help themselves, you fat bitch! Get out of the car and do what you came to do! You've come too far! You gonna back out now? You gonna let Mallory fuck your husband every night? If you're not gonna do it, then pick up the gun and kill yourself, you disgusting waste of life! **Kill yourself!**

Naomi was shocked to hear the condescending voice was back in full force. It was so real, it sounded like someone was speaking to her from the back seat. She continued to wail as her tears flowed even harder.

She *was* disgusting. She was a waste of life.

She reached to the passenger seat and picked up the gun.

● ● ● ● ● ●

Naomi got a running start, starting midway down the sidewalk. By the time she reached the porch, she had built up enough speed to hop the steps with hardly any effort. She impacted the front door shoulder first. She hit it hard enough to tear the deadbolt from the frame. The door flew open and crashed into the adjacent wall.

BOOMP!

Naomi nearly fell as she staggered into the living room. She brought her gun up as she regained balance. When she did, three full seconds passed, during which nothing at all happened.

Naomi saw Angelina standing near the couch, looking back at her in wide-eyed horror. Naomi saw a child on the floor next to the couch. He or she wore nothing but a diaper. Naomi saw another child who looked to be six years old. This one was sitting on the couch. Naomi saw a *fourth* person in the room. It was an older woman standing in the hallway. She could tell it was Angelina's mother – and most likely her live-in babysitter. That would explain how Angelina made it to the clinic without her rug rats in tow.

Everyone in the room was Hispanic. They weren't light-skinned Hispanics. They all had brown skin. Now that she was closer, Naomi saw that Angelina's skin was light brown as well. There was no doubt the baby in her womb would look like everyone else in the family.

Someone screamed, breaking Naomi out of her paralysis. She trained the gun on her baby donor, thinking she could still salvage this. The children shouldn't put up much of a fight. If they did, there were six bullets in the revolver and four people who needed a bullet. Naomi would have a couple of bullets to spare.

"Get on the ground!" she yelled at Angelina.

The woman threw her hands up and continued to scream. Naomi realized she wasn't only screaming, she was saying something – completely in Spanish. The grandmother was yelling too, and she was heading back down the hallway. Naomi swung her gun in that direction. One of the children made a move, and she had to adjust her aim again.

Kill 'em. Kill 'em all!

"What the fuck?"

Naomi's eyes darted in every direction. She didn't know which voices were real anymore. She looked up and saw a man emerge from the hallway. He looked to be Angelina's age. He was bald-headed and tatted up, wearing a tank top. Naomi pointed her trigger finger at him, but he ducked out of sight. She heard more Spanish coming from the back of the house – and some English too.

"Run!"

That suggestion was probably not meant for her, but it was the only thing Naomi had heard in the past thirty seconds that made sense. She turned and sprinted out of the house just as quickly as she'd came. Despite her retreat, the screams behind her became louder and more insistent.

It didn't seem like she was in the house long enough for the family to gather the troops, but the neighborhood was now twice as active as it was when Naomi first got there. There was a man in the front yard across the street. There were two people on the sidewalk next to her car. A woman stepped out of the front door of the house next door. Naomi's heart pumped harder than her legs as she ran.

Oh God, what have I done? Jesus, what have I done?

The neighbors were more confused than afraid of what they were seeing. No one made a move to stop Naomi as she jumped into her car, until a man rushed from Angelina's house yelling, "*Stop her! Somebody stop her!*"

Naomi threw her car in gear and stomped the gas with all her might. The sound of her engine screaming drowned out everything, including the demons whispering in her ear, but her car didn't move at all. It took several precious seconds to realize she'd put it in Neutral, rather than Drive. By then Angelina's brother had caught up. He yelled through the open passenger window.

"*Get out, bitch!*"

Outside of Mexican gangster movies, Naomi had never seen anything more frightening. She didn't realize she was screaming as she got her car in the correct gear. She took off just as the brother yanked the passenger door open. The force of her acceleration slammed the door closed again.

Ten blocks down the road things had quieted down enough for her to hear the voices again. One was screaming, somewhere deep between her ears.

Kill yourself! Why are you still breathing? You have nothing! Nowhere to go! You're not gonna get away with this! Do the right thing, for once in your miserable life!

Naomi's wails were soulful and eerie. She slapped the side of her head as hard as she could, but the voice wouldn't shut up. In fact, it became louder.

Do it! Just one bullet, and it'll all be over! Do it!!

Her eyes were so blurry with tears, she couldn't find the firearm on the passenger seat. She pawed for it blindly. She knew it was the right thing to do when her hand came in contact with the cool metal. She continued to howl as she brought the barrel to her temple.

Do it!!

Do it now!!

BAM!

The jolt was so hard, Naomi thought she pulled the trigger. Instead, in the real world, her car impacted the curb like a wrecking ball when she failed to stop at a T-bone intersection. Naomi's sedan sat low to the ground. Her axle snapped in two before the front wheels bounced over the curb. Everything in the car flew forward viciously, including the driver. If not for the airbag, Naomi would've broken every bone in her face when her head smashed against the steering wheel.

As it was, the sudden stop and impact of the airbag knocked her silly. She had no idea where her gun went, just as she had no idea two cars had been pursuing her since she left Angelina's house. She expected the police when someone yanked her driver and passenger doors open, but the men wore street clothes. They cursed her in Spanish and dragged her from the vehicle.

Naomi found herself sprawled on her back, looking up at brown faces, a pretty, blue sky. The clouds were puffy and perfect. She was reminded of what a beautiful day it was a moment before the first fist came crashing down.

After that, there was only darkness.

EPILOGUE

On Friday March 10th, four days after Naomi followed Angelina (whose real name was Sylvia Ramirez) from an OB/GYN clinic, RN William Harkins arrived for his morning shift in the Meredith Building. For him, working mornings sucked. After clocking-in on third shift for so many years, he considered himself a bonafide night owl. Now he had to go to bed by 11 and get up at 5am.

The sun wasn't even up by then, and he didn't think he should be either. But to save his marriage, he was willing to reconstruct his lifestyle. He loved his wife and children. After what he'd done to disrespect their holy union, he was fortunate that Jennifer gave him an opportunity to make things right. Lord knows he didn't deserve it.

He stood on the ground floor with a group of employees waiting for an elevator. A few of his colleagues were wide-eyed and animated at that hour. William wouldn't have that kind of spunk until at least one cup of coffee.

He didn't perk up when the elevator dinged, announcing their ride had come. But his eyes widened when the doors opened. His group stepped aside to make way for a few people stepping off the elevator. Among the night-shifters who were headed home, William was surprised to see Sherry. He realized this shouldn't come as a shock to him. When he worked third shift, he and Sherry took the same route when they exited the hospital together.

He hadn't laid eyes on her since he ended their affair. Locking eyes with her stirred up emotions he was trying to subdue – emotions that had broken his wife's heart. Looking into her eyes, he could tell Sherry was struggling with the same passion.

Her face reddened as she stepped off the elevator. She looked away, met William's eyes again, and then she lowered her gaze.

It was clear she didn't expect to run into him either. William knew she would take steps to avoid this encounter in the future, even if her new route added a couple of minutes to the time it took to get to her car. He knew that was for the best, but the pain in her eyes impacted him differently. His heart clenched and wept for her.

He reached and touched her hand as she walked past. If she kept going, he would leave it at that. This would be the last time he'd attempt to communicate with her. But Sherry hesitated and looked back at him. Her eyes filled with tears as she studied his expression. He knew she was mentally at war with herself, just as he was. Righteousness was currently winning, but sin was always a formidable foe.

William couldn't find the words to express the stirring in his heart. His body seemed to move on its own accord. He wrapped his hand around hers. A strong pulse of energy passed from one to another, giving both of their souls a jolt. She gasped. But she reciprocated. Her fingers tightened around his.

William pulled her into him and wrapped his arms around her. She immediately felt safe and wanted in his embrace. The sensation was much stronger than it had ever been with her husband. She couldn't stop a startled whimper from escaping her. The sound was mostly muffled against his chest. Her tears spilled freely. She became lightheaded, her legs unsteady.

"I am so sorry," William moaned. "I never meant to hurt you. I'd do anything to make you happy. I'm sorry, baby."

"I'm sorry too," Sherry cried. "We were wrong. We never should've let this happen."

"No," William told her. "No, no. No that. Being with you was the best thing that ever happened to me." He sniffled. "I'm sorry I let her tear us apart. I don't wanna be without you. I'd give anything to have you back."

Sherry's heart froze. Her life, her hopes and dreams dangled in the air. She looked up at him – not believing what he said.

"I mean it," he said, looking into her eyes. "I wanna be with *you*, Sherry. I can't live without you. I thought I could, but I can't. I can't go another day without knowing you're my girl."

Sherry only thought she was weak before. Her legs felt useless now, as the lobby of the Meredith Building spun around them. It took all she had to maintain a standing position. She fought for enough breath to respond to him.

"That, that's what I want too, William. But, but what about your wife?"

"I don't know," he said. "I don't know what's going to happen with Jennifer, but I know I can't stop seeing you. If she finds out, and she leaves me, I guess I have to accept that."

The blood rushing through Sherry's veins turned ice cold. "Me too. I don't want to stop seeing you," she breathed.

"Oh, baby! That's all I needed to hear." Tears of joy filled William's eyes.

He kissed his mistress passionately; for all to see. The employees and visitors in the area were polite enough not to stare at the bold display of affection. They walked around the couple as they deepened the kiss, seemingly oblivious to their surroundings, as if they were on a private island with just the two of them.

Jeez, get a room, Lola thought as she stepped past them on her way to the Patient Transport department. Inside she encountered a dozen men and women; all dressed in black scrubs. A couple of them said, "Morning, Dr. Barnes," as she walked by, on her way to their manager's office.

"Morning," she replied with a smile. She did not ask how they were doing, because the last time she did, one of them responded with brutal, long-winded honesty. It took five minutes to tear herself away from that conversation. Plus there was the issue of a couple of the transporters flirting with her.

Her husband had told her, "It's not every day they get to see a young, fine, black doctor."

Lola agreed that was true, but it didn't make it right. She was careful not to complain too much, because she knew Larry would fire them in a heartbeat.

She smiled when she approached his door. The placard on the front read

LARRY BARNES
TRANSPORT MANAGER

When she met him, Larry wore black scrubs, like the crew out front. Lola was a medical student at the time. To this day it amazed her that he had the gall to ask her out while she was working alongside her father, Dr. Dego. Larry's unshakable belief in himself was one of the things she found most endearing. It took her dad a while to come around, but that was to be expected. Larry was working an entry-level position, and Lola was Dr. Dego's only child. He didn't want *just anyone* to court his baby girl.

Larry's door was closed. Lola knocked, rather than barge in, though she knew he wouldn't have minded. After a second, the door opened. Lola's smile widened, in anticipation of her husband, but a transporter with a sullen expression appeared instead.

"Excuse me," he told Lola on his way out.

"Excuse me," she said. When she turned back to the door, her tall, dark mate approached her. Her smile returned as he wrapped an arm around her waist and drew her into the office.

"Morning, beautiful."

His touch warmed her body, mind and spirit. His kiss in the crook of her neck made her giggle. He reached past her and closed the door.

"Morning," she said. "Are you ruining someone's day already?" she asked, referring to the transporter who just left.

"He's ruining his own day," her husband replied. "He's lucky to still have a job. He might not be able to say that in a couple of weeks, if he keeps it up."

Larry wore dark slacks with a blue button down she picked out for him. Lola wore her lab coat over a sensible blouse and a pencil skirt that accentuated her curvy figure. Larry backed toward his desk, pulling her closer. Lola placed a hand on his chest when his hands dipped down to her backside.

"Your door's not even locked," she said and kissed his warm lips.

He returned the affection and told her, "No one's gonna come in here without knocking."

"Sure they won't." She took a step back and brought her arm up, blocking him with a half full plastic bag. "Sorry, honey, but I don't want to put on a show – like the two nurses I passed on the way in here."

Larry took the bag and allowed her to back away. He grinned as he checked out the treats she brought him. "What two nurses?"

"I don't know." Lola stood next to him. They both leaned with their butts on the desk. "Some man and woman. They were going at it like they were on their honeymoon. People were walking around them, trying not to look, but it was hard not to."

Larry grinned. "Love's always in the air at this hospital. What have we got here?" he asked, reaching into the bag. "I hope you saved me some of that Kasha."

"*Kashata*," she corrected him. "And yes, I did."

Lola was born in America, but her family was from Ethiopia. Her mother was insistent that she learn the culture of her homeland. One of the lessons Lola took pride in was her ability to bring a taste of Africa into her home. Larry appreciated that as well. Lola wouldn't share her Kashata when she made it yesterday. She said it was for a potluck dinner at her hospital. She promised to bring her husband the leftovers.

"I brought food from some of the others too," she told him. "It's more than enough for your lunch today."

Judging by the weight of the bag, Larry agreed with her.

"Thanks, babe." He placed the bag on his desk and turned to kiss her cheek.

Lola's skin was golden brown, like a honey bun. Despite having worked a 12-hour shift already, she smelled sweet to him.

"How was the party?" he asked.

"I ate too much," she said, reaching for her belly. "Everyone got full, and then we got lazy afterwards."

He placed his hand over hers. "That's okay. The baby needs sustenance."

"The baby's not big enough for that yet," she said with a giggle. Lola wasn't showing, but the life growing inside her had been confirmed. They were both excited about their first child.

"When are you gonna come work here?" Larry asked, not for the first time.

When Lola graduated from medical school three years ago, he thought it was a given that she'd work at the same hospital as her father. But Jackson Memorial didn't have an opening when she sought her first assignment. She accepted a position at Baylor, less than five miles away. She'd been employed in their ER ever since.

Lola worked third shift, while Larry was on first shift at Jackson Memorial. The young couple only saw each other in passing on some days. Today, for instance, Lola had just gotten off, while Larry was at the start of his day. Despite their lopsided schedules, they spent a lot of time together. Lola made sure to never neglect him in the bedroom. The new life blossoming in her womb was proof of that.

"You know I can't leave now," she told him. "I'm settled. Things are going great at Baylor."

"Things would be great here too," he countered. "Plus, the longer you stay there, the harder it'll be for you to leave."

"I may never want to," she acknowledged. "I work with a great team."

"We got great people here too."

"You don't want to have me so close," she said with a smile. "Absence makes the heart grow fonder."

Larry knew there was some truth to that. They were home together so infrequently, he looked forward to each precious moment they shared. Lola sometimes marked the dates they were both off on their refrigerator calendar.

"I don't even know if I wanna work here," she said jokingly. "Y'all got more drama than a little bit."

"Ah, it's not so bad," Larry replied.

She looked at him sideways. "Yeah, right. One of your PCT's got jumped in the parking lot on Monday."

"Yeah, that was bad," Larry acknowledged. "But they didn't get away with it."

"You said the police didn't get all of them."

"They got the ringleader," Larry said, "the one that used to work here. Her name is Danielle. I know they got her for sure."

"Mmm hmm," Lola commented. "Not to mention people actually get *murdered* here."

"Um, yeah," Larry said, his mood darkening. "That was bad. Everyone's messed up about that. Wait, did you say *people*, like *plural*? We only had one murder."

"*Only had one murder?*" She shook her head with a smirk. "That's like saying your house only burned down once."

He grinned. "No it's not."

"And there were *two* murders," Lola reminded him. "You had the one inside the hospital, and you had the one around the corner."

"Wait-wait-wait. The one in the hospital, yeah, that's on us. But the one around the corner – and *around the corner* is a bit inaccurate, by the way. It was more like a few miles away. But that had nothing to do with us."

"You said that boy worked in your department."

"He did," Larry confirmed. "I didn't know Bobby well. He worked third shift, usually in the ER. It's sad that he died, but don't add his story to our problems at the hospital. People get killed every day. Just because some of them have jobs doesn't mean you can blame their employer."

"Did they figure out what happened?" Lola asked.

Larry shook his head. "It could've been anything. People are saying it might have been a drug deal gone bad." He shrugged. "I don't know. I wish black men would stop killing each other, though. It's sad."

"It is sad," Lola agreed. "And what about the crazy man that snapped; beat his coworker with a mallet? Any word on what that was about?"

Larry shook his head again. "Not that I've heard. He's still in jail, or a mental hospital. I don't understand how someone could work here for so long without anyone realizing he was crazy. Jalen didn't deserve that. He was – wait, are you using these incidents as examples of why you don't wanna work here?"

Lola grinned. "Baby, you have to admit it's a lot. The people at your hospital are cray-cray."

"No, they're not. Just because a couple of–"

"*A couple*? Umm, what about the lady that tried to kill someone and take their baby."

"You don't know if she was trying to do that."

Lola's eyes widened. "Really, Larry? Do you wanna defend your hospital that badly? She had a gun – a bag full of medical instruments that would've been very helpful if she planned to cut someone open. She had an *umbilical cord clamp*. There's only one use for that. Not to mention she was telling everyone she was pregnant."

"Okay. You're right. She was trying to take that lady's baby."

"No..." Lola shook her head. "A *kidnapper* takes someone's baby. She was going to kill that woman and slice her open." Her hand subconsciously returned to her own stomach.

Larry sighed. "That lady is pure evil. I hope they never let her out of jail. But if you're saying all of that to explain why you don't want to work here, that's silly. All hospitals have drama."

"Not as much as this one. The things that happened here in the past few weeks... It reminds me of that nurse who OD'd while I was doing my residency here. You remember her? She stole meds from the pixus machine and passed out in the parking garage..."

Larry thought for a moment and said, "I think her name was *Sandra*."

"Did you ever hear what happened to her? I'll never forget her story. It was sad."

"She went to rehab, rather than jail," Larry recalled. "They're treating addiction like a disease nowadays. I heard she got to keep her license."

"She still works as a nurse?" Lola was shocked.

"Yeah, I think so," he said. "But not here. Maybe she's a *Baylor*," he said with one eyebrow raised.

"Yeah right. We don't hire junkies at Baylor!"

Larry's mouth fell open. "Wow. First her story's all sad and stuff. Now she's a *junkie*."

"Her story's sad," Lola said. "But she's still a junkie – or at least she was."

"The doctors at Baylor aren't very compassionate, I see..."

She elbowed him in the arm. "Shut up. I've got plenty of compassion."

"I can tell," he said sarcastically as he rubbed his arm. "Anyway, I know all of these stories sound bad, especially when you mash 'em up like that. But I assure you this hospital is the same as any other."

She rolled her eyes at that.

"I bet Baylor's just as bad," he continued. "You just don't tell me about the wild things that go on there."

"I tell you about them when I hear about them."

"That's another thing," he said. "No one sits around gossiping with a *doctor*. If you were a tech, you'd know a lot more about how sleazy your hospital is."

"Maybe," she agreed. "But *my* hospital's not sleazy. The stuff that happens here makes the news – *national news*, in some cases. If our sleaze isn't worthy of a news report, I'd say my hospital is better. As a matter of fact, you should come work at Baylor. I know some people. I could get you in."

"I'll think about it," he said.

He wrapped an arm around her waist and pulled her closer. She rested her head on his shoulder.

"You tired?" he asked.

She nodded and then yawned unexpectedly. "Excuse me."

"Come on," he said, pushing off the desk. "I'll walk you to your car."

She stood as well. "You don't have to do that."

"Sure I do. I can't have anyone hitting on you on your way out."

She grinned. "You don't have anything to worry about, Mr. Barnes. No one's gonna steal me away from you."

"That's nice to know, Dr. Barnes. But I'd still like to walk my lady around; show her off a little."

"Oh, well by all means..."

She offered him her hand. He reached to pat her ass before he took it.

"You off tonight, right?" he asked.

She nodded. "I'll have a nice dinner waiting for you."

"No, don't bother," he said. "It's Friday. I'll take you out."

Her eyes brightened. "That would be wonderful. Olive Garden?"

"You can't get enough of that eggplant parmesan," he noticed.

"Well, I am eating for two."

Larry's smile was wide and proud as they exited his office. "Anything for my baby – both of you."

KEITH THOMAS WALKER

ABOUT THE AUTHOR

Keith Thomas Walker, known as the Master of Romantic Suspense and Urban Fiction, is the author of nearly two dozen novels, including *Life After, The Realest Ever,* the *Brick House* series and the *Finley High* series. Keith's books transcend all genres. He has published romance, urban fiction, mystery/thriller, teen/young adult, Christian, poetry and erotica. Originally from Fort Worth, he is a graduate of Texas Wesleyan University. Keith has won or been nominated for numerous awards in the categories of "Best Male Author," "Best Romance," "Best Urban Fiction," and "Author of the Year," from several book clubs and organizations. Visit him at www.keithwalkerbooks.com.